ANYONE GOT A MATCH?

Max Shulman:

Anyone Got a Match?

HARPER & ROW, PUBLISHERS

New York, Evanston, and London

TO WALTER I. BRADBURY

ANYONE GOT A MATCH?

Chapter 1

Never mind what they tell you on Madison Avenue. It was not one of those thin-lapelled Ivy League copywriters who composed the immortal jingle. Oh, they will wink and look wise, but do not be deceived. It was *not* one of them. It was Jefferson Tatum himself. Yes, Jefferson Tatum, who came barefoot off a burley patch at the age of twelve and worked and gouged and scrabbled and finally built the great Tatum Cigarette Company with his own two callused hands, who caused people the world over to step up to tobacco counters and ask for Tatums as often as they ask for Camels or Marlboros— Jefferson Tatum, unlettered and unschooled, who was magically touched by the Muse in his office late one night and wrote the jingle —he, himself—on the back of a bill of lading:

> Tatums smoke mild,
> Like an innocent child.

"Land's sake!" said the late Mrs. Tatum to Jefferson when he brought the jingle home. "How *ever* did you think of it?"

"Love," he replied simply.

Well, there it is. Nobody ever loved the cigarette business as Jefferson Tatum did—not Buck Duke, not R. J. Reynolds, not Pierre Lorillard—nobody. And hence the jingle. If love can make the world go round, why can it not make a poet of a hard-fisted brawler like Jefferson?

A brawler he is, and always was. To illustrate, take what happened in the town of Owens Mill, headquarters and home of the Tatum Cigarette Company, on last March 24th. It was the date of Jefferson's seventy-fifth birthday, but he was far from festive. For one thing, he was cutting a wisdom tooth. For another, he had a thrombosed hemorrhoid. For still another—and this was the most painful of all—the annual fiscal statement of the Tatum Cigarette

Company, issued that day, showed sales running a full 3 percent behind the previous year.

But age and distress notwithstanding, Jefferson arrived at his desk at his usual hour of seven A.M. and put in his customary twelve hours of work, and then later at the birthday party the employees gave him in the company cafeteria he drank an entire Mason jar of white mule and danced the two-step with every lady worker present, bar none, and then he hand-wrestled the shredding-room foreman, Will Watson, a 235-pound Negro who almost went the distance in the Golden Gloves a few years ago. Then Jefferson cut his birthday cake and ate a chunk the size of your head and then went home with Millie and Esther McCabe, the twins from packaging. True, he only made it with Millie, but even so—*seventy-five years old!*

And after such a night he arose before dawn the next day—it was a Saturday—and set out with Virgil, his son, to climb the ridge and have another try at Old Slewfoot, a large and cunning black bear which Jefferson hated as Ahab had hated the whale. For twelve full years Jefferson had stalked Old Slewfoot without so much as one clean shot, but this year he felt it was going to be different; he felt it in his bones.

Jefferson and Virgil, guns ready to hand, squatted about a hundred yards from a cave sunk in the wooded hill. "He's in there, I know it," Jefferson said to Virgil. "That's got to be where he winters. I figured it out. And I figured out something else. He always comes out exactly the same time—just three days after the sweet William buds. And that's *today*, boy. I been keeping track. You watch. You watch. Before you know it, he'll drag himself out of there blinking and yawning and rubbing his old pelt on them rocks, and then I get him. *Then!*"

"Pa," said Virgil mildly, "I hate to mention it, but the bear hunting season isn't open."

"Don't I know that?" snapped Jefferson. "Ain't I the game warden?"

Virgil smiled. "Yes, Pa," he said. Virgil was forty-three years old, a large rugged man, yet scholarly in appearance. He had a gimpy leg, the result of another bear hunt long ago, but the limp was so slight that a stranger would fail to notice it.

The old man suddenly grabbed Virgil's arm. There was a stirring in the cave, dim but definite. "I told you, didn't I?" whispered Jefferson. He raised his gun and waited.

And while he waited, spring betrayed him. Without warning, a north wind howled over the ridge and thick white flakes of snow came pelting down. Inside the cave—for Jefferson had rightly diagnosed the bear's whereabouts—Old Slewfoot opened one gummy eye, regarded the snow, and decided to resume his long winter's nap.

Jefferson cussed, and it was a thing to hear because Jefferson, by common consent, was one of the three or four truly great cussers of the Border South. He could cuss lengthily, pithily, chromatically, and even creatively. He did not, however, cuss often. Knowing the awesome power of his profanity, he saved it for occasions when it was unquestionably indicated—like when a black bear refused to come out and be killed, or when some fool suggested cigarettes could cause lung cancer.

Virgil laid a soothing hand on his father. "Let's go to the lodge, Pa," he said. "Nobody will be there yet."

A half-hour's climb to the top of the ridge brought them to the Tatum hunting lodge—or, as people insisted on calling it, the Owens hunting lodge. The Owens family, founders and gentry of Owens Mill, had in fact built the lodge originally, but along with everything else in Owens Mill the lodge had eventually accrued to Jefferson. Still, habit dies hard, and people, including the surviving Owenses, continued to think of it as the Owens hunting lodge.

It was a big, handsome, comfortably furnished place commanding a magnificent view of the valley below. In the beginning there had been only a single building, sixty feet by thirty, made of varnished logs and fieldstone. Now this structure was surrounded by a colony of small cabins, rude but not without plumbing and innerspring mattresses. Every weekend a group of Owenses, plus guests, arrived to enjoy a healthful two days of alcohol and sex. The drinking was done in the main lodge; the other was accomplished in the cabins, generally in pairs.

Regarding the Owens family, Jefferson had curiously mixed feelings—loathing and respect. The ratio was roughly 96 percent loathing and 4 percent respect. He hated them for their spanking-new Abercrombie and Fitch woodsmen's outfits, for their costly and unfired guns, for their Princeton educations, for the outlandish guests they brought to the lodge, many of them Yankees and some almost certainly Jews.

But mostly Jefferson hated the Owenses because they were rich, and it was all his fault. In the early precarious years of the Tatum Cigarette Company, Jefferson had had to borrow heavily to stay in business, and in Owens Mill nobody had had money to lend except the Owenses. As a financial risk, Jefferson had been spectacularly unsafe, but as a borrower, he had been a veritable Demosthenes. The Owenses, spellbound, had granted the loans and accepted stock in the Tatum Cigarette Company as security. When Jefferson had defaulted—and he could do no other in those first bruising years—the Owenses, willy-nilly, had wound up owning big blocks of Tatum stock—par value, $1.00. Today, after three splits, the stock stood at $96.50, and the Owenses, to Jefferson's everlasting chagrin, were all rich. They were not as rich as Jefferson—even in his worst days Jefferson had taken care to keep control of his company—but they were rich nonetheless.

Yet in spite of all of his grousing at the Owenses, Jefferson retained a sneaky respect for them. He could never quite forget that he was a backwoods boy of uncertain lineage, while they were what the South calls *quality*. So he made them executives of his company—naturally in posts where they could do no harm—and he allowed them to gambol each weekend at his lodge.

It was only ten o'clock in the morning when Virgil and Jefferson reached the lodge and, as Virgil had predicted, the Owenses had not yet arrived. Jefferson sank into a big leather chair. Virgil touched a match to the logs in the fireplace, fetched the Jack Daniel's, a pitcher of water, and two glasses. He poured three fingers for his father, two for himself, and added a finger of water to each. Then he sat down across from Jefferson, filled a pipe, and lit it.

"Do you have to smoke a goddam pipe?" said Jefferson irritably. "I happen to make cigarettes, remember?"

Virgil grinned and puffed.

"You're a disappointment to me, boy," said Jefferson. "You always been."

"Drink your drink, Pa," said Virgil.

Jefferson sipped, but his melancholy did not abate. "Disappointments," he said lugubriously. "That's all life is. Disappointments. There's you. There's Old Slewfoot. There's that last statement of the cigarette company with sales down three percent in a single year. There's them pantywaist Owenses with their lifted pinkies. There's my wisdom tooth and my piles. . . . Disappointments, disappointments. And yet folks are all the time saying, 'That Jefferson Tatum —man, has he got the world by the short hairs!' Ha! That's all *they* know about it. *What* have I got, boy? Will you please tell me?"

"Yes, sir," said Virgil. "You've got eighty or ninety million dollars.

You've got the biggest cigarette plant in the world. You've got the town of Owens Mill and everything in it. You've got two churches, one cemetery, one public park, one country club, one hunting preserve, one skyscraper, one—"

"You damn right, boy!" interrupted the old man, banging down his glass. "And nobody gave me one stick of it. I made it all. *Me!* All alone. *Me!*"

He leaped to his feet, waving a finger, but before he could begin to declaim, Virgil rose quickly. "Pa, if you're about to do the speech about how you came to Owens Mill barefoot and fought your way to the top—and let me make it clear, sir, I do enjoy that speech thoroughly; I mean it's right up there with Mark Antony and Patrick Henry and Lincoln's Second Inaugural—all I'm saying is if you're going to do that particular address, you always get terrible thirsty, it being so long and all, so how about if I fix a drink first?"

"I have nursed a viper in my bosom," said Jefferson with a resentful glare at Virgil. But the glare abruptly turned to a laugh, and the father embraced the son and clapped his back with hard, noisy, painful thumps to prove that the emotions flooding his breast were not, Heaven forfend, less than manly.

Jefferson, a shameless melodramatist, complained loud and often of the many disappointments in his life, but the truth is he had only one: Virgil. Everything else had broken Jefferson's way, not easily, but ultimately. There had been hungry years in the beginning, precarious years of battling the tobacco trust, but he had prevailed. He had seen his Tatum Cigarettes zoom to the top and stay there. He had, against all counsel, courted and won Miss Hallie Owens, a genuine Owens of Owens Mill. (The acquisition of Miss Hallie, it must be said, was not an unflawed triumph. She was a bustly, cheery, gossipy, homey little creature, a compulsive preserver of preserves and quilter of quilts, who bored Jefferson almost to the edge of shrieking. Still, she *was* an Owens, and she *did* bring forth a fine, intelligent son, and she *had* had the grace to die quickly and young. Viewed judiciously, she could not, on balance, be called a disappointment.)

No, the sole clear disappointment was Virgil. An only son, strong, smart, determined, a son on whom Jefferson lavished all the pent-up, unused, untapped, and even unsuspected love within his heart, and who, in his turn, repaid Jefferson's love in the same honest coin— such a son, such a logical successor to the stewardship of the Tatum Cigarette Company and to the personal barony Jefferson had made

of Owens Mill, such a gratifying, satisfying, totally qualified heir
said no.

Virgil had nothing against the cigarette business: he just did not
want to be in it. Nor did he want to own the town of Owens Mill. He
wanted—and this stabbed Jefferson like a knife—to devote his life
to the pursuit of learning.

"Where do you get such nutty ideas?" Jefferson had yelled when
Virgil, then aged eighteen, had first announced the dread news.
"Not from me, that's for sure. And not from your mother, up there
making piccalilli with the angels. So where?"

"I don't know, Pa," Virgil had replied. "I've always liked books
and plays and school and stuff like that."

"I don't understand," Jefferson had said, honestly bewildered.
"I know you're not a pansy, not the way you're leaving pecker
tracks all over town. I know you're in a fist fight behind the drugstore at least once a week, gimpy leg and all. I've seen you hunt
and fish. I just don't understand."

"Well, maybe you will someday. Now, Pa, if you'll excuse me, I've
got to pack."

"Where do you think you're going?"

"I haven't quite decided. Harvard, maybe. Or else Yale."

"Like hell!" Jefferson had thundered. "If your hard head is set on
college—which I will *never* understand—you'll damn well go to
Acanthus!"

Like any other tobacco tycoon, Jefferson naturally owned a college. It was a denominational school, staffed by elders of the Don't-
Fiddle-With-The-Gospel Brotherhood, and the campus was located
right in Owens Mill where Jefferson could keep a watchful eye on it.

"Aw, Pa," Virgil had groaned.

"Aw, balls!" Jefferson had retorted. "It ain't going to be all *your*
way, boy. If I give, you give. You won't go into the business, okay,
I guess I got to accept it even if it breaks my heart. But you're not
running away and leaving me here alone. You're my family, boy,
my *only* family. What's the matter with you? Don't blood count for
nothing?"

To this argument there was no answer, so Virgil had enrolled at
Acanthus College. And today, twenty-five years later, as he sat with
his father before the fire in the hunting lodge, Virgil was still at
Acanthus. He was, of course, no longer a student; he was, in fact,
president of the college, having advanced in two and a half decades

from undergraduate to teacher to dean to provost and, finally, to prexy.

"Here, let me freshen your drink, Pa," Virgil was saying.

The old man shook his head morosely.

Virgil shrugged. "All right. You want to pout, go ahead and pout."

"Ain't I got a right to?" demanded Jefferson. "Ain't I got miseries enough? Cigarette sales down three percent in one single year!"

"So what? Tatums are still the leading brand in the country."

"That ain't the point!" cried Jefferson in a righteous rage. "Point is that so-called Surgeon General is scaring people off cigarettes, and it's getting worse all the time."

"You'll handle it," said Virgil lightly.

"Yeah? How? I been studying this thing day and night, and I swear I don't know how to stop it."

"Don't fret, Pa. You'll find a way."

"When?"

"Maybe after your nap," said Virgil.

"*Nap?*" cried Jefferson incredulously. "Are you unhinged, boy? Do you imagine I could sleep with all this trouble on my mind?"

"Try," urged Virgil.

"Won't do no good," declared Jefferson. Nevertheless he walked into the bedroom, removed his boots, stretched out, closed his eyes, and fell asleep—elapsed time: 31 seconds.

Virgil meanwhile made ready for the arrival of the Owenses and their guests. It was a fairly involved procedure. For example, preparing the bar was not a simple matter of setting out bourbon and branch water, as might be assumed from this rustic Southern locale. One of the Owenses wintered in Italy and drank nothing but Strega. Another summered in France, and for him Virgil had to break out a bottle of Amer Picon. A third lived half the year in Galway and required numerous bottles of stout, room temperature.

After he finished at the bar, Virgil went to the piano and rummaged through the sheet music in the bench. Late or soon, the Owenses always got musical. First in their recitals came nostalgic tunes of the 1930's. These were followed by traditional airs in the manner of Joan Baez. Then, as the alcohol began to take hold, they switched to Ivy League hymns. Finally, good and gassed, they finished with Confederate marches. Virgil chose a substantial number in each category and arranged them in order on the piano desk.

As he headed for the kitchen to make a selection of hors d'oeuvres, Virgil heard a groaning from Jefferson's bedroom. He opened the door and looked in. The old man was threshing and rolling in his sleep. "Disappointments," he kept mumbling, "disappointments."

Virgil closed the door and smiled wryly. "He thinks *he's* got disappointments," he said to himself and continued toward the kitchen.

Virgil was a man who shunned self-pity as unproductive and unvirile. Yet, being human, he could not avoid it altogether. Now as he prowled the kitchen gathering cheeses and biscuits, he allowed himself one of his infrequent lapses. Yes, he thought, embracing dolor, I know a thing or two about disappointments.

He did. There was the death of his mother when Virgil had been twelve. There was the gimpy leg, caused by one swipe of a black bear's paw when Virgil had been fifteen. And there was Acanthus College when Virgil had been eighteen, and today, with Virgil forty-three years old, there was still Acanthus College.

Acanthus was a small place, only twelve hundred students, but it was renowned throughout the nation for two reasons: first, because credits and degrees earned at Acanthus were recognized by no other American college; and second, because the Acanthus football team had not lost a game since Nineteen Meyers—called Nineteen because that was the size of his collar—took over as head coach.

There were other noteworthy aspects of Acanthus College. For example, it led the entire country in the age of its faculty, the weight of its undergraduates, and the slenderness of its catalogue. For further example, the largest building on the Acanthus campus, a neo-Gothic edifice with two spires and three stained-glass windows, was not, as a visitor might suppose, the chapel; it was the residence of Nineteen Meyers. The three stained-glass windows, made in Augsburg, depicted the wing-T formation, pass interference, and the red dog.

Virgil had been only twenty-three years old when he assumed his instructor's duties at Acanthus, and being only twenty-three he was full of burning zeal to raise the level of scholarship. The burning zeal underwent an instant hosing upon encountering Nineteen Meyers' book-proof athletes. He could not teach them, nor could he expel them because they were protected by Nineteen, who was, in turn, protected by Jefferson. Nor could Virgil leave town because he was the only family Jefferson had, as Jefferson never tired of reminding him. Nor could Virgil quit his job because he had chosen to devote his life to learning, and in Owens Mill, Acanthus College, save the mark, was it.

So Virgil stayed, and as his aged colleagues on the faculty were

called, row on row, to Abraham's bosom, Virgil perforce climbed up
the academic ladder. It was not Jefferson's influence that raised Virgil
from instructor to prexy with such rapidity; it was a simple failure of
geriatrics.

Through all his tenure at Acanthus Virgil never stopped making
sorties against the minds of the undergraduates. His record of failure
was perfect. But even now as he stood in the kitchen of the hunting
lodge loading a platter with Camembert, Oka, Brie, and Huntley
and Palmer's Export Assortment, he still nursed a tiny, faint, flickering hope that somehow, someday, he would pry loose the brute grip
of Nineteen Meyers and turn Acanthus into a sure-enough temple
of higher education.

He carried the cheese and crackers into the living room, placed
them on a coffee table, and sat down to resume riffling through the
tragedies in his life. Abruptly he stopped. *"That,"* he said sternly to
himself, "will be enough of *that!"* Self-pity begets self-pity, and it
was definitely not Virgil's line of work. Resolutely he put misfortune
out of his mind and picked up a volume of James Conant. After a
moment he laid the book aside. As long as he was doing a census of
his traumas, he thought, he might as well do it properly. He had not
yet touched the biggest setback of all, the crowning disappointment
in a career of disappointments: the lady known as Boo.

Boo was the great and only love of Virgil's life. Naturally, with his
kind of luck, she did not love him back. She was called Boo because
she had been born Barbara Ogilvie Owens, a member of the Owens
family and vaguely a second cousin to Virgil on his mother's side. It
was not, however, consanguinity that made Boo reject Virgil; she
just plain did not want him.

For a long time the feeling had been mutual. Boo was a few years
younger than Virgil, and as children in this family-minded community they had, of course, seen one another often. Virgil had not
then regarded her as a love-object. He had, in fact, thought of her
more as a jockey. She owned a horse from whose back she would
descend only at bedtime; even her meals were taken in the saddle;
when she forgot to bring along a sandwich, she simply grazed with
the horse.

To the undisguised relief of her immediate and distant kin, she
went away to school in her teens. She was spindly, pimpled, and
bustless when she left; she returned transfigured—tall, slender, elegant, rounded, gracious, poised, and, most important, dismounted.
Virgil looked upon the new Boo and was instantly smitten. She,

on her part, was friendly to Virgil, even cordial, but she dated him no more often than she did a dozen other eager swains of the town.

Even after Pearl Harbor when the young men of Owens Mill enlisted wholesale and Virgil, 4-F because of his leg, had Boo all to himself, he made no perceptible progress. "I love you, Virgil," she kept saying, "but not *that* way." (She was still saying it.)

But Virgil, back in those first months after Pearl Harbor, was not dismayed. He clung to the conviction that if he could keep courting Boo without competitors for just a little while longer, he would surely wear her down.

It was not to be. Competitors appeared in droves around the beginning of 1943. The Army Air Force set up a base outside Owens Mill, and luckless, dauntless Virgil again became one among many.

Virgil still pursued Boo, and so did an impressive number of the officers and men of the Army Air Force, but in the end it was a rank outsider who lapped the field. The Okinawa campaign was raging in the Pacific, and news arrived that Owens Mill had its first war hero. A local attorney's son, poor but of good bloodlines, by name Gabe Fuller, a lieutenant commander in naval aviation, won a posthumous Navy Cross for knocking a kamikaze out of the skies at the cost of his own life. The town buzzed with tales of Gabe's gallantry. The town buzzed even louder when Boo made the astonishing announcement that she had quietly gone to San Francisco and married Gabe just before he sailed overseas to meet a hero's death. By way of proof she produced a gold wedding band and a marriage license. If further proof were needed, she produced a baby boy some months later.

The baby boy—Gabriel, as Boo named him—in no way dampened Virgil's ardor. "It doesn't matter about the baby," he declared. "I will cherish him and raise him as my own. Boo, listen, you just got to marry me."

"I love you, Virgil," she said, "but not *that* way."

Today Gabriel was eighteen years old, and Boo, though still a beautiful woman, was no longer a prime target for the blades of Owens Mill. Only Virgil remained constant, and no amount of discouragement could extinguish his hopes. Just as he believed he would one day infuse culture into Acanthus College, he believed that he would finally lead Boo to the altar. A stubborn man.

He stirred now in the chair before the fireplace in the hunting lodge. He uttered a four-letter word and then he said it louder. He poured a stiff jolt of bourbon and knocked it back. At the moment he disapproved thoroughly of himself, not for playing a mugg's game with Boo, or with Nineteen Meyers either, but for letting himself wallow so long in the slough of self-pity. Insidious, that's what it was. Habit-forming. Fiber-destroying. Had blind Homer whimpered and whined? Or epileptic Caesar? Or stumpy Napoleon? Of course not. Well, neither would lame Virgil.

Feeling better, he went to the window. The snow had stopped falling. The sky was washed bright, and on the horizon there suddenly appeared a long, white, double-rotored, banana-shaped helicopter. It approached rapidly, hovered for a moment directly overhead, whirring and beating, and then it descended to a clearing in front of the lodge.

The Owenses had arrived.

Chapter 2

Flint Granite was a cowboy star who had played the lead for five years in one of America's most beloved television series, *Gut-Shooter*. Flint was six feet, eight inches tall, all of it sinew.

Ira Shapian was five feet, seven and one-quarter inches tall, and nearly strong enough to swim two laps in a forty-foot pool—sidestroke. Ira was a television executive, the West Coast vice-president of the Star Spangled Broadcasting Network.

They sat now, Ira and Flint, in Ira's Hollywood office, a room thirty by thirty, handsomely furnished in Early American chromium. Ira sat on one side of his spirochete-shaped desk, Flint on the other.

"Stand up, Ira," said Flint.

Ira rose.

"Take off your glasses," said Flint.

Ira removed his black-rimmed spectacles.

Without haste, Flint reached across the desk and punched Ira in the nose.

Ira sighed.

"Think I broke it?" ased Flint.

"I don't think so," Ira answered. "You usually hear kind of a cracking sound when it breaks. This was more like a *splat*."

"You're bleeding pretty bad," said Flint. "Want my handkerchief?"

"No, thank you," said Ira. "Just tell Miss Goldberg when you leave."

"Right, pardner," said Flint. He walked out of Ira's office, and within seconds Miss Goldberg entered, carrying a basin of ice cubes and several hand towels. Ira stretched out on a sofa, his head hanging over the edge. Miss Goldberg, a stocky, gray-haired spinster of sixty, knelt beside him and went to work without comment or delay.

"It's stopped," she said after five minutes of applying ice.

"Thank you," he said and stood up.

"He should of killed you," said Miss Goldberg.

"Yes," Ira agreed. "Get me Clendennon in New York."

Miss Goldberg nodded. She made a quick survey of the bloodstains on Ira's clothes. "Better you should change the whole garments," she said.

"Good thinking," said Ira, and when Miss Goldberg left to place the phone call, he walked into his executive dressing room that led from his executive office to his executive bathroom. Here was a fully stocked wardrobe containing a wide selection of shirts, all of them white; a large gallery of neckties, all of them black; a generous assortment of cashmere hose, all black; and a half-dozen suits, all with vests, all with jackets having two vents in the rear and vestigial lapels in the front, all in various shades of black: dark black, coal black, total-eclipse black, Stygian black, pitch black, and stove black. Ira's employer, Mr. Harry Clendennon, president of the Star Spangled Broadcasting Network, cherished a conviction that people are more inclined to believe you when you lie to them in black.

Ira stripped to his shorts, which were made of peach-colored nylon and embroidered with a flight of monarch butterflies. "Oy!" said Miss Goldberg, who had appeared unannounced at the dressing room door. "Would Mr. Clendennon ever give it to you if he saw those drawers!"

"A man's crotch is his castle," said Ira with dignity. "Is Clendennon on the line?"

"In conference. Call you back in half an hour," she answered. "But hurry up dressing. Scarpitta is waiting outside."

"Oh, God!" groaned Ira.

"Well, at least he only cries," said Miss Goldberg philosophically. "That's better than hit."

"I wonder," mused Ira. "Okay, tell him I'll be right with him."

She walked out and Ira began to dress. Despite Mr. Scarpitta waiting in the outer office, Ira dressed slowly, pausing often to ruminate while he buttoned buttons. Once, as he was thinking, a little smile flitted across his face. He was remembering a question Ezra and Leo had asked him long ago. Ezra and Leo were Ira's twin sons, and normally he did not smile when he thought about them. They were eighteen years old now, and they passed their days chiefly in lifting. They lifted barbells, girls, friends, acquaintances, passers-by, boulders, small automobiles, and most anything else that came to hand. Occasionally they stopped lifting long enough to go surf-riding or scuba diving, or to kick sand in the faces of ninety-seven-pound weaklings—not maliciously, let it be emphasized, only playfully. It never occurred to Ezra and Leo to be malicious. In fact, almost nothing ever occurred to them. They were dumb as a set of matched posts and beautiful as a brace of Greek gods. They were large, bronzed, vacuous, untroubled, muscular, and semiaquatic, as endemically Californian as the dateburger.

When the twins had been small boys, before Ira realized the Los Angeles sun was baking their brains out, he had doted on them. It was those days Ira was thinking of now as he dressed in his executive dressing room. He was recalling an evening he had come home from work, and the twins had looked up at him trustingly with their lovely, liquid Armenian eyes, and they had asked, "Daddy, what do you do at the office?"

"I *nice*," he had answered.

"Oh," they had said, satisfied.

Ira selected a black necktie and knotted it. "Yeah," he said to himself grimly, "and that's what I still do: nice."

In television *to nice* is a verb, generally transitive. It means to inspire confidence, which is no small thing in television because, in the main, actors are paranoiac, agents are mendacious, and advertising men are haunted by the harrowing knowledge that if they should disappear, nobody would notice it.

To deal with this distrustful lot, tv producers search diligently for somebody who can nice. Producers, of course, cannot do it themselves, for who would trust a producer? Therefore they must seek out men so shiningly honest, so unchallengeably aboveboard—in short, so *nice*—that their statements will be accepted on faith even by actors, agents, and ad men.

Ira Shapian was such a man. He never lied. That is to say, he lied all the time, but he never *knew* he was lying while he lied. The punch in the nose by Flint Granite, described earlier, will serve to illustrate.

Every television series, even one so dear to the hearts of the nation as *Gut-Shooter*, must someday reach the end of the trail. A year ago *Gut-Shooter* was canceled after five seasons on the Star Spangled Broadcasting Network, and Flint Granite found himself at liberty, much to the delight of ABC, CBS, and NBC. ABC offered Flint the role Robert Horton had left on *Wagon Train;* CBS offered him the deputy's part in *Gunsmoke;* NBC proposed writing him in as a fourth son in *Bonanza.*

While big Flint mulled these mighty attractive offers, Harry Clendennon, president of Star Spangled and a much better muller, did some mulling of his own in his New York headquarters. He rapidly broke the problem into its two component parts: first, he had to keep Flint at Star Spangled because it was flatly not thinkable to let a rival network grab off such a valuable piece of flesh; second, Star Spangled was completely booked for the year and consequently Clendennon had no series to offer Flint.

What, then, was the solution? Why, it was simplicity itself, thought Clendennon, cackling in his black suit, and he picked up the phone and called Ira Shapian in Hollywood.

"Ira baby, it's Harry," said Clendennon, smiling over three thousand miles of AT&T wire. "How does it march?"

"Just peachy-keen, Harry baby," said Ira. "Just tickety-boo."

"How's that lovely Molly of yours, you lucky dog?" asked Clendennon.

"Also peachy-keen," said Ira, "but I think her name is *Polly*. I'll ask when I get home."

"You stone me!" cried Clendennon, laughing silverly. "You're a regular Joe Penner!"

"Flatterer!" said Ira.

"Ira, I'm calling about the big horseapple kicker. How do you stand with him—still A-OK?"

"Flint Granite? Well, sure, we're friends, I guess."

"*Friends?*" said Clendennon deprecatingly. "He *loves* you!"

"All right, he loves me."

"And who does not? . . . Now, listen, doll buggy, I want you to tell Flint to say no to the other networks and sign with us."

"Why?" asked Ira sharply. "We have no series for him—none that I've heard about, anyhow."

"I'm sorry, Ira. I'd give my left gonad to tell you what we've got, but when you luck onto something this big, it's lock-and-key time."

"Harry, one favor. Please, *please* don't ask me to give the cowboy a finger. It's shooting birds on the ground."

"*Finger*, he says! All my friends and loved ones should get such a finger! This just happens to be the biggest thing that ever hit television, that's all."

"Harry, you're lying. You and I both know there's no time left on the network."

"For this one, chickie, we'll *make* time."

"So what is it?"

"Pal, I swore I wouldn't breathe a—oh, hell, who can hold out on a pussycat like you? All right, I'll give you two words, but that's all: John Steinbeck."

"*John Steinbeck* is going to write a series for Flint Granite?" shouted Ira.

"Cool it, cool it!" Clendennon whispered urgently. "The walls have ears."

"Sorry," said Ira. "John Steinbeck? The Nobel Prize? Wow!"

"I leave it to you, sweetie-face," said Clendennon and hung up the phone softly.

First thing next morning Ira met with Flint and proposed the deal. "Pardner," said Flint, his blue eyes looking straight into Ira's black ones, "I never heard tell of this here Mr. Steinbeck, but if'n *you* say I should do it, why, that's good enough for me."

So Flint signed Ira's contract, never so much as glancing at it, and he notified ABC, CBS, and NBC to make other plans because he was not available.

For the next thirteen weeks Flint called Ira daily to find out how Mr. Steinbeck was progressing with the scripts. Ira, in turn, called Clendennon, who reminded Ira that Mr. Steinbeck was, after all, a genius and could not be chivied like some television hack. Ira then relayed this information to Flint, who said he reckoned it must be so.

At the end of thirteen weeks, Flint's first option came up. Clendennon phoned Ira and announced sadly that Mr. Steinbeck had bowed out of the project in order to travel with Charley through Mexico and Yucatán. Nobody could be sorrier than Clendennon, said Clendennon, but in view of the circumstances, there was nothing except for Ira to notify Flint that his option had been dropped.

"You bastard," said Ira, and then he said other things, about a half-hour's worth, but finally he summoned Flint and broke the bad news. The punch in the nose followed immediately.

During his years at Star Spangled, Ira had received a round dozen punches in the nose. There had also been a sizable number of kicks in the shin. From female stars there had been cascades of tears, sometimes followed by fingernails in the face. On one gaudy occasion involving a Parisian *chanteur*, Ira had even been challenged to a duel.

It may be fairly asked why Ira, if he were such a nice man, allowed himself to be used so wickedly. The answer is quickly given: Ira was paid $3,000 a week.

He loathed himself for what he was doing. He felt like a man swimming through a sewer. But all the same, he kept swimming because three thousand a week, after taxes, was not quite enough to cover his house and pool in Bel Air, his house and pool in Palm

Springs, his Negro butler, his Japanese gardener, his Jaguar Mark VII, his wife's Buick station wagon, his twins' Austin-Healey, his Chagall, his Rouault, and a Beverly Hills dentist who had somehow persuaded him that uncapped front teeth were infra dig.

About these accretions—the houses, pools, servants, cars, paintings, and porcelain jackets—Ira's feelings were ambivalent. Or perhaps tri-bivalent. Possibly even quadri-bivalent.

There were times when he surveyed his possessions and was suffused with a glow of pride. "Not bad for an Armenian kid from Tenth Avenue," he would tell himself, swelling. At other times, looking over the very same possessions, he would actually tremble with rage. "Chains!" he would yell, silently or aloud. "Diamond-studded chains —that's what I got!" Then there were times when he felt both pride and rage simultaneously, often accompanied by an obbligato of disgust, desolation, and spastic colon.

Naturally he blamed his wife for his entrapment. "You!" he would cry, pointing a quivering finger. "You had to have the fancy houses, the fancy pools, the fancy cars, the fancy kids! You, you, *you!*"

"In your hat," Polly would reply mildly and leave the room. In twenty years of marriage she had learned the futility of arguing with Ira when the blackness was upon him. There was nothing to do but wait until rationality returned—often a matter of months.

But on those rare occasions when sweet reason informed Ira, he knew well that the blame was not Polly's but his. In 1949 Ira had been a director in the New York theater, not an important one, and certainly not a rich one, but a busy one. He staged a cycle of Bertolt Brecht plays that year, one of which was seen by an M-G-M executive who happened to be junketing in New York. The M-G-M man understood fewer than ten words of the play; nevertheless he hated to go back to Hollywood without some kind of souvenir, so he signed Ira to a contract.

Ira lasted six months at M-G-M, during which time he gave several producers sweaty palms by proposing to make movies of *Erewhon, Varieties of Religious Experience,* and the Alger Hiss case. Finally they loaned him to Monogram to direct a Bowery Boys picture. Following that, Ira and M-G-M parted company with honest tears of joy on both sides.

Television beckoned. It was a lusty youngster then, not afraid to experiment, and Ira made a quick reputation. But while he was making a reputation as a director, he was making another kind of reputation too. Eyes in high places were observing him, not because of his

directorial talents—after all, any damn fool in puttees can direct—
but because Ira could definitely *nice*. Volatile he was, blunt, hyper-
thyroid, given to swarthy outbursts, but everyone trusted him on
sight. So the silken trap was set.

Undreamed-of sums of money were gently urged on Ira. Fabled
homes were opened to him; living legends invited him to golf. Blinking with enchantment, Ira was eased off the sound stages, issued a
black suit, and installed in a small but well-appointed office on the
executive floor. A period of training followed—training for *what*, Ira
did not quite understand—and then he was given a bigger office.
Then he was given still a bigger office and still a bigger office and
still a bigger office, until today his office measured thirty by thirty
and he was West Coast vice-president of the Star Spangled Broadcasting Network.

Ira buttoned his black vest, slipped on his black jacket, and
touched, ever so gingerly, the nose that Flint Granite had splatted.
That is what was left now—not enchantment, but a sore nose.

He walked to his desk and pressed the intercom button. "Miss
Goldberg, I suppose Scarpitta is still there?"

"Where then should he be?" said Miss Goldberg.

"Send him in," said Ira without joy.

Scarpitta, a fifty-year-old man weighing 103 pounds, was not actually crying when he entered. His lower lip was fluttering, his tiny
shoulders were heaving, but his eyes were, as yet, dry.

"You lied to me," he said without preliminary.

"Yes, Mr. Scarpitta," said Ira.

Scarpitta clutched Ira's lapels. "Look, I know I run a lousy little ad
agency. Young and Rubicam I'm not. BBD&O I'm not. I'm a crappy
little agency with crappy little clients nobody else will touch—laxa-
tives, deodorants, depilatories, false teeth stickum. I know all this.
. . . But still and all, I've got feelings. I'm a human person. Attention
must be paid!"

The tears were rolling now, drop after steady drop.

"You *promised* me!" he wept. "And I promised the Jollybowel
people. 'Don't worry,' I told them, 'Ira Shapian personally gave me
his word you could buy three sixty-second spots for Jollybowel on
the *After Midnight Movie.*' . . . Mr. Shapian, you should have seen
their faces! Like kids on Christmas morning!"

Ira gently disengaged Scarpitta's hands from his lapels. "Please,
sir, compose yourself," he urged.

Scarpitta manfully stemmed his tears. "All right. So what happened with Jollybowel?"

"New York said no."

"But you checked with New York before you promised me, and they said *yes*. Why all of a sudden *no?*" he asked. "And, oh, what a foolish question," he continued without pausing. "Somebody offered Clendennon more money for those three spots. Who?"

"U.S. Steel," Ira confessed.

"Great!" said Scarpitta bitterly. "Got to be lots of people buying ingots at one o'clock in the morning."

"I'm sorry," said Ira.

"You're always sorry," said Scarpitta. "You're always lying and you're always sorry."

"True," sighed Ira.

"But I ain't mad," Scarpitta assured him. "I got *my* job—trying to get my crappy products on tv—and you got *your* job—telling lies."

"True," repeated Ira.

"Only my job is harder on account of I can't get my crappy products on any network, not even in the middle of the night when nobody's watching. And, believe me, my crappy clients brood about it. I mean it's like a *stigma!* They're getting a whole inferiority complex, these clients, and you know what happens when people feel inferior? They look for somebody even more inferior to take it out on. Me, for instance . . . Mr. Shapian, please help me before I get the ax. I'm a married man with kids."

"I'll do what I can," said Ira.

"Can you get me two minutes for Gamy-Gone?"

"I'll try."

"How about No-Klack?"

"I'll try."

The intercom buzzed, and Ira flicked the switch.

"Mrs. Shapian calling," said Miss Goldberg.

"I'll call her back," said Ira.

"You'll talk," said Miss Goldberg firmly. "She says it's altogether an emergency."

"I'm leaving, I'm leaving," said Scarpitta hurriedly. "But just one thing: can I tell my deodorant people and denture people you promised me some air time?"

"I can't make any such promise, Mr. Scarpitta."

"So *lie* to me," Scarpitta implored. "I always believe you."

"Good-bye, Mr. Scarpitta," said Ira.

Scarpitta slank, crying softly, to the door. Ira was perilously close to tears himself as he watched the tiny, hunched figure make his exit. To give the finger to a man like Flint Granite was, of course, reprehensible, but at least Flint was six feet, eight inches tall, and could bash your nose. How much more despicable, thought Ira, to diddle a poor defenseless schnook like Scarpitta. Was three thousand a week worth it? Was *five* thousand? Was *ten* thousand?

"What's the matter?" said Miss Goldberg through the intercom. "You don't want to pick up the phone? You don't care your wife's got an emergency, the house is maybe burning, God forbid?"

Ira roused himself and snatched up the phone. "Polly? What's the trouble?"

"It's the twins," said Polly.

"Ask a foolish question," muttered Ira. "All right, what now?"

"Promise you won't holler."

"Why should I holler? Does a man holler when he's blessed with a couple of sons like mine? Why, it's like having John Stuart Mill in duplicate."

"Never mind the sarcasm. I'm keeping *my* temper, and I'm a lot madder at those two louts than you are."

"Possibly that's because you know what they did, and I do not. Will you tell me already?"

"Okay, okay. Now, follow me carefully. Today is the last day to qualify for the annual surfboard derby. The Athletic Commission is holding the final trials at Long Beach this afternoon."

"Just a minute. I'm making notes."

"Shut up and listen. The twins must get out to Long Beach and qualify or else they won't be eligible for the derby. . . . Now, Ira, you know I never bother you at the office, but this is really a crisis. Those big dumb kids of ours will simply curl up and die unless they get into that surfboard thing."

"So what's the problem? They've got a car. Let 'em drive out to Long Beach and qualify."

"Well, that's the point. They *don't* have a car."

"Oh, yes, they *do*, and I got the bills to prove it."

"What I'm trying to tell you—"

"And very badly."

"Yes, very badly. Anyhow, what I'm trying to tell you—oh, boy, are you going to holler!—is that last night they were lifting their car on the pier at Santa Monica and they dropped it in the ocean."

"*They dropped it in the ocean?*" hollered Ira so loud that all the Emmies on his shelf trembled.

"See?" said Polly. "What did I tell you?"

"Sorry. Lost my head. Please go on."

"Thank you. Now, I'd let the twins use my car, only I'm going to be a Gray Lady this afternoon."

"Maybe sooner," said Ira. "How about the butler? Couldn't he drive them to the beach?"

"He's at a Black Muslim meeting."

"I have a distinct feeling I'm going out of my mind," said Ira.

"So my idea is this: if you could get away from the office for an hour or so—"

"I cannot get away from the office for an hour or so," said Ira, "but I have a brilliant idea of my own. Remember those English bicycles we bought the twins a few years ago, the ones that have been gathering rust in the garage since the day they were delivered?"

"Smashing idea, Ira—bicycles down Highway 101 with an eight-foot surfboard under their arms and their girl friends, also eight feet, sitting on the handlebars."

"Polly," said Ira wearily, "could we say good-bye now? Please? Huh?"

"I think perhaps we better," said Polly, clipping her words carefully.

"Good-bye."

"Good-bye."

Ira replaced the phone. He looked at his watch and decided to allow himself a groan of ten seconds. But Miss Goldberg buzzed before he was halfway through.

"Mr. Clendennon returning your call," she said through the intercom.

Ira's hand darted savagely toward the phone. "Just the man I want to talk to!" he said to himself. "Boy, will I burn that sneaky sonofabitch! Boy, will I tell that lying rat fink!"

Suddenly, just an inch away from the phone, Ira's hand stopped—stopped and then wilted. The anger drained from Ira's face; the erectness dribbled out of his spine. What, exactly, was he going to say to Clendennon? That he was sneaky and a sonofabitch and a liar and a rat and a fink? But Ira had told him all of this before, and a great deal more besides. It all rolled off Clendennon, or under him, or over him, or around him. It never got *inside* him.

There were only two words Ira could use that would *pierce* Clendennon—two short words: "I quit."

And the time was ideal to say those two little words: in just a few weeks Ira's seven-year contract would lapse, and the network had already let him know he would be offered a new one.

But was Ira prepared to say those two fateful words? He ran a quick trial balance.

On the debit side were Flint Granite and Scarpitta, and all the Flint Granites and Scarpittas who had preceded them. There was the crowd of friends Ira had lost, the debris of trusts he had betrayed, the mass of lies he had told, the dungheap of self-loathing he had accumulated. There was a wife gone testy and a pair of sons gone lame-brained.

Ira looked at the credit page of the ledger. There he saw one large, loud, unblinkable entry: *$3,000 per week.*

But, Ira asked himself, did a man *need* three thousand a week? Did he need houses and pools in Bel Air and Palm Springs? Did he need a Black Muslim chauffeur and a Japanese gardener? Did he need three expensive automobiles (actually, only two now; one lay on the bottom of the Pacific)? Did he need a Chagall and a Rouault and porcelain caps on his front teeth?

As for the porcelain jackets, these seemed to be an abiding part of Ira's life no matter how he opted. The rest, however, could surely go. Ira could shuck his black suit and resume his career as a director. He was, of course, a little rusty, so he would have to work for short money at first. But so what? He would still make enough to live in modest comfort. He could move his family to a little bungalow in the Valley. Polly could do the housework, Ira could help out around the yard, and the twins could get a newspaper route. Ira could drive a Corvair, buy his suits at Robert Hall, close his account at Chasen's, switch from J & B to Imperial, give up cigars, and wear stretch socks.

Ira slammed both hands on his desk disgustedly. Come on, Ira baby, he thought, stop playing with yourself. A little house in the Valley indeed! Stretch socks indeed! Why such halfway measures? Why not go whole hog? Why not move into a cave and live on roots and berries? Maybe he could trap an occasional muskrat for meat and fur. Maybe Polly could pick up a little cash money hustling in front of the post office on Saturday nights. Maybe the twins could sell their brains to the Scripps Institute of Oceanography.

You are *hooked,* Ira baby, he thought. Face the facts, he told himself, face the bitter undeniable facts. If he quit his job and went back

to directing, *what* would he direct? *The Virginian? McHale's Navy?*
Donna Reed? Is this how he would rebel against the system, by
grinding out the same sausages, only for less money?

As for quitting television to direct feature pictures, who wanted
him? As for returning to Broadway, who needed him?

No, Ira baby, he thought with a plummeting heart, you are stuck
in television, and if a man has to spend his life in the vast wasteland,
he might as well get top dollar for it. Sybaritism was not the issue;
it was a matter of plain logic.

"Miss Goldberg," said Ira to the intercom, "tell Clendennon I don't
want to talk to him."

"What are you crazy?" asked Miss Goldberg with authentic curiosity.

"Tell him," said Ira and switched off the box.

He leaned back in his executive chair. Yes, he thought approvingly, I did the right thing. But in something under one second, the
approval was replaced by a new blast of self-condemnation. Like hell
I did the right thing, Ira snarled at himself. I chickened, that's what
I did. For the umpteenth time, I chickened. I've got no character,
no principles, no values, no guts. I can't do one goddam thing right—
not at work, not at home. I've let my kids turn Cro-Magnon and my
wife grow peckish—all because I was too bloody busy to be a proper
father and husband. Busy doing what? Busy telling lies. I've butch-
ered whatever talent I ever had. I've sold my birthright for a mess of
Chasen's pottage. I am trussed, plucked, and packaged. I am *theirs*.
My life is a stench. Nothing I do is any damn good; nothing I ever
have done was any damn good—nothing, nothing, nothing.

Wait! thought Ira, sitting upright suddenly. Once upon a time, he
was remembering, something good had come his way—one indubi-
table good—the single, unquestionable, unerodable, untarnishable,
timeproof good of his entire life, and he had need to dwell on it now.

He threw the intercom switch. "Miss Goldberg, I don't want any
phone calls. I don't want anybody coming into the office—you especially. I am not to be disturbed, is that clear?"

"Well, pardon me for living!" huffed Miss Goldberg.

Ira closed the switch again. He rose and drew the blinds. He
locked the door. Then he sat down, pulled the desk lamp close for
better illumination. He took a wallet out of his inside breast pocket.
He found a flap in the wallet so cunningly hidden that only Ira and
the manufacturer knew its location. From this secret crevice he re-

moved a yellowing newspaper clipping. He spread the clipping on the desk, directly under the lamp.

The clipping showed a photograph of a tall, slender, handsome woman holding a bouquet of flowers and smiling directly into the camera. Under the photograph was a short caption: *"Mrs. Barbara Fuller—better known to her many friends as Boo—opens the annual Owens Mill Peony Festival."*

Ira looked at the picture. First he looked intently, closely. Then he looked lingeringly, sweetly. He looked and he was healed. His face was young. His eyes were bright with undead dreams.

Chapter 3

The Owenses of Owens Mill disembarked from their helicopter in the clearing before the hunting lodge, ran inside with many a laugh and cheer, and fell joyfully upon the food and spirits there arrayed. For three hours they ate and drank and gamed, and then the mood for singing seized them in its playful spell. Mrs. Barbara Ogilvie Owens, better known to her many friends as Boo, therefore moved to the piano to take her accustomed position as accompanist.

Boo moved gracefully; she sat erectly on the piano bench. The years had not sprung her fluent carriage nor thickened her willowy waist. Her breasts were high, her throat was smooth, her back was straight, her belly was flat, her legs were long, strong, and marvelously articulated. A whisper of gray in the tips of her ash-blond hair, a faint tracing of lines beside the patrician mouth, were time's only discernible testimony. Yet she looked her age. No man mistook her for twenty, or even thirty; but neither did any man fail to feel a pleasant itch upon regarding her.

As Boo arranged the sheet music, Virgil Tatum sat down beside her. "Would you like me to turn pages for you?" he asked.

"I don't believe so, thank you," she replied pleasantly.

"In that case, would you like to marry me?" said Virgil.

"Tell you what," said Boo. "You can turn pages."

"Ah, good! Then you're not angry at me?"

"For what?"

"For this unseemly haste, of course," he said. "I mean proposing marriage when your late husband has been gone scarcely eighteen years."

"On second thought, you can't turn pages," said Boo, shoving him hard with her lean, trim buttocks.

Virgil sat firm. "Boo, dear Boo," he said earnestly, "all these years without a man! What are you trying to prove?"

"Virgil, dear Virgil," she mocked. "What are *you* trying to prove?

How many times have I offered to take you to my beach house for a
mad weekend of sinful pleasure?"

"Very amusing," he said. "Come on, let's get back to marriage."

Boo laughed. "Oh, Virgil, you're too perfect. All you need is a but-
ternut uniform, a sash, and a sword. . . . Southern ladies, suh, are for
marryin', suh, not dallyin'. For *that* there's places in Memphis. . . .
Right, cousin?"

"All right, so I'm a little old-fashioned."

"Try *obsolete*."

"Well now, look who's talking! Come out from behind that Span-
ish moss, Miss Melanie, and answer me a question: this beach house
of yours—have you ever invited anyone who might really go?"

"Well—"

"Well, *no!* Next question: in the last eighteen years have you
ever once seriously considered a proposal of marriage? Never mind
mine. I mean all the others you've had."

"All right, Virgil, I'll admit it. I'm obsolete too."

"Maybe *extinct*," he said. "And it's got me worried."

"That's very kind of you, but I'll be just fine, thanks."

Virgil shook his head gravely. "I'm not so sure. I've been reading
this article on prolonged sexual continence. Do you know it's one
hundred percent fatal?"

"Oh, dear me!" exclaimed William Ransom Owens, first cousin to
Boo and third cousin to Virgil, who had just walked up behind them.

William Ransom was plump, smooth, pink, trusting, thirty-two
years old, and a virgin. Some uncharitable people said he was a
homosexual, but he was not. Perhaps he *would* have been, only he
had never heard of it. He stood now in a costume he had carefully
selected for this woodsy weekend of roughing it—a suede Lincoln-
green jacket that was almost a doublet, narrow Lincoln-green trou-
sers that were almost hose, and ankle-high, laceless Lincoln-green
boots of glove-soft leather. He had toyed with the idea of adding a
deep-throated blouse with ruffled pleats but abandoned the notion
out of an accurate fear that Uncle Jefferson Tatum would seize him
by the ruffles and flang him down the mountain.

William Ransom, like the other Owens men, was a kind of executive of the Tatum Cigarette Company. He had an imposing title, a
Bigelow on the floor, and a total lack of authority. William Ransom
was listed on the corporate roster as Director of Education and
Morale, which meant he chose the country-and-western music that
was piped through the factory by Muzak all day.

"You're just funning, aren't you, Cousin Virgil?" said William Ransom nervously. "I mean about the article you were discussing? About prolonged sexual continence will kill you?"

"Yes, William Ransom," Virgil assured him. "A little joke is all."

"Whew!" said William Ransom, vastly relieved. "Course, I'm not really worried. I mean I'll *surely* find a girl soon. . . . Won't I?" he added doubtfully.

"No question about it," Virgil answered firmly.

William Ransom beamed. "Cousin Boo," he said, "what say we sing some good old songs of the thirties?"

"By all means, Cousin William Ransom," she said. "But would you mind gathering the others? It's so much nicer when we start together."

"Why, sure, Cousin Boo," said William Ransom and scurried around the room and collected his various kinfolk, all of them officers of the Tatum Cigarette Company, all holding executive positions equal in responsibility to William Ransom's.

William Ransom next proceeded to round up guests who were not members of the family, for no more Owenses remained to be tapped. There *had* been one more Owens present, but only briefly. This was Gabriel Owens Fuller—Boo's boy—who had dropped everyone off at the lodge and then flown the helicopter back home to Owens Mill so he could finish work on a digital computer he was building. Aeronautics and physics held no riddles for eighteen-year-old Gabriel. Only the ultimate mystery baffled him: girls.

"Hurry, William Ransom," called Boo from the piano bench, for the singers had assembled and were clamoring for a downbeat.

"Yes, Cousin Boo," cried William Ransom and hastened to gather the remaining voices. He spied a grotesquely large neck hunched over the bar and laid a timid finger on it. "Mr. Meyers, sir," he said, essaying a tentative smile, "would you care to go over to the piano and sing?"

"Sing my ass," replied Nineteen Meyers, glowering so fiercely that William Ransom went almost Lincoln-green.

"Just thought I'd ask," stammered William Ransom and backed rapidly away.

Nineteen, muttering, returned to his bottle—no glass; just a bottle. He hated his weekends at the hunting lodge, and the fact is, everybody hated having him there. All the same, a deal was a deal, and Nineteen was not about to give up one single speck of one single thing that was coming to him.

Nineteen's contract clearly called for free board and room at the
Tatum hunting lodge on every weekend outside the football season.
It was the least of the benefits in Nineteen's agreement with Acanthus College. He had the huge marble house on campus, the one
with the stained-glass windows, rent-free and staffed with three Negro servants. He had an annual salary of $40,000 as head coach, plus
two new Cadillacs every year—a red sedan and a red convertible.

For all of this Jefferson Tatum footed the bill without complaint.
He was content with his coach. Year after year Nineteen disappeared into the canebrake and emerged with an awesome bag of
huge, infrangible, mouth-breathing young men who loved bodily
contact better than anything you could name. Sometimes Jefferson
suspected that Nineteen could not simply be *finding* such people; he
had to be *breeding* them in some secret place—a hollow mountain,
most likely. But Jefferson never inquired; all he cared to know was
that the Owens Mill Municipal Stadium was jammed with 55,000
ecstatic fans at each game. Jefferson was aware, as others in comparable positions have been aware before him, that to rule a city you
must provide circuses as well as bread.

"Gentlemen, gentlemen!" cried William Ransom, detecting the
final two guests skulking in the pantry. "Why, I do believe you're
hiding!"

They shuffled their feet guiltily, for hiding is precisely what they
had been doing. They were dressed in blue suits, vests, starched col-
lars, dark ties, and rimless glasses, and they had not come to the
lodge to make wassail. In fact, they were guests only in a manner of
speaking. Both were officers of the Tatum Cigarette Company, but
neither was an Owens, and consequently they were answerable
for their conduct. T. T. Wilcox, an accountant aged sixty-six years,
was vice-president of the firm, and Noah Fenster, a chemist aged
fifty-nine years, was Director of Research. Jefferson Tatum had summoned them this weekend—*summoned*, not invited—to justify the
company's last fiscal statement, and if there was one thing in the
world they did not feel like, it was singing.

But William Ransom would brook no objections. "Pishtush!" he
said blithely as they tried to tell him they could not carry a tune, and
besides they had laryngitis, and moreover they were tone deaf, and
in any case, the only song they knew was "Trees."

"I found the rascals, Cousin Boo!" crowed William Ransom as he
hauled them, kicking feebly, to the piano.

Boo smiled approval, ran an arpeggio, and the songs of the 1930's commenced.

First came "The Music Goes Round and Round" as a kind of flexer for the chorale. Next came "The Hut-Sut Song" in case the first flexer had not quite flexed everybody. Then, confident they were flexed, Boo trusted them with "Small Hotel" and "Funny Valentine." Then came "Isle of Capri," during which a nostalgic shimmer appeared behind T. T. Wilcox's spectacles and he actually hummed two and a half bars before he was silenced by a glare from Noah Fenster. Then Boo, shifting moods, swung into the rousing rhythms of "Strike Up the Band" and "Louisiana Hayride."

Then the bedroom door opened and Jefferson Tatum appeared and looked upon the revels as Charlton Heston had looked upon the children of Israel when he surprised them doing a hora around the Golden Calf.

"STOP THE MUSIC!" roared Jefferson in a voice so loud that William Ransom jumped squealing into the arms of Nineteen Meyers.

The other Owenses fell into a timorous silence, except for Boo. She was the only Owens not frightened of Jefferson. In fact, she was quite fond of the old pirate. Jefferson liked Boo too and would have been delighted to have her as a daughter-in-law. Failing that, he would have thoroughly enjoyed jumping on her elegant bones.

But he had no eyes for Boo as he advanced, dark as a thundercloud, into the room. "If you got to sing," he snarled at the huddled carolers, "how about 'Nearer My God to Thee'? That's customary, ain't it, when the ship is sinking?"

"What ship, Uncle Jefferson?" asked William Ransom.

"The Tatum Cigarette Company, that's what ship, you ninny!" shouted Jefferson. "We're going under like an anvil!"

Virgil concealed a grin. For a man facing a watery death, he thought, old Jefferson was sure a sound sleeper. He had napped through three hours of merrymaking just outside his door, not to speak of the landing and takeoff of a two-rotored helicopter. But Virgil discreetly kept his thoughts to himself.

"You've all read the last financial statement," Jefferson went on. "That so-called Surgeon General is ruining us, and you stand here and sing! Ain't nobody, for Chrisake, got no ideas?"

"I have, Uncle Jefferson," said Robert E. Lee Owens. Lee, at twenty-nine the youngest of the Owenses, was also the most serious. His title was Director of Public Image; what's more, he believed it.

He was all the time consulting motivational researchers, writing memos, drawing graphs, and carrying a briefcase.

"I have some ideas," said Lee, unzipping his briefcase.

"You have oatmeal for brains, is what you have," said Jefferson. He turned to T. T. Wilcox. "You—you're supposed to be the vice-president. What the hell have *you* been doing?"

"Everything I can, sir," said Mr. Wilcox, licking his dry lips. "We've dropped all our crime shows on television and switched entirely to wholesome family comedies. And, if I may say so, sir, it seems to be effective. Tatums are still the No. 1 cigarette in the country. . . . Of course I know sales were down last year, but *all* cigarettes fell off."

"And a good thing," rumbled Nineteen Meyers, looking up from his bottle. "Them lousy cigarettes play hell with your wind. Brother, I catch any of my athletes smoking, it's two hundred laps around the track!"

Jefferson clenched his hands tightly. If he did not need this cretin, he would have fired him long ago. But he did need him, so he squinched down his temper and forced a smile. "Nineteen, old buddy," he said winsomely, "how would you like to go outside and dig a few stumps?"

"Later maybe," said Nineteen. "I got some whisky to finish."

"You do that," said Jefferson. "It's good for you. Not like cigarettes."

"Sir," said Noah Fenster, Director of Research, "I'll be glad to dig some stumps."

"You stay right here," said Jefferson, grabbing Mr. Fenster by the necktie. "What the hell's been going on in that lab of yours? Where's the new filter you said you're developing, the one that's so all-fired effective?"

"Well, I *did* develop it, sir," answered Mr. Fenster, perspiring, "and it *is* remarkably effective. Trouble is, you can't get any smoke through it."

Jefferson released Mr. Fenster's necktie and heaved a long, racking sigh. "So we're licked, is that it? We just lay back and wait for the so-called Surgeon General to put us out of business."

"Uncle Jefferson," said Lee Owens, "I have made a survey of our problem—a study in depth, you might call it."

"Shut up," said Jefferson.

"I won't shut up!" declared Lee with a rush of determination. "You just listen to me, Uncle Jefferson. I have talked to dozens of experts in psychology and motivational research, and I have gathered all the findings of the Tobacco Industry Research Council, and you are going to listen to me!"

The Owenses looked up with trembling as Jefferson's color rose.

"Listen to him, Pa," said Virgil quietly.

The old man's color subsided. "All right, sonny," he said to Lee. "Go ahead."

Lee reached into his briefcase and removed a sheaf of papers. "First of all, let's take the work of the Tobacco Industry Research Council, to which we all belong. The Council, as you know, provides generous grants, with no strings attached, to any reputable, independent research organization, public or private, that wishes to make studies of smoking. So far we have spent eight million dollars through the Tobacco Industry Research Council, not to mention the ten-million-dollar grant we just gave the American Medical Association to make a four-year study of the effects of tobacco."

"By all means, sonny, let's don't mention the ten-million-dollar grant to the AMA," said Jefferson. "That's a simple horse-trade, like you'll find in any political back room in the country. I'm only guessing, of course, but it seems to me you don't need to be a genius to figure that one out. We hand the AMA ten million to play with for four years; what they get back is a pledge from all the tobacco state Senators and Congressmen to keep Medicare bottled up in committee for four years. Looks to me like an ordinary, everyday piece of logrolling. . . . No, sonny, forget AMA and get back to the deal with no strings—the eight million dollars we've handed the Tobacco Industry Research Council. What have we got to show for it?"

"I am glad you asked that question, Uncle Jefferson," said Lee, opening a folder. "I have here reports from nearly one hundred unimpeachable scientists which completely exonerate cigarettes."

"*Exonerate!*" shouted Jefferson. "*Unimpeachable!* Eight million dollars we give away, and for this we get *exonerate!*"

"But that's the word—exonerate. Nobody at Johns Hopkins or Sloan-Kettering or anywhere else has yet found a carcinogen in tobacco."

"*Carcinogen!*" mumbled Jefferson. "Dandy!"

"And here is the Berkson report," Lee continued, waving a paper. "Dr. Joseph Berkson, no less—the chief of biometry at Mayo Clinic!"

"Biometry," said Jefferson. "Very nice . . . Yes, sonny, let's talk about Dr. Berkson's report. Happens I know it real good. He said a *casual significance* had been *erroneously assigned* to a *statistical as-*

sociation. He said—and I quote—'*It is a notorious example of what Alfred North Whitehead has called the fallacy of misplaced concreteness.*' . . . Sonny, I got to admit it: there now is one hell of a battle cry!"

"But, sir—"

Jefferson, livid, was pacing back and forth, waving his arms wildly, and Virgil whispered to Boo, "Here comes the black hat."

"The *what?*" said Boo, mystified.

"Listen," whispered Virgil.

"For God's love!" cried Jefferson. "Why are we talking about Alfred North Whitehead when we ought to be out looking for a black hat?"

"Who ought to?" asked William Ransom Owens.

"We!" answered Jefferson. "The cigarette industry. We got to find a black hat."

"I see," said William Ransom, who did not.

"You all been to the cowboy movies," said Jefferson. "When the bad guy comes in, what's he got on his head? A *black hat!* You know right away he's the bad guy, and you're properly scared."

"Why, that's true!" exclaimed William Ransom. "Like in *Shane* and *High Noon* and like that."

"Thank you," said Jefferson with a tight smile at William Ransom. "A black hat means *bad,* means *dangerous,* means *death!* And that's what the so-called Surgeon General got going for him—a black hat: cigarettes. Coffin nails, gaspers—a black hat if ever there was one. Is it any wonder people are scared of cigarettes?"

"Damn well ought to be," muttered Nineteen Meyers. "Terrible for your wind."

But Jefferson was too wound up to notice. "A black hat!" he cried. "That's what we got to find. We're in a war to the finish with this so-called Surgeon General, and we ain't going to win it with ten-dollar words. That guy is trading in *fear,* and fear is something you can only fight with fear, not with Alfred North Whitehead. . . . Say, who the hell is he anyhow?"

"A famous Western badman," said Virgil.

"Oh, clever," said Jefferson balefully. "We'll have many a chuckle about that after the bankruptcy hearing."

"Uncle Jefferson," said Lee, "I quite understand what you mean by the black hat. There is no doubt that the Surgeon General has fear on his side. For instance, I have here a report—" he produced another folder— "which was done for me by a prominent motivational research organization. This report proves conclusively—now mark this well!—that 96 percent of all Americans associate cigarette smoking with *sin!*"

Jefferson accepted the intelligence calmly. "How much did this report cost you?" he asked. "I mean cost *me?*"

"Fifteen thousand dollars," answered Lee. "Or was it fifty thousand? I could look it up."

"Why, you twelve-thumbed idiot!" roared Jefferson. "I could have told you *for free* that people think cigarettes are the road to perdition. Ain't you never heard one of them Bible-thumpers? . . . Naw, I guess you're too young. . . . Well, I heard plenty of 'em—old-time bull-voiced hellfire-shouters. Cigarettes, they said, are the instruments of the devil. . . . And make no mistake, sonny, people believed it. Course they didn't stop smoking, no more than they stopped drinking or humping, but every time they took a puff, there was a little pinch of guilt—the same kind of sinful feeling they felt the first time they snuck a smoke behind the barn. Down deep in their gut they *knew* the Lord would call for a reckoning someday. . . . Well, sonny, this makes pretty easy pickings for the new breed of hellfire-shouters. Oh, it's a new breed, all right. They ain't Christ-bitten country boys this time, not backwoods bumpkins with hay in their hair. Now they're all nice, smooth-talking fellows with white smocks and medical degrees. And they ain't threatening damnation on that far-off Judgment Day. They got it for you right here and now. I mean lung cancer."

"I *do* wish you'd read my memos, Uncle Jefferson," said Lee with an edge of exasperation. "I covered all this months ago. We're up against a scare campaign; I know that. But the other side has all the scare techniques; we have none. So let's stop looking for a black hat. Let's instead try a brand-new approach to the smoking public—a campaign of *moderation.* Let's go part way with the Surgeon General's committee. Let's concede that too much smoking might hurt you."

"Never!" thundered Jefferson, the cords popping out on his neck. "Never!"

"For heaven's sake, Uncle Jefferson, too much *anything* might hurt you—apples, milk, even vitamins."

The old man opened his mouth to shout again, but suddenly he closed it. A flicker of interest danced over his eyes. He addressed Lee quietly: "What did you say, sonny?"

"I said too much *anything* might hurt you," Lee repeated.

"Apples?" asked Jefferson. "Milk? *Vitamins?*"

"Why, sure," said Lee.

Jefferson turned to Noah Fenster. "Fenster, you're a chemist. Is this true?"

"Well, not normally, of course," answered Mr. Fenster, "but in excessive amounts, I'd have to say yes."

"How come?" asked Jefferson. His voice was calm, but there was a mounting brightness in his eyes.

"In the case of apples," said Mr. Fenster, "they are generally sprayed with pesticide, which is a poison. Milk is a prime source of cholesterol and, in many areas, it also contains a heavy concentration of strontium-90. Even vitamins, in a massive overdose, have been known to kill people."

"Well, well," said Jefferson thoughtfully. "Go on, Fenster, tell me some more stuff that'll poison you."

"Practically anything, if you take too much of it."

"Water?"

"Yes, provided the fluorine level is above the permissible limit."

"Bread?"

"Possibly. It depends on the bleach and the emulsifiers."

"What's that?"

"Additives," explained Mr. Fenster. "Almost any food you eat today has a certain amount of chemicals added to it. To begin with, there's fertilizers to make it grow. Then there's pesticides to keep the bugs off. Then when the food gets processed, there's additives—coloring agents, flavoring agents, softeners, preservatives, things like that. They're all chemicals, and they're all poisonous if you go beyond the allowable levels."

"But don't the government keep a watch on all this?"

"Golly, Uncle Jefferson," said Lee impatiently, "what's all this talk about food? Let's get back to my plan."

"Shut up, you Arnold Benedict," said Jefferson. "Go ahead, Fenster. What about the government?"

"Yes," said Fenster, "FDA—that's the Food and Drug Administration—sets the permissible dose for all the chemicals that go into our food, but there's some who say FDA is much too lenient."

"*Who* says so?" asked Jefferson sharply.

"Well, of course, the health food addicts—"

Jefferson made a gesture of dismissal. "Scratch them. Bunch of nuts. Probably Communists too . . . What I want to know is does anybody *reliable* knock FDA."

"Oh, yes. Rather a large number of doctors, scientists, nutritionists, chemists. For example, a few years back a woman named Rachel Carson, a highly respected biologist, wrote a book called *Silent Spring* in which she claimed our food is loaded with deadly pesticides."

"People believe this book?"

"Quite a few, including the President's Science Advisory Committee."

"But nobody stopped eating, did they?"

Mr. Fenster began a little smile, thinking perhaps Jefferson was making a joke. But Jefferson's face was serious—in fact, *glazed*. He turned abruptly away from Mr. Fenster and walked to a chair in the corner of the room. Completely oblivious of his guests, he sat as though sculpted by Rodin, thinking silently, furiously, *passionately*.

Everyone watched with astonishment, but they stayed quiet, not daring to intrude on such monumental concentration. Their astonishment doubled when, after a moment, Virgil, who was seated on the piano bench with Boo, suddenly assumed precisely the same look and the same pose as old Jefferson.

Fully five minutes went by while the Tatums, father and son, were locked in their separate reveries. The only sound in the room was the steady, rhythmic glug of Jack Daniel's from the bottle to the glottis of Nineteen Meyers.

It was Boo who spoke first. "Virgil," she whispered, plucking at his sleeve, "what's going on?"

"Hush," said Virgil absently.

"I will not hush," said Boo. "What are you thinking about? What's Uncle Jefferson thinking about?"

Virgil emerged from his trance. He sat up straight on the piano bench. On his face there was a wide, happy grin. "What was it you asked?" he said to Boo.

"I asked what you and your father were thinking about."

"And I shall tell you," said Virgil, his grin widening. "My father is thinking that he might have found himself a black hat. . . . And me—" he laughed aloud, pulled Boo to him, and planted an exuberant kiss on her cheek—"me, I'm thinking I might have found one too!"

Chapter 4

Jefferson came out of his trance only a few seconds after Virgil did. His eyes swept the room, seeking his son. He found Virgil looking directly at him. The old man tilted his head toward the door of the lodge, indicating he wanted to see Virgil outside. Virgil nodded acknowledgment. "Excuse me, honey," he said to Boo. He kissed her again, loud and hard, and rose and joined his father in the clear air outdoors.

They did not speak. They sat down side by side on a big tree stump. They sat easily, calmly, like two riverboat gamblers each holding four of a kind.

"Boy," said Jefferson casually, "I got kind of an idea."

"About a black hat?" asked Virgil, just as casually.

Jefferson shot him a respectful look. "You ahead of me, boy?"

"Not ahead, Pa. Just *with* you. You're thinking food could be the black hat."

"Why not? It's all poison, ain't it?"

"Well, it *can* be."

"Damn right it can! You heard what my chemist said about all them scientists who claim our food is poison. But people don't seem to get worked up about it, and I'll tell you why: because food ain't like cigarettes. I mean food's got a good name. I mean you never heard of nobody sneaking behind the barn to have their first slice of bread, did you?"

"So you think you can give food a bad name."

"I *know* I can! I'll show that so-called Surgeon General a thing or two about scaring people! I'm going to *blast* food! I'm going to rip it to pieces! I'm going to do such a smear job on food that this country will end up thinking the safest thing you can put in your mouth is a cigarette!"

"But to make this anti-food crusade convincing," said Virgil, "you'll need some scientific backing—which is where I come in."

44

"Say, you are *with* me," said Jefferson admiringly.

"Right on top of you, Pa. I see it all now. You want me to take the chemistry department at Acanthus College and put them to work finding the poisons in food."

"Right!"

"Right. And then you'll get your high-pressure publicity boys to spread the word all over the country!"

"On the television, that's where I'll put it! Dab smack on the television where even the idiots who can't read will get the message!"

"Great!"

"Yeah! And people will get so nervous they won't just start smoking again, they'll start *chain*-smoking!"

"Brilliant idea, Pa. Too bad it won't work."

The elation oozed out of Jefferson's face. "Why not?"

"Two reasons: first, no network would carry such a program unless they had someone from the food industry to present *their* side of the argument. After all, the networks sell a hell of a lot more time to food companies than to cigarette makers."

"Boy, don't you think I know that? Sure, they'll have somebody on the program to take the defensive, and that suits me just perfect! I'd like somebody else on the defensive for a change. Me, I want to attack! Because that's what folks believe—the attack, not the defense!"

"Probably true," agreed Virgil. "But that doesn't begin to answer my second objection. You'll need scientific research to back up the charges you intend to make against food. Where's this research coming from?"

"Why, you said it yourself, boy: Acanthus College."

"And that's why you're stone-cold dead," said Virgil. "Acanthus College is without doubt the rectum of the academic world. Who is going to believe any scientific report coming out of a school with the lowest admission standards, the poorest scholarship level, the highest teacher incompetence, the oldest equipment, the smallest library, the thinnest curriculum, and the fewest textbooks in the United States of America?"

"That bad, huh?" said Jefferson morosely.

"Well, Harvard it's not."

"Hey!" cried Jefferson, brightening. "That's it! If them reports come out of Harvard, people will believe 'em. So why don't I give Harvard the money and start 'em working?"

"You can give Harvard money, Pa, but you can't tell them how to use it."

"Oh," said Jefferson. "Yale?"

Virgil shook his head. "No, Pa. Nor Princeton, nor M.I.T., nor Cal Tech. There's only one place you can run the show, and that's at Acanthus, and how are you going to get a legitimate scientist to come to Acanthus?"

"Boy, listen to me. I swear I ain't looking to pull a swindle. I don't want to disadvantage potatoes or beans or anything else. All I want is honest facts from honest men. Ain't there no possible way we can get some of 'em down to Acanthus?"

This was the question Virgil had been waiting for; this was the trap he was itching to spring. "Well, there might be, Pa," he said, managing to keep the eagerness out of his voice. His face, however, betrayed him.

The old man's sharp eyes narrowed suspiciously. "I don't like the look of you, boy," he said.

Virgil put on his most innocent stare. "Oh? What's wrong?"

"I don't know," said Jefferson, "but maybe you better give me a kiss because I think you're about to screw me."

Virgil abandoned deception. "All right, Pa, I do have a plot in mind, but it's for your good as well as mine."

"Let's hear."

"I can get you the chemists and nutritionists you want, if you'll do one simple thing: you must turn Acanthus into a decent, respectable, bona fide college."

"And how do I do that?"

"Well, first we've got to raise our College Board scores to the Ivy League level."

"Okay, I'll do it. I don't know what the hell it means, but I'll do it."

"Second, you have to clean out those fossils on the faculty and bring in a bunch of new men—big men, big names. This means raiding Harvard, Stanford, Chicago—places like that."

"You're saying I got to offer 'em more money, Okay, money I've got. What's next?"

"Wait a minute. I'm not through talking about the faculty. It takes more than a few chemists to make a top college. You need to go after the best men in the humanities too."

"What's that? Never mind, you got it. Go ahead."

"Also the best men in the arts, the social sciences, the languages, the classics, and so forth."

"Fine, fine. Proceed."

"I want a library that will compare with Widener."

"I'll buy you Widener. Next?"

"Desegregation."

Jefferson frowned. "Don't push your luck, boy."

"This is important, Pa. Most of the teachers we want have strong convictions on the subject. We'll need *real* desegregation, not the way you did it in Owens Mill—nine Negroes in the high school and twelve in the grammar school."

"All right. How many do you want in Acanthus?"

Virgil took a deep breath. "Five hundred," he said.

Jefferson was silent for a long moment. Then he said calmly, "Boy, I suppose you thought I'd yell and holler and carry on."

"Yes, sir," said Virgil truthfully.

"I'm surprised. Don't you know your old Pa? Are you forgetting I was the first man in the cigarette business to put black foremen in charge of white workers? Are you forgetting I desegregated all the buses, hotels, restaurants, and movie shows in Owens Mill without anybody ever asked me to?"

"That's true."

"And wasn't it just last month I got a plaque for racial tolerance from them Hebes at B'nai B'rith?"

"Yes, sir."

"And ain't it practically a dead certain cinch that the William Lloyd Garrison Foundation, which is the oldest and most respected race relations outfit in the country, is going to give their annual Community Relations Award to Owens Mill this year?"

"Yes, Pa," said Virgil. "Then I can have five hundred Negroes at Acanthus?"

"You can have fifty."

"All right," said Virgil promptly.

Jefferson gave him a puzzled look. "Ain't you going to argue?"

"No, sir. I was figuring I'd get twenty-five," replied Virgil.

"Damn," said the old man sadly. "To think of wasting a mind like yours in a college! Well, go on. What's next?"

Virgil swallowed. "You won't like this."

"I ain't liked a goddam thing so far. Let's have it."

Virgil swallowed again. "No more football."

Jefferson blinked. "You know, boy, for a minute there I thought you said no more football."

"No more football," Virgil repeated, mustering strength. "No more

Nineteen Meyers. As long as that big-necked baboon is around, Acanthus is going to be a joke. No self-respecting teacher—or student, for that matter—will come near the place. So make up your mind, Pa: you can have either a football team or a black hat."

Jefferson smiled mirthlessly. "You been waiting a long time for this moment, ain't you, Virgil?"

"I won't lie to you. Yes. But I'm telling you a plain fact: it's Nineteen or the black hat, one."

"Don't leave me no choice, does it?"

"I'm sorry, Pa."

"Like hell you are."

"Like hell I am," Virgil agreed.

"Okay," said Jefferson. "What else?"

"That's it."

"Well—" said Jefferson.

"Well?" said Virgil.

"Done," said Jefferson.

"Done," said Virgil and shook his father's hand.

Chapter 5

Polly Shapian hung up the telephone and turned to her sons, Ezra and Leo, who stood on the flagstone patio of the Bel Air house, each holding a surfboard. The boys were naked except for skintight, iridescent, latex swim trunks. Their bodies, mantled with rippling muscles, shone like burnished copper. The tips of their dark hair had been sun-washed to the color of maize. Their black eyes, fixed on Polly, were motionless with hope held in abeyance. Twin frowns creased their tiny brows.

"Your father says he can't take you to Long Beach," Polly reported.

They sighed and continued to stare at Polly, their eyes now quite empty of hope.

Polly looked at their sweet, silent, dumb, disappointed faces and felt the usual rush of guilt. "See here," she said defensively, "your father is a busy man. He's running a network, remember?"

"We know, Ma," said Ezra without rancor.

"It's okay," said Leo in the same tone.

Polly's guilt mounted. "And you know you can't have *my* car," she continued. "I have a million things to do today."

"It's okay, Ma," said Leo.

"Sure," said Ezra.

Their gaze was steady, obedient, and stricken, like two well-trained hounds who have been told they cannot come to the hunt.

"Oh, take my car!" cried Polly, utterly routed. "I'll get a cab or something. Take my car. Take it, take it!"

Big white smiles lighted the twins' faces.

"You're a great American," said Ezra.

"You're a hundred percent," said Leo.

They leaned over to kiss her, but she pulled away irritably. "Get going," she snapped. "And try very hard not to drop my car in the ocean, will you? And when you come home—*if* you come home—I want you to clean your room, understand?"

"Yes, Ma," they said and ran ecstatically from the patio.

Polly looked after their great, tawny, disappearing bodies, lit a cigarette, and proceeded to do some thinking. She did her thinking as she did everything else—*con brio*. She was a small, swift, graceful woman, never at rest. Her hands were dexterous and eloquent. Her legs—not long—were rounded, shapely, and utile: light when she danced, certain when she walked, strong and thrusting when she made love. Her hair was russet, healthy, glistening. Her skin was dark, not swarthy like Ira's, but black Celtic with an underlay of high color. Her face—mobile mouth, short nose, unterrified chin, clear brow, flashing blue eyes—could range from Giaconda serenity (rare) to spark-showing outrage (frequent).

Expression chased expression across her face as she smoked and paced and thought. Why had she given the twins her car? A clout in the chops is what they deserved after dropping their Austin-Healey in the drink last night, and after bringing home those sickening report cards the previous semester, and after all the other numberless, endless, reasonless displays of stupidity. Yet, instead of forty lashes, or even a thorough chewing-out, she had given them her car. Why?

A possible explanation occurred to her. She was remembering a lecture on child psychology she had heard some weeks ago at UCLA. (What with Ira seldom getting home from the office before ten P.M., Polly had had to choose between night courses at UCLA or taking a lover; the second had, upon consideration, seemed less entertaining.) The lecture Polly recalled had been delivered by a youngish man with tweeds, thick glasses, thin hair, and a pitying manner toward anyone who questioned his propositions. When children go wrong, he had said in a way that brooked no rebuttal, always blame the parents. Misbehavior in children is nothing more than unconscious wish-fulfillment in parents. Parents—on an unconscious level, of course—seduce children into acting out their own suppressed desires.

Well, maybe so, maybe so, thought Polly. Maybe she and Ira, who had both endured hard, poor childhoods, had unconsciously pushed the twins into becoming idlers and beach bums. There was surely evidence to support such a hypothesis: Polly and Ira had both grown up on the New York pavements, had both known the pinch of empty pockets, had both wanted their children to have it easier than they did, and, when Ira's fortunes improved, had both been proud to see their kids enjoying the same advantages as the neighbors' kids (the neighbors, in this case, being Gregory Peck, Bing Crosby, and Aristotle Onassis).

But no, thought Polly. Parental wish-fulfillment, if ever it were a factor, had stopped early. As soon as Polly had realized the twins were turning into a set of sun-baked slobs, she had tried with all her considerable resources to reverse the tide. And, in fairness, she had to admit that Ira had done his sporadic best too. Polly had supplied an intelligent amalgam of love and discipline; Ira had contributed Levantine outbursts and mouth-to-mouth kisses.

Nothing helped. The twins greeted all assaults with the same open, level-eyed, unastonished agreeableness. If they were asked for an apology, they would apologize. If they were required to swear to reform, they would so swear. If they were punished, they would make no protest. Slobs they remained—*good-natured* slobs, to be sure, but slobs.

With a quick wave of her hand, Polly dismissed parental wish-fulfillment. She had a simpler answer, the same answer that accounted not only for the twins' slobbery, but for Ira's misery and Polly's mopery: television.

Everything had been fine in the Shapian family until television intruded its big ugly eye. The boys had been averagely bright; Polly and Ira had enjoyed a felicitous union. Of course, they had had occasional spats. . . . No, make that *fights.* . . . Also change *occasional* to *regular.* . . . But the fights had been good, healthy, air-clearing fights about important topics—like Henry Wallace, or fruit-symbolism in *The Cherry Orchard.*

The Shapians had been very serious thinkers back in the early years of their marriage; in fact, they had been cerebrators of consequence even before. They first met in 1940. Ira was nineteen years old, and Polly—then Miss Polly McLeod—was sixteen, and the world needed saving. To this worthy end they pledged their youth and their brimming passions. They joined the Group Theatre.

Of course, they were not full-fledged members of the Group. They did not figure importantly in major productions, or exchange opinions with giants like Odets, Clurman, Strasberg, and Cheryl Crawford. Polly and Ira served a more lowly, more peripheral function. They painted scenery, rigged lights, rehearsed classroom scenes, did improvisations in mime, worked as grips, prompters, ushers, and, occasionally, walk-ons.

But they were not kept forever on the edges. When the Group held general meetings, Polly and Ira were privileged to attend and

to listen, fascinated, as the giants held forth on topics like Stanislav-
sky, Ibsen, Adam Smith, Prester John, the Missouri Compromise,
and Newton's Third Law—all of which, in the minds of the giants
(and in the minds of Polly and Ira too), were clearly interrelated.

And, in addition to their long, stimulating days at the Group,
Polly and Ira were frequently detailed to go out and distribute leaf-
lets or march with pickets or hiss at rallies of the German-American
Bund.

Perhaps the most gratifying of all were the postmidnight sessions
at Riker's Cafeteria. Here the hot-eyed Groupniks would gather by
the dozen and sit the whole night through discussing life, art, politics,
science, metaphysics, beauty, and truth, their fervor unflagging,
their cigarettes burning so low that a toothpick was needed to hold
the butt, their single cups of coffee developing a cold, viscous scum.

These were busy, challenging days for Polly and Ira, but, nonetheless, love crept in. One spring day in 1941, about six months after
they had met, Ira turned to Polly as they were marching with a striking cloakmakers' local and said, "Listen, I think I love you."

"Me too," said Polly.

"All right," said Ira briskly. "We'll activate our impulses when we
get time. Right now there's work to do. Right?"

"Right!" said Polly.

They exchanged a fast handshake and resumed chanting, "Down
with the bosses!"

The activation of their impulses was not quickly accomplished.
As soon as the cloakmakers' strike ended (won by the bosses) Ira
got his first chance to direct. It was only a small classroom exercise,
a scene from *Othello*, but it was Ira's maiden effort and he shook like
an aspen.

His trembling accelerated when he learned which three actors
had been assigned to him for the scene. There was Polly, there was
a man named Eric Lindstrom from Minnesota, and there was a man
named Linus Calloway from Georgia.

He loved Polly and had a lover's normal nervousness about directing his beloved, but she was the least of his problems. She would,
of course, play Desdemona. But casting the other two parts, Othello
and Iago, gave Ira fits of anguished vacillation. The dilemma was
that Lindstrom was a thin, pale, frail, blond Swede, whereas Linus
Calloway was a big, deep-chested, woolly-cropped Negro.

How could Ira, a certified left-liberal equalitarian, cast a Negro as Othello? Wasn't it a bit *de trop?* Wasn't it too obviously white-massa?

And yet, what kind of theatrical sense did it make to blacken pallid, piping Lindstrom and whiten booming, black Linus? How would the giants of the Group feel if they saw such a gaffe? But, on the other hand, how would they feel if they saw Ira exploiting—that was the word: *exploiting*—a Negro?

Ira agonized and came to a decision: civil liberties superseded art. "Linus," he said as rehearsal drew near, "I've been thinking."

"I know what you've been thinking," Linus interrupted with a smile. He was a handsome man, imposing, bass-voiced, easy in his bearing, quick to smile. "I know exactly what you've been thinking," he said. "Forget it."

"But—"

"Ira," said Linus gently, "you're directing a scene from Shakespeare, not organizing a lynch mob. Do it right. That means me as Othello and Lindstrom as Iago."

"I can't!" cried Ira.

"Why not? Were you thinking of having Othello enter eating a watermelon? Do it *right,* Ira. They'll all be watching. This could mean something to you."

"Do you think," asked Ira hotly, "that I would advance my career at the cost of exploiting a fellow human being?"

"Tell you what," said Linus. "Send a dollar to the NAACP, but do this scene the way it needs to be done. Now can I please go tell Lindstrom he doesn't have to play the Moor, because he's out in the wings peeing in his pants."

Linus laughed then, a big, booming, infectious laugh, and he held Ira in a bear-hug until Ira was laughing too. The scene was performed with Linus as Othello, and later some restrained but definitely flattering words were murmured to Ira by the paladins of the Group, and Ira took Polly and Linus to Riker's to celebrate.

So festive was Ira that he ordered pound cake with the coffee. "To you, Linus," said Ira, raising his cake like a goblet of champagne. "You did me one hell of a favor."

"That I did," admitted Linus without immodesty. "And I'll tell you why: because you're a bleeder, and that's good. You never send to find for whom the bell tolls. . . . Nor you either, Polly," he added, turning to her.

"Thank you," she said. Then she said earnestly, "I appreciate what you did for Ira. I think you're a fine, decent person, and I'm proud to be your friend."

"Not so fast," cautioned Linus. "We're not friends yet, good Caucasian lady. I'd like to be your friend—yours too, Ira—but there's a question that has to be answered first. I mean answered by me, not you. Trouble is, neither of you will ever ever be able to ask it."

"What's that?" said Ira.

"You want to know what it feels like to be black," replied Linus.

"Well—" said Ira and Polly, exchanging a guilty glance.

"Let me try to tell you," Linus continued. "It's bad mostly. It's a kick in the belly mostly. But there's part of it that's awful good. It's like when you were a kid and you had a secret nobody else had. Maybe the secret was measles, but it was *yours*. Do you understand?"

"Yes," said Polly.

"No, you don't," said Linus. "You don't understand at all. But try to understand this: I don't need or want or appreciate pity. If you feel like putting your little pink hand in my big black one, well, I'd like that. But don't pull away, sweet child. Once you put it there, you must go where I go, and it could just possibly be to the barricades."

Polly held out her hand without pause or reservation. Linus hesitated a brief moment, then took it. Ira reached over and closed his hand on both of theirs.

"Kind of misty, ain't it?" said Linus. Then he threw back his head and laughed deeply. "Yes, I *do* like you palefaces," he said. "Let's hope none of us ever has to stand up and be counted."

"I know which side I'll be on," declared Ira.

"And I!" added Polly stoutly.

"I believe you," said Linus truthfully. "But let's hope the day never comes. Let's all hope real hard, because I don't want to be there either."

From then on, Polly and Ira went nightly to Riker's with Linus. He was a good talker, wry, funny, and authentically erudite (B.A., Fisk—M.A. and Ph.D., Columbia). He was in the Group not because he was stage-struck—in fact, he thought show business was largely ridiculous—but because he was investigating the theater as an instrument of propaganda. The betterment of race relations was the goal and fixation of Linus' life, and he proposed to explore every possible means.

Pearl Harbor put an end to the seminars at Riker's. Linus went immediately to enlist. He tried first to join as a line soldier, but when he learned he would have to serve in a segregated outfit, he signed on instead as a mess boy in the Navy. "If Uncle Sam says I'm second-class, well, goddam it, I'll *be* second-class," he explained to Polly and Ira, laughing loudly but without mirth.

Ira, too, rushed to his nearest recruiting office, for he yearned mightily to do battle with the forces of reaction. "Polly," he said after he had filled out his Air Force enlistment papers, "I think maybe we should get married right now. . . . Who knows," he added with a kind of twisty Ronald Colman smile, "if I'll be coming back?"

"Oh, my darling!" cried Polly, clutching him.

Polly's father's consent was reluctantly given. Her father, a member of the New York City Police Department, disapproved thoroughly of Ira (as a matter of fact, Polly gave him kind of a pain too), but as a veteran of the Fighting 69th, he could hardly say no to a young man on his way to fight the Hun.

There were very few Huns and no Japs at all where Ira was stationed after his induction. He was sent South to an Air Force base in the town of Owens Mill.

Polly joined him there, which might have been pretty dismal for a girl born and bred in New York, except that she found three powerful antidotes to boredom: first, she had Ira, who was then a fiery young buck; second, she made friends with two attractive people—a young woman named Barbara Ogilvie Owens and a young man named Virgil Tatum; and third, she got pregnant, which women love to do.

Not trusting the local doctor, who doubled as a veterinarian, to preside over her confinement, Polly went back to New York to give birth to Ezra and Leo. By then the war was in its final months, so she never returned to Owens Mill. Instead, she rented a flat on Mac-Dougal Street and waited for Ira to be demobilized.

Ira sought work as a director when he returned to New York in early 1946. Being the avant-gardist he was, he encountered a knotty problem: Off-Broadway had not yet started, so he was forced to stage Off-Broadway type plays on Broadway. He enjoyed a succession of resounding flops, and each night he came home screaming like a wounded thing. Polly screamed right back, but only because Ira required it. She knew that in his heart he was not unhappy for his reach was exceeding his grasp.

The fluke invitation to join M-G-M was as disastrous for Polly as for Ira. They sat in Hollywood for six months and screamed for

real. Then Ira went into television, and the bluebird of happiness
came flying back.

Ira, as a director, had the guts of a steeplejack. He would try
anything—Sophocles, Robinson Jeffers, Cardinal Newman, documen-
taries on whores and junkies—and television, still too young to know
fear, let him.

But Ira's halcyon days, and therefore Polly's, were numbered. He
had been marked as a man who could *nice,* and his seduction was
accomplished in short order.

Polly was honest. *Her* seduction, she admitted, was accomplished
at the same time. While the paunchy, plausible executives bamboozled Ira, their smooth, lacquered wives worked on Polly. First they
disarmed her by telling her they were smooth and lacquered and
they hated it. Then they extended invitations to her, not invitations
to canasta or long lunches at Scandia, but invitations to serve on
committees for the symphony and the hospital and the fair treat-
ment of Mexicans by the Los Angeles police force.

They did their work well, and Polly was properly snowed—not
for very long, of course, but long enough to take her eye off Ezra and
Leo while they slipped, irretrievably, into the soft, shiftless life of
the California rich.

Yes, thought Polly, pacing her flagstone patio in Bel Air, it was
television that did it. No need to get fancy about parental wish-fulfillment. It was just plain old television that turned her kids into oafs,
her husband into a sponge, and herself into a hatchet.

For years she had wanted out, *desperately* wanted out. But how?
Ira was mired, and all her piety and wit could not budge him.

She dialed a Yellow Cab to take her on her errands. God is love
there is no death, she repeated rapidly to herself as she spun the dial.
Look at the bright side. Things could be worse. The twins could
have become juvenile delinquents instead of lovable dunces; Ira
could have gone into daring daylight robberies instead of television;
and herself—

Polly paused. What worse could have happened to her? She concentrated fiercely, but nothing came to mind.

Chapter 6

Making a first-rate college out of Acanthus was a task roughly comparable with turning Tia Juana into the Acropolis, or the Three Stooges into Learned Hand. Yet Jefferson Tatum and Virgil Tatum accomplished the metamorphosis in the incredibly short period of six months. They embarked on the project in March; they were finished in time for the fall semester.

They divided the work of transforming Acanthus into two parts: Jefferson rang out the old; Virgil brought in the new.

Jefferson's chore was, in the main, easier. To get rid of the incumbent student body, a simple literacy test was sufficient. To shuck the resident faculty, all elders of the Don't-Fiddle-With-The-Gospel Brotherhood, Jefferson offered these alternatives: either they could sail on a three-year mission to the Jivaros, or else they could retire on full pensions. All chose the pensions, save for one, who declined both offers and went into the aluminum siding game.

One task remained—firing Nineteen Meyers—and Jefferson approached the moment with trepidation. He was convinced that Nineteen, as a free agent, would be instantly grabbed by Wake Forest or Duke, and the thought of his coach carrying the colors of R. J. Reynolds or American Tobacco filled the old man with profound melancholy.

But Jefferson was wrong. Nineteen sighed mightily when he was dismissed and wiped his eyes and blew his nose on his sleeve, and then he said, "Well, Mr. Tatum, I guess that's the end of me as a coach."

"Nonsense, Nineteen," Jefferson protested. "Plenty of places be glad to have you."

"Naw, it wouldn't be the same," said Nineteen, shaking his head sadly. "Way the college business is going these days, wherever I went I'd be hind tit to a bunch of deans. What's the use kidding?

I'd never find a touch like I had here. Acanthus, God bless it, is—
was—the last of the football schools."

"What will you do, then?"

"I don't know," said Nineteen, scratching his tree-sized neck. "Politics maybe. Lots of folks around here like me, don't they?"

"Almost nobody," said Jefferson gently. "It's best that you know."

"Oh," said Nineteen. He lapsed into silence, furrowing his minus-
cule forehead with concentration.

"Listen," said Jefferson. "You must have gone to school at one
time. You didn't, by chance, learn some kind of a trade?"

"By God, I did!" cried Nineteen, his face lighting up like a sun-
burst. "Clean forgot about it. I've got a diploma in dentistry!"

"Why, that's real nice, Nineteen. I'll set up an office for you right
away."

"Gee, I better not," said Nineteen doubtfully. "I ain't what you'd
call real good at it."

"Who'll know?" asked Jefferson.

"Yeah, that's right," said Nineteen upon reflection, and within
weeks he was conducting a decently lucrative practice.

While Jefferson was cleaning the deadwood from Acanthus, Virgil
packed his bags and crisscrossed the nation, seeking the eminent
professors of nutrition and food chemistry who were needed to prove
that anything you eat will kill you, plus distinguished teachers in
the arts, the humanities, and the social and natural sciences who
were needed to make Acanthus a top-caliber college.

Virgil's excursions failed more often than they succeeded, but he
persevered, and by midsummer he managed to bag 135 teachers,
every one of them with impeccable credentials. It was a faculty that
would have done honor to Harvard, Yale, M.I.T., or Stanford—which,
in fact, is where Virgil stole most of them.

Stealing was not Virgil's line of work, but, as he kept telling his
rumbling conscience, how else could he get a good teacher to come
to Acanthus? Someday, he assured himself, eminent academicians
would *beg* for appointments to Acanthus—would *trample* each other.
But for now—conscience, be still!—robbery was the only answer.

So he snuck from campus to campus with a three-pronged bur-
glar's tool: first, of course, money—salaries not even dreamed of in
the collegiate world; second, contracts insuring lifetime tenure; third
—and most alluring to his quarry—binding, ironclad, loophole-proof
guarantees of academic freedom.

Having snared a faculty of 135 luminaries, Virgil then proceeded to gather a student body worthy of sitting at such illustrious feet. Toward this end, he scattered full scholarships like autumn leaves, and in short order he enrolled twelve hundred undergraduates with straight "A" averages and glasses.

On the evening of the second Wednesday in September, just one day before the fall semester officially began, the new members of the Acanthus faculty were invited to the common room for an informal get-together co-hosted by the president of the college, Virgil Tatum, and the chairman of the board of trustees, Jefferson Tatum.

The common room was beamed and paneled in oak. At each end was a massive refectory table on which long-stemmed glasses and crystal decanters of sherry were arrayed. A generous scattering of leather couches and chairs provided seating. The end tables were numerous, sturdy, and stacked with learned journals.

One hundred and thirty-five teachers were present in the common room, eddying sluggishly as people do in the opening minutes of a party. Against the wall stood the co-hosts, Virgil and Jefferson, together surveying the assemblage. Virgil's face was filled with pride, Jefferson's with open apprehension.

"What's the matter, Pa?" asked Virgil. "Nervous?"

"Me? What for?"

"Well, meeting all these strange people for the first time—"

"There now, boy, you have spoke the truth," said Jefferson. "*Strange* is just what them people are. Never saw the like. Where *did* you find such a mess of loony-birds?"

"It wasn't easy," said Virgil.

"Couldn't have been."

"Hush," said Virgil. "Here comes the first."

Approaching was a tweedy apparition named Professor Joel Kane, a milky-pale, unshorn man who, though not yet thirty years old, knew more about Wordsworth's sister Dorothy than Wordsworth had known himself. "Evening, Prexy," said Kane.

"Evening, Kane," said Virgil. "I'd like you to meet my father."

"How do," said Jefferson and grasped the professor's hand.

Two tears popped into Kane's eyes and rolled slowly down his cheeks. "How do you do," he whimpered.

"Help yourself to sherry, Kane," said Virgil.

Kane bit his lip, nodded gratefully, and scurried away.

"What the hell?" said Jefferson, dumfounded.

"Pa," said Virgil, "this is not an Elks convention. Watch those manly handshakes."

"Maybe I ought to curtsy," said Jefferson.

"Evening, Prexy," said a newcomer, a round, pink, elderly, bald, twinkly man with suede patches on his elbows.

"Evening," said Virgil. "Pa, I'd like you to meet Professor Linden-Evarts."

Jefferson took the professor's hand, gave it a delicate press, returned it carefully, and said, "How do, Mr. Evarts."

"That's Linden-Evarts," said Linden-Evarts. "With a hyphen."

"Fine," said Jefferson.

"You might say," continued Linden-Evarts with a merry chuckle, "that almost everything about me is hyphenated. Some call me a sociologist-historian. Others say that I am an anthropologist-economist. Still others contend that I am a psychologist-archaeologist. And no doubt you have heard Irving Howe's epigram describing me as a medievalist-modernist. . . . Rather a better phrasemaker than a critic, don't you think?"

"Who?" said Jefferson.

"Howe," said Linden-Evarts.

"Oh," said Jefferson.

"Robert Penn Warren called me a philosopher-photographer," said Linden-Evarts. "In his cups, of course. Meant no harm. Decent sort, Warren. Quite often *too* decent. I refer to the Ezra Pound business naturally."

"Virgil," said Jefferson, perspiring lightly, "fetch me a glass of that sherry wine."

"Yes, Pa," said Virgil, concealing a smile as he left.

"Still," Linden-Evarts went on, "he was not too wide of the mark."

"Howe?" said Jefferson.

"Warren," said Linden-Evarts.

"Oh," said Jefferson, looking rapidly around to see whether he could not find a more likely partner for conversation, specifically one of the food and nutrition experts Virgil had hired. But he could discover no way to distinguish them from their colleagues. He frowned in bewilderment. One hundred and thirty-five teachers were gathered in the room, teachers of all sizes, shapes, and sexes, yet, to Jefferson's eye, there was an indefinable sameness about all of them. Tall or short, thin or fat, bald or hairy, silent or garrulous, aloof or forward—they somehow seemed to be cut all from the same bolt.

Wouldn't you think, thought Jefferson, that food chemists would just naturally look different from poetry teachers? Yet they did not. The mark of Academe was mysteriously on all of them.

Jefferson did not understand it, and what Jefferson did not understand, Jefferson did not like. A vague uneasiness gripped him, a sudden feeling that maybe this whole project had been a mistake. It had all sounded so foolproof when first he and Virgil began, but now as he looked upon this flock of loony-birds, he was not sure at all, not the least little bit sure.

"But a fig to them all!" cried Linden-Evarts, breaking into Jefferson's reverie. "Let them call me historian or anthropologist or sociologist or just plain Nosy Parker! I am all of those, and more. What I want is to *know!* So I look. I listen. I poke. I pry. I prod. I burrow. . . . And that, Tatum, is why I am most awfully glad to meet you."

"Likewise, I'm sure," said Jefferson politely.

"Did you, by chance, read my latest monograph, *The Nostalgia for Feudalism?*"

"Durn!" said Jefferson. "Must have missed it somehow."

"Pity," said Linden-Evarts. "Well, no matter. We'll just start at the beginning. Tatum, why do you think I accepted this post at Acanthus?"

"Money?" ventured Jefferson.

"Perfect! Perfect!" exclaimed the professor, clapping his hands together. "How precisely in character! Bless you, Tatum, you are a living fossil!"

"Come to that, you ain't exactly a beauty winner yourself," said Jefferson with a chilly smile.

"Sorry, Tatum," said Linden-Evarts placatingly. "We'll start again. I recently published, as I said, a monograph called *The Nostalgia for Feudalism*. Well, of course, the left-liberals were up in arms before you could say 'knife'! Oh, what did they not call me! Reactionary! John Bircher! Fascist! Me, mind you, who still carries a picture of Adlai Stevenson in his billfold!"

"Hmmm," said Jefferson darkly.

"But a fig, I say. I shall answer my critics, for I am right. There is among us a most definite nostalgia for feudalism—yes, here in America in the second half of the twentieth century. Nor is it so difficult to understand. When in all history, I ask you, were things better ordered than during the age of feudalism? There was one unchallenged, preordained leader, and all the rest were followers. Each man gave obeisance and received, in return, his pallet, his hut, and his pittance. He saw no horizons and hence did not aspire. Having no ambition, he suffered no frustration. A closed, complete, congruous, consonant world . . . Not, of course, my own cup of tea, but not nearly so dismal as some would have it."

"So how come folks got rid of it?" asked Jefferson.

"Ah, but they did not—not entirely. It still exists, sometimes perfectly intact, and that, Tatum, is why I have come to Acanthus."

"I don't get your meaning."

"Isn't it obvious? Here is where I will gather material for my next paper, because this town of yours, this Owens Mill, is an almost classic fief, and you, my dear fellow, are an almost flawlessly prototypical lord of the manor!"

"Now, just a durn minute," said Jefferson, reddening. "This here is a town of free-born people who can live how they like, work where they please, vote for who they want to, come or go, stay or leave— and not one of 'em beholden to me for nothing."

"It's no such thing, you rogue, and you know it," chuckled Linden-Evarts, nudging Jefferson playfully in the ribs. "But the question is," he continued, turning serious, "how do you manage it? How—in such an unlikely place? The barons of the thirteenth and fourteenth centuries were, after all, imposing serfdom on basically homogeneous units of population. But you, Tatum, have successfully made vassals not only of the indigenous stock, but also of a group which is both numerically significant and ethnically quite alien. I refer, of course, to the Negroes of Owens Mill."

"What the hell are you talking about?" Jefferson demanded hotly. "For your information, it just so happens that it's practically a dead certain cinch the William Lloyd Garrison Foundation is going to give the Community Relations Award to Owens Mill this year."

"I shouldn't count on it," giggled Linden-Evarts merrily. "It also just so happens that I am chairman of the board of trustees of the Garrison Foundation." Then, turning serious again: "But back to my question, Tatum. How do you get your Negroes to accept vassalage with such docility?"

"Now, see here," rumbled Jefferson, his color deepening.

"It's all right, it's all right," said Linden-Evarts, patting Jefferson's arm. "I didn't really expect you to give away your secrets. It's a puzzle I have to solve for myself, and, by Jove, I shall! I am going to dig, dig, dig, and dig some more until I find the answer!"

"What you are going to do, you little pissant," said Jefferson ominously, "is take your picture of Adlai Stevenson and scoot right back where you came from."

An urgent tugging at his sleeve turned Jefferson around. "Pa," said Virgil, "here's your sherry."

"Don't want it!" snapped Jefferson and started to wheel back on Linden-Evarts.

Virgil held. "And this, Pa," he said, indicating a large, erect, steady-eyed, handsome, gray-haired lady of fifty years who stood at his side, "is Dr. Clara Silenko."

Jefferson nodded and tried once more to turn away. Virgil's grip tightened. "Dr. Silenko is head of our new department of nutrition and public health," he said pointedly.

Jefferson paused, untensed, made a smile. "How do, Doctor," he said, offering his hand.

She gave it one firm pump. "Evening, Tatum," she said. She spoke in level, clipped tones, her eyes meeting Jefferson's dead-on. "Prexy here tells me you're interested in food adulterants."

"More than anything in the world," said Jefferson. "Shall we set?" He took her elbow gallantly and steered her to an empty sofa.

"Food adulterants," mused Dr. Silenko. "Strange thing for a cigarette maker to be concerned about. I mean you're not exactly peddling health yourself, are you?"

"Never said I was," said Jefferson, looking appraisingly at her handsome, intelligent features. No fool, it was obvious. Some careful footwork would be needed here.

"Never said I was peddling health," he repeated. "All I'm peddling is cigarettes to people who enjoy smoking. Can't do 'em no good I can think of. On the other hand, can't do 'em no particular harm either."

"Oh?" said Dr. Silenko. "Are you aware, Tatum, that I was a member of the Surgeon General's Panel on Smoking?"

"Yes, ma'am, I know that," said Jefferson. "Happens you was dead wrong in your report, but that's got nothing to do with the business at hand. You're at Acanthus to study food, not cigarettes."

"True," she said. "And that brings me to my next question: the big money you're paying me—the fine staff you've gathered—the beautiful labs—the marvelous equipment—what's in it for you?"

"That don't rightly concern you, if you'll excuse me, missy," replied Jefferson courteously. "As I understand it, you've been warning people for years that they're pouring poison down their gullet by the cubic ton. Now I've given you the wherewithal to prove it. While you're proving it, if some benefits should fall my way—I ain't saying they will, mind you—but if they do, why should it matter to you?"

"Fair enough," nodded Dr. Silenko.

"You *can* prove it?" asked Jefferson sharply. "I mean about all the poisons in our food?"

"With these facilities, this staff, these funds, no doubt whatsoever," she said with perfect positiveness.

"Good, good!" said Jefferson, rubbing his hands gleefully. "Mind telling me how you're going to start out?"

"Glad to. I've divided the staff into five teams. One will research permissible doses."

"And what might that be?"

"The Food and Drug Administration—FDA—allows food processors to dose their products with more than four hundred different chemical additives—things that make bread soft or butter yellow or corn flakes crisp or milk smooth, emulsifiers, preservatives, coloring agents, things like that. Every last one of these four hundred chemicals is, in itself, a deadly poison. Moreover, according to the Public Health Service, also an agency of the federal government, one-quarter of the additives can definitely cause cancer. But FDA maintains that if the additives are used in permissible doses, they are absolutely harmless."

"Well, well," said Jefferson, eyes shining. "And how does FDA arrive at this permissible dose?"

"With the LD-50 test," replied Dr. Silenko. "*L* stands for *lethal,* *D* stands for *dose,* and *50* means 50 percent. Each chemical is added to food in doses of varying strength and then tested on different groups of laboratory rats. When the technician finds a dose that will kill only one-half of the group of rats being tested, it is then certified by FDA as a permissible dose for humans."

"But people ain't rats!" said Jefferson indignantly.

"No. Nor rabbits, nor hamsters, nor dogs. Each organism has its own system of tolerance for poisons. And, even assuming that FDA's permissible dose is safe for one human meal or two or ten or fifty or a hundred, who knows what the *cumulative* effect may be over a period of years?"

"*Murderers!*" whispered Jefferson. "Good Lord, that FDA ain't nothing but a nest of murderers!"

"Gently, gently," soothed Dr. Silenko. "The researchers of FDA are all highly trained scientists—all honorable men who believe implicitly in what they are doing. . . . Of course, it *is* true that FDA is woefully understaffed—and their budget isn't a *tenth* of what it ought to be—and they don't attract any of the really *bright* young college graduates—and their equipment *is* obsolescent—and they *are* under constant pressure from the lobbyists of the food industry who swarm all over Washington—but, all the same, I would hardly call the FDA *murderers.*"

"Manslaughterers?" said Jefferson hopefully.

"Oh, no."

"Will you settle for pee-poor guardians of the public gut?"

"*That* I'll accept."

"Fine. Now, about these additives—would you say they get squirted into very many kinds of food?"

"I would say they get squirted into *every* kind of food."

"No kidding?" said Jefferson, grinning hugely.

"Let's take, for example, what you had for lunch today. Can you remember?"

"Ought to remember," he answered. "Been having the same thing every day for fifty years: one bourbon old-fashioned, one roast beef sandwich, one tossed salad, one glass of milk."

"All right," said Dr. Silenko. "We'll take a quick look. Your bourbon old-fashioned contained, in addition to the alcohol, an antifoaming agent called dimethyl polysiloxane; an orange slice sprayed with pesticides and dyed with coal tar; sodium o-phenylphenate and ammonia—both preservatives; and a maraschino cherry preserved with sodium benzoate, bleached with sulphur dioxide, and then reddened with coal tar.

"The roast beef contained DDT, chlordane, heptachlor, aldrin, and probably several other pesticides that the steer accumulated while he was grazing. It had, besides, one or two female hormones with which the animal had been injected, a residue of aureomycin from the cattle feed, and a film of mineral oil from the wrapping paper.

"The bread contained a dough conditioner called ammonium chloride; softeners called diglyceride and polyoxyethelene; an antioxidant called ditertiary-Butyl-para-Cresol; artificial vitamins to replace the nutrients lost in milling; and, of course, a wide assortment of pesticides.

"The butter contained nordihydroguaiaretic acid, which is an antioxidant; magnesium oxide, which is a neutralizer; AB and OB Yellow, both coal tar dyes; and diacetyl, which inhibits stinking."

"Do tell!" exclaimed Jefferson happily.

"And, in addition, the butter had a heavy concentration of pesticides. And, naturally, the milk did too."

"How about the salad?" asked Jefferson hopefully.

"*Crawling* with pesticides."

"Good, good!"

"Also in the salad, there was sodium alginate, which is a stabilizer; monoisopropyl citrate to prevent fat deterioration in the dressing; and—shall I go on?"

"No, that's fine. I got the picture." He regarded her with admiration. "You know something? You're an awful smart lady. Pretty too. Not young, of course, but still tolerable good to look at."

"Thank you . . . The first team, as I said, will research permissible doses. The second team—"

"What are you doing tomorrow night?" interrupted Jefferson.

"Dissecting a monkey," said Dr. Silenko.

"I see," said Jefferson. "The second team?"

"The second team will investigate hormones. More and more livestock and poultry are being fattened for market with injections of female hormones—stilbestrol and other estrogens. And in recent years, even fruits and vegetables have been widely dosed with growth hormones derived from plant life—the gibberelins. The object, of course, is to add bulk and therefore increase the price."

"Scandalous!" said Jefferson happily.

"More than you know," said Dr. Silenko. "The endocrine balance in the human body is extremely delicate. This indiscriminate use of hormones may have significant, perhaps *disastrous*, consequences. It's not inconceivable, for instance, that we could turn into a nation of oversexed women and impotent men."

"A bad arrangement," said Jefferson solemnly. "*Very* bad."

"Very," agreed Dr. Silenko.

"Look," said Jefferson, "tomorrow night you're dissecting a monkey. What are you doing the night after?"

"Grinding his kidneys," said Dr. Silenko.

"Oh," said Jefferson. "Please continue."

"My third team," said the doctor, "will investigate pesticides. Of course, the late Rachel Carson did a brilliant job in this field, and for a time her book had a very real effect. But there has, I fear, been considerable backsliding. The pesticide makers are pretty determined fellows, and the farmers, quite understandably, prefer spraying to weeding. We must preserve Miss Carson's gains."

"And you're the kid who can do it," said Jefferson, patting her knee. "Next?"

"Team number four will look into food packaging."

"What's the matter with food packaging?" he asked curiously.

"We're not sure, but we have well-formed suspicions. I'm talking of the new plastic packages—polyethylene, squeeze bottles, and all the other substances made of long, synthetic molecules which do not occur in nature. How stable are those molecules? What happens when a plastic package has been on a grocer's shelf for six months or a year? Do the molecules in the package begin to unravel? And if so, do they enter the foodstuff? And if so, how do they affect the human who eats the foodstuff? Not favorably, is my guess."

"You're scaring me half to death," said Jefferson, his face a study in delight. Oh, sweet Lord, what a pile of ammunition this pretty lady doctor was going to give him! Great balls of fire, what a barrage he was going to turn loose on the country! He would get people so shaky that every tobacco counter in America would be positively mobbed! He might, in fact, bring back cigarette rationing.

"And your fifth team?" he asked, beaming on the pretty lady doctor.

"The fifth team will study drinking water, which, to be perfectly honest, is not my field. Dr. Levine is in charge of the project. He's the short man with the large red beard over there. Would you like to talk to him?"

"Directly, missy, directly. First let me ask you something: when you prove all these things we've been talking about, how do you go about telling folks?"

"We publish our findings in the *Quarterly* of the American Nutritional Society," she answered.

"*Oh, swell!*" said Jefferson silently. Aloud, and with his most fetching smile, he said, "Missy, I got some powerful good news for you. When you finish your experiments, I am going to put the results on the television—coast-to-coast!"

"Television!" exclaimed Dr. Silenko, taken aback. "Good heavens!"

"Why not?"

"Well, I don't know," she said hesitantly. "Isn't it a bit *gaudy?*"

"Yes, it is," said Jefferson, putting on his most earnest expression. "I'll admit it. . . . And I know it's strange to you and all the good people you're working with. I mean, you're nice, quiet, studious ladies and gentlemen, and you don't cotton to hoopla and stuff like that. . . . But remember, missy, what you're doing here is trying to warn the United States of America that it's getting poisoned to death. Now, can you think of a better way to spread the alarm than the television?"

"I suppose when you put it that way—" said Dr. Silenko.

Jefferson rose and shook her hand. "I want to thank you for your time and patience, Doctor, and I'd certainly admire to call on you some evening—when you finish with the monkey."

He bowed, turned, and started toward Dr. Levine, the short man with the large red beard. But Virgil intercepted him in mid-passage.

"You're looking mighty pleased, Pa."

"I am, boy, I am. Had a fine talk with Dr. Silenko."

"First-class scientist," said Virgil.

"First-class!" agreed Jefferson. "Got a pretty fair set of knockers too. She spoken for?"

"Well, I've heard some talk about her and Linden-Evarts."

"That settles it," said Jefferson decisively. "Boy, you pay off that hyphenated loony-bird and pack him in."

"No, Pa," said Virgil.

"Boy, this is your Daddy talking."

"Daddy, this is the president of Acanthus talking. To get these people here, I promised them tenure."

"What's that?"

"That means an unbreakable lifetime contract. They can *not* be fired."

"You're one hell of a sharp trader," said Jefferson, shaking his head. "Praise God you stayed out of the cigarette company."

"Amen," said Virgil.

"Okay, you made a promise and we got to stick with it. We can't fire that loony-bird, but we sure as death can keep him from nosing around in my business."

"No, Pa. I promised them academic freedom too. They can teach, speak, research, write, and publish anything they please."

Jefferson smiled uneasily. "You mean within *reason*, of course, don't you, boy? You surely didn't give 'em license to teach like Communism, for instance? Or *atheism?*"

"I surely did. Also, if they are so minded, free love, racial equality, and safecracking."

"A little joke, huh, boy?" said Jefferson, his smile increasing in size and nervousness. He looked into Virgil's eyes for confirmation. He found none. His smile faded. "My son, my son," he said hollowly, "what is happening here?"

"What is happening here," Virgil answered, "is what you call a university."

"No, a bird sanctuary," said Jefferson. "That's what is happening here. A bird sanctuary—for loony-birds."

Virgil grinned. "Maybe so, Pa," he said, "but *useful* loony-birds." He reached out and stopped a short man with a large red beard who was heading toward the sherry. "Levine," he said, "I don't believe you've met my father."

The gloom scudded from Jefferson's face. "How do," he said winsomely, clasping the doctor's hand. "I understand you're our expert on water."

"Water! Feh!" sneered Levine. "That stuff'll kill you!"

"Is that a fact now?" said Jefferson, taking the doctor tenderly by the arm. "Come, let's set, and you tell me all about it."

Chapter 7

While Jefferson and Virgil Tatum poured sherry into the new faculty of Acanthus College, Barbara Ogilvie Owens Fuller—Boo—sat at home and thought about sex.

Her home was a Southern manor house with a portico and columns, surrounded by spotless white outbuildings, a paddock, a meadow, a lawn, and a fragrant sprinkling of magnolias, honeysuckle, and jasmine. Boo sat on the portico wearing blue jeans and a checkered shirt, yet somehow looking as perfectly the mistress of the manse as though she were decked in a picture hat and a flower print dress of silk. She sat easy, her long, elegant bones comfortably arranged in a wicker chaise. A bourbon-on-the-rocks stood on a wicker table beside her. The evening breeze was cool, a nightingale sang in a bay tree, and visions of coition passed sweetly through Boo's mind's eye.

It would have come as a shock to Owens Mill, and most especially to Boo's constant suitor Virgil, to learn how much time she gave to thinking about sex. The consensus locally was that she had little or no interest in the subject. In the eighteen years since Boo's son Gabriel had been born, tireless espionage by her devoted friends had uncovered not one single lapse of chastity. All were satisfied now that she was a woman of admirable virtue, and all were properly depressed.

All were mistaken. Boo's sex life, though far from rambunctious, was quite suited to her needs. On those rare occasions when she felt her juices boiling over, she made a discreet trip to New York City and spent a discreet weekend with a discreet admirer. He was an eminently eligible man, which is to say he had no wife, no foreign accent, and, most significant, no mustache. He was clean-living, gainfully employed, potent, considerate, agreeably scented, and he regularly proposed marriage to Boo. She just as regularly said no thank you. He accepted her rejections calmly. Although he honestly wanted to take Boo to wife, or at least to multiply her infrequent visits by ten or twenty, he grew increasingly comfortable in this unencumbered, nonbinding liaison.

Boo always left New York feeling slightly besmirched, but in time the guilt would pass. Was this trip really necessary? she would ask herself, and the answer, if somewhat hesitant, was always affirmative. The trips *were* necessary. They kept her pores open and her reputation intact. Also they gave her a chance to get to Bergdorf-Goodman's.

Every so often Boo toyed with the idea of severing her New York connection and taking up with Virgil instead. But in the end, she always abandoned the notion. Two things were against it: first, though she had genuine affection for Virgil, it was not *that* kind; second, Virgil would flatly refuse to consider unsanctified coupling with the lady he loved. His rigid ante-bellum code demanded marriage or nothing, and marriage is precisely what Boo did not want.

She did not want to marry Virgil or her New York friend or any of the other hopefuls who kept appearing. Boo, in her own fashion, had an underlay of chivalry every bit as stout as Virgil's: she regarded it as a manifest breach of honor to become one man's wife while she was still in love with another. And she *was* in love with another. Now, tonight, eighteen long years after he had left her bed, she remained deeply, immutably, rhapsodically in love with the father of her son Gabriel.

It was Gabriel's father Boo was thinking of as she sat in the wicker chaise on the columned portico. Looking back over a gap of eighteen years, she could still feel, physically feel, lips on lips, body on body, hands on breasts and buttocks. She could hear his voice; she could see his eyes; she could smell his hair. The old rapture was upon her, fresh, undiminished, good as new.

As these things are reckoned, thought Boo, I am a lucky woman. I have a perfect memory of a perfect love. I have enough sexual activity to forestall dry rot. I have here in Owens Mill a busy, productive life—an estate to run, horses to breed, dozens of kinfolk and scores of friends to visit and entertain. I have a raft of worthy projects—the hospital, the orphanage, the symphony orchestra, the art gallery, the Red Cross, the League of Women Voters, and *The Mermaid*.

Of all Boo's good works, *The Mermaid* was her very favorite. It was a quarterly of poetry, hand-set and deckle-edged, in which the bards of Owens Mill and its environs could find release for their lyric urges. To be sure, nobody ever actually *read* the magazine; still, it was prominently to be seen in the homes of all the local bon ton. Boo was *The Mermaid's* editor, publisher, and sole financial backer. And, in addition, writing modestly under the simple pseudonym *Leda,* Boo contributed to each issue a love poem brimming with ladylike, but definitely sexy, symbolism.

But over and above sweet memories, beyond busyness and family and friends and civic virtue and the sowing of culture, Boo had one soul-salving, marrow-deep, heart-warming delight: her eighteen-year-old son Gabriel. He was a beautiful, mercurial boy, a challenge and a comfort, an authentic genius in science and no fool in the arts and the humanities. Only one small aspect of Gabriel's character gave Boo occasional pause: he was something of a hermit. He vastly preferred machines and books to friends, especially to female friends. Boo, of course, did not like to see his life so circumscribed, but at bottom, she was not dismayed. She felt sure that gentle, persistent prodding on her part would rectify his social underdevelopment, because Gabriel, stormy though his temperament and dazzling though his mentality, was at the same time a dutiful, obedient boy whose first thought was ever to please his mother.

Yes, thought Boo again, I am a lucky woman. I am a happy woman. . . . And, save for one omission, I am a *fulfilled* woman.

Inside the entrance hall of the house Boo heard the grandfather clock chime the quarter-hour. She rose and went in the front door. She headed toward the television set in the library, passing, as she walked, through a succession of gracious, uncluttered, tranquil, tastefully appointed rooms. Any woman, coming for the first time into these rooms, would be moved to admiration so great that envy would be shamed; any man, no matter where his origins, would feel instantly and peacefully at home.

As Boo entered the library she found the television set not in its accustomed place in the cupboard. It had been dismantled into what looked to Boo like several million little tubes and wires and coils and gizmos, which were now arranged in a neat circle on the library floor. Seated in the center of the circle was Boo's son, Gabriel Owens Fuller.

"Gabriel!" she cried, clasping her bosom.

"Hush!" he said, not looking up. He was a tall, slender boy with a shock of raven hair, an olive complexion, a mobile mouth, a straight patrician nose, and black, smoldering, restless, enormously intelligent eyes. The eyes darted now over the ring of television parts around him, giving each one a short but intent examination. Sometimes he emitted little grunts of satisfaction, sometimes snarls of annoyance. His face, like a blinker light, turned alternately dark with frustration and bright with joy.

"Don't tell me *hush*," said Boo sternly. "I'm your mother, remember?"

Gabriel looked up. "Oh, hi, Ma," he said pleasantly.

"That's better. Now would you mind explaining what you're doing with the television set?"

"Oh, sure. I'm adapting it for UHF."

"But there's no UHF in this part of the country."

"Bound to come along in another five, six years."

"Dandy!" said Boo with a wintry smile. "Gabriel, I hate to be a bore, but there's a program I want very much to look at in fifteen minutes."

"So look at the set in your bedroom."

"Thank you."

"It's okay."

"And while I am watching television, do you know what you will be doing?"

"Picking up these pieces and putting them together?"

"Precisely!"

"No, Ma, I don't believe I will," he said with the air of a man who had given the question long consideration. "I've been sitting here kicking around an idea. Maybe I'll drop the UHF after all. I've got a hunch—" his voice rose in excitement—"that with a little more equipment, I can turn this stuff into an X-ray machine!"

"Which no home should be without," observed Boo.

"I'll need to take the condenser out of the air-conditioner. Okay?"

Boo put on her gentlest, tenderest face. She laid a loving hand on Gabriel's shoulder. "Son," she began, "dear, dear son, I—"

"Gawd!" he groaned. "Here it comes again!"

"Here it comes again," agreed Boo, still tender, still gentle. "You know there's a freshman dance at Acanthus tonight. Why are you home fiddling with machinery instead of at the college having fun?"

"*Fun*, she says!"

"Yes, fun," Boo insisted. "Meeting people *is* fun, you know. Conversation *is* fun. Even *girls* are fun. . . . You want me to get you some testimonials?"

"Girls are *hell!*" he cried, flinging up his arms.

Boo stayed sweetly calm. "Gabriel, you are a normal, healthy, attractive young man. Why this morbid fear of girls?"

"It's not fear," he declared. "It's like I keep telling you, Ma, I just don't know how to talk to them."

"Nonsense. Anybody who can build an X-ray machine and fly a helicopter and make his own digital computer surely shouldn't have any trouble talking to a teen-age girl."

"Ha!" he exclaimed tragically. "That's *exactly* the trouble. I talk to them about pi-mesons and they get glassy. I try Doppler, Rutherford, even John Glenn. So what happens? They get glassier and glassier till finally they actually forget to chew their gum. . . . This is *fun?* This is hell! This is a holocaust! Ma, let's face it: girls are just too damn dumb!"

"I see. So what's your plan, Gabriel—to go through college without a date?"

"I'm glad you asked that question," he replied seriously. "Because I've given it a lot of thought. This'll come as a surprise, Ma, but it happens I *do* like girls . . . only there's one small proviso: they've got to have a brain. Not a scientific brain necessarily; just a brain. So here's what I've been thinking: maybe I've been looking in the wrong age bracket. Maybe I ought to find me a more *mature* type girl."

"*How* mature?"

"Oh, I don't know. Like thirty. Thirty-five maybe."

"Dear God!" gasped Boo. "Son," she said, deftly recovering her composure and her benevolent smile, "listen to your mother who gave you birth and loves you very dearly. Forget this plan of yours. Find a girl your own age."

"They're too dumb."

"Then educate her. *Mold* her."

Gabriel shook his head. "They won't stay molded."

"Try."

"Aw—"

"For me. For your mother."

He sighed. "Well, if you say so—"

"I say so."

"Okay, I'll go to Acanthus tonight."

"Thank you."

"It won't work, you know."

"That's what I like—confidence. All right, pal. Hit the road."

"Now? But the dance doesn't start for another half-hour. I'll stay with you and watch this tv show you're so keen about."

Boo hesitated a tiny moment. "If you want to," she said, "but I don't think you'll like it. It's an old documentary, a rerun, made seven or eight years ago. I'm afraid you'll think it's pretty old-fashioned."

"Let's find out. Come on."

He offered Boo his arm. She concealed a flicker of nervousness, managed a smile, took his arm. They went to Boo's room—chintz, airiness, pastels, softness, delicately wrought furnishings. Gabriel switched on the television set. They sat in a pair of handsome little armchairs.

The tv set crackled. A forest of lines appeared, waved, then formed themselves into a picture. It showed a mean street on Los Angeles' skid row. Background music was heard: a drum softly stroked with brushes, an understated bass fiddle, a sad, goosy clarinet. The opening titles crawled over the picture: *"IRA SHAPIAN presents THE SUN-BAKED SLUMS."*

Gabriel frowned. "I know that name," he said.

"Watch the program, dear," said Boo.

"Ira Shapian," said Gabriel thoughtfully. "Why does that name stick in my mind?"

"Shh!" said Boo.

He fell silent. For thirty minutes mother and son sat quietly and watched a stark, staccato documentary about Los Angeles' sun-bright nether world—the winos, the junkies, the whores, the drifters, the perverts: the losers and the lost. It was a tough, laconic film, blessedly lacking in artiness. The commentary, brief and pointed, was spoken by Ira himself.

As the program finished, the end-titles began to crawl over the picture. Boo rose to switch off the set. "Wait!" called Gabriel, his eyes riveted to the screen. *"PRODUCED AND DIRECTED BY IRA SHAPIAN"* was the final credit before the fade-out.

"Better get over to the dance, dear," said Boo with an overbright smile as she turned the television set off.

"Ira Shapian, Ira Shapian," Gabriel repeated slowly. "I *know* I know that name. Why?"

Boo carefully kept her tone casual. "It's perfectly simple, dear. There was an Air Force base in Owens Mill during the war, and Mr. Shapian was stationed here. No doubt you've heard Virgil or somebody mention it."

"That's right," he nodded. "Yeah, that's right."

"Good night, son. Have fun."

"But there's more," he said, not moving, his forehead furrowed in thought. "A photo!" he exclaimed with sudden certainty. "There used to be a photo of Shapian in this house!"

"Really? I don't remember."

"Not a photo of Shapian alone. I mean a group picture. There was Shapian and you and Virgil and another lady. Yeah, four of you . . . And it was in this room! In fact, right *here!*" He walked over and pointed to a spot on the wall directly above Boo's small white desk.

"Why, I do believe you're right. Now that you remind me, yes, I distinctly remember that picture. . . . But," she added quickly, "I got rid of it a long time ago."

"How long ago?"

"Ten years."

"It's crazy," said Gabriel. The lines in his brow deepened. "How come I remember Shapian's face so clearly? Not so much his face, just the eyes. It's like I've been seeing those eyes every day, every hour! Now why should I feel that way?"

"My dear boy," answered Boo, "if I knew why you feel the way you feel, I would have to be a genius like you are, and *that* I most definitely am not. True?"

"True."

"Thank you."

"Forget it."

"A genius, as you so gallantly agree, I am not. But there is one thing I can do: tell time. The dance at Acanthus has started. So saddle and ride, my boy."

"Look, Ma, about that dance—"

"Which you are going to, and no excuses!"

"Listen, let me stay home, and we'll look for the picture of Shapian. I'm *positive* it's still here."

Boo took a deep breath. "And I'm positive it's not," she said firmly. "Because ten years ago I personally put a match to it."

Gabriel searched her face. "You're not kidding, are you?"

"I am not."

"No, you're not," he said, nodding. "You really burned it. You really did, I can tell. . . . But why?"

"Because every once in a while I get an irresistible urge to set fire to things—like old photographs, or young boys who don't mind their mothers."

"I'm going, I'm going!" he said with a shuddering sigh. "Oh, Gawd!" he wailed as he lurched toward the door.

"No kiss, huh?" said Boo. "We're all washed up, is that it?"

Gabriel stopped. He grinned, an abrupt, dazzling slash of white across his swarthy face. He hugged his mother hard, gave her a loud kiss on the cheek, hugged her again, kissed the other cheek.

"*Bonne chance,*" she murmured, aiming him toward the door.

"*Ça sera un débâcle,*" he warned.

"*Va-t'en.*" She pushed him gently, then stood in the doorway watching him as he left the house. Then she went to her bedroom window and watched him some more as he walked briskly down the driveway, vaulted into a sports car he had built himself, gunned the engine, and zoomed away with a spray of gravel.

Tears, warm tears of felicity, stood in Boo's eyes as she watched her son. How beautiful he is, she thought, her breast swelling with love. How like his father! Of course, there were some physical differences: Gabriel's height, for example, came not from his father but from Boo, as did the leanness and the short Anglo-Saxon nose. But all the rest derived from his father—the startling black eyes, the brooding darkness, the quicksilver passions; melancholy followed instantly by euphoria; serenity chased by frenzy; despair hard on the traces of hope.

Oh, yes, thought Boo. Oh, yes, dear Gabriel, you are Ira Shapian's son. You are his heart's heir, his soul's spit and image. But you will never know it, my good sweet beloved bastard Gabriel. Nor will Ira ever know it. It will always be my secret and nobody else's.

The photograph is safely burned now. It was weakness, it was folly, to keep Ira's picture on my wall as long as I did. But I needed to look at Ira's face, and you, dear Gabriel, were still a little child. How could I recognize so soon that you had the mind and memory of a genius?

Well, the picture is gone now. The only time you will see Ira's eyes again is when you look into a mirror. You will be haunted, yes. There will always be a rustling of unease at the back of that incredible brain of yours. But you will not *know*. That's the important thing: you will not *know*. Ira will not know. Nobody will know.

Boo's eyes gazed out the window of her bedroom, across her estate, across two miles of sloping countryside, and came to rest on the lighted skyline of the town of Owens Mill. A wry half-smile suddenly appeared on her lips. The Owens Mill skyline—if such it could be called—was a cluster of shops and houses, one and two stories tall;

a tobacco warehouse, three stories tall; a cigarette factory, four stories tall; the Stonewall Jackson Hotel, six stories tall; and, finally, standing in solitary, phallic splendor, the Tatum Tower, headquarters and home office of Jefferson's cigarette company, thirty-one stories high with a red beacon slowly revolving on the capstone.

How ironic, thought Boo. Indeed, how comic, if such a thing could be called comic. Not a leaf dropped, not a sparrow fell, in Owens Mill except that Jefferson knew of it. There was no secret in town to which the old man was not privy—except the biggest, deepest, darkest secret of all: Gabriel's paternity.

Chapter 8

True, Jefferson Tatum was not aware of Gabriel's paternity, but he was nonetheless the cause of Gabriel's being, just as he was the cause of everything else that came to be in Owens Mill.

In 1939 the business offices of the Tatum Cigarette Company were jammed, helter-skelter, in odd corners of the factory and the warehouse. Then, in the autumn of 1939, Jefferson went to Winston-Salem to discuss industry matters with his colleagues at the R. J. Reynolds Company, and he saw their home office for the first time—the R. J. Reynolds Building, twenty-one imposing stories of Indiana limestone.

Jefferson was pensive when he returned to Owens Mill. He summoned his executives to a meeting. "Fellers," he said, "I'm going to build me an office building."

The executives beamed. Even the most senior of them had never had an office to himself.

"How big a building are you planning?" asked the vice-president in charge of sales.

"I don't care," said Jefferson. "Just so it's bigger than the R. J. Reynolds Building."

The comptroller blanched. "But sir," he protested, "the Reynolds Building is twenty-one stories."

"Mine will be *thirty*-one," said Jefferson.

"What in the world do we need with all that space?" asked the comptroller, getting nervouser.

"Shut up," said Jefferson.

"Yes, sir," said the comptroller.

"What costs more than limestone?" asked Jefferson.

"Oh, lots of things," said the vice-president in charge of engineering. "For example, if a man really wanted to go crazy, there's marble."

"That's it," said Jefferson. "Make it out of marble. Thirty-one stories tall. And way up on top I want a big red light that goes round and round and round."

"But, sir—" said the comptroller.

"Meeting adjourned," said Jefferson.

Ground was broken for the Tatum Tower six months later. By the end of 1941 the skeleton of fourteen stories had been completed. Then the contractor came to Jefferson, shuffling his toe with embarrassment. "Mr. Tatum," he said sheepishly, "I can't get no more steel."

"Why the hell not?" asked Jefferson.

"On account of the war."

"We'll see about *that!*" said Jefferson grimly and caught the first train to Washington.

He called on his Congressman, the Honorable Mr. Pettigrew, a portly gentleman of seventy, now serving his twelfth term, who wore a black suit, a white waistcoat, a string tie, a long hair-do, and a perpetual smile.

"Jefferson," said Mr. Pettigrew reasonably, "you know I'd like nothing in the world better than to help you, but there's a war going on."

"I know there's a war going on, you overweight peckerhead," said Jefferson to the Honorable Mr. Pettigrew. "Ain't my factory working three shifts to help out our boys in the trenches?"

"I do not minimize, mark you, the importance of cigarettes to the morale of our gallant young warriors," replied the Congressman, "but to obtain steel these days you must have a reason that is, shall we say, more *military.*"

"All right then, find me some military outfit that can use the Tatum Tower—only for the duration, of course."

"A military outfit in the *Tatum Tower?* I don't see how I can swing it, Jefferson."

"Too bad," said Jefferson. "Washington ain't going to seem the same without you next term."

"I'll swing it, I'll swing it," said Mr. Pettigrew hastily.

The Congressman promptly paid visits to the Army and the Navy, but all his rolling oratory failed to persuade them that the tide of victory clearly depended on completing the Tatum Tower. At the Army Air Force, however, Mr. Pettigrew struck pay dirt.

The Air Force, for so many years the neglected orphan of the services, had suddenly become the pampered darling. It had only to ask, and it was given. Naturally, like any spoiled brat, the more it was given, the more it asked. Thus, when the winged generals heard about thirty-one stories of marble available in a place called Owens Mill, their eyes grew as bright as the stars on their shoulders. A new area command was created within minutes—headquarters, the Tatum Tower. And, of course, one can hardly have an Air Force area command without an airfield, so Jefferson Tatum patriotically sold the United States five thousand acres of bog just outside the town.

Quickly there was steel to complete the Tatum Tower. There was also concrete to lay the runways for the shiny new airplanes, and there was wood to build the barracks to house the troops who kept 'em flying.

A certain Private Ira Shapian, assigned to Special Services because of his theatrical experience, was given the task of delivering a series of lectures on "Why We Fight." This he did with such skill and fervor that every soldier present was passionately aware of why he fought. Nobody ever learned, however, *who* he fought.

While Ira and his colleagues manned their posts with exemplary zeal, others in Owens Mill also contributed their bit to the war effort. Each Sunday the gentry of the town opened their great houses to the lonely soldier boys at the base, except for Jefferson Tatum, who never allowed visitors in his house, unless you count Millie and Esther McCabe, the round-heeled twins from packaging, but they were always required to leave before cock-crow.

Virgil Tatum, however, held open house every Sunday. (Virgil, of course, was not in the service; he was 4-F because of his gimpy leg.) William Ransom Owens also opened his house on Sundays. (William Ransom was 4-F too because his testicles had never descended.) And another who entertained on Sundays was Boo.

Boo had been eighteen years old, a second-semester freshman at Wellesley, when she had received the shocking news that both her parents had died in an automobile accident. She rushed back to Owens Mill in time for the funeral. Afterward she stayed a couple of weeks for the grim legal necessaries that follow death. Then she prepared to return to Wellesley. But, to her astonishment, she found she did not want to leave. It came to her suddenly that she was an Owens of Owens Mill. Her place was here. She had no brothers or sisters, and it seemed all wrong—she could not say exactly why—to trust executors with duties and obligations to which she had been born.

She unpacked and stayed. She became—it happened effortlessly —the mistress of her house and estate, a clubwoman, a doer of good

82

deeds, a worker for civic betterment and cultural enhancement. And, one year later, when the Air Force moved into town, Boo, like her friends and kinfolk, held open house each Sunday.

Ira Shapian met Boo at one of her Sunday at-homes. Ira was with Polly and several other G.I.s and their wives when he arrived. At first he did not see Boo; he was too overcome by the house itself to notice anything else. Never had he seen a home so expensively appointed, yet so warmly inviting. He knew the chairs were priceless, but he would not have hesitated to flop in any of them. Nor would he have shrunk from plunking down a drink on one of the irreplaceable tables. He, Ira Shapian, the Armenian kid from Tenth Avenue, felt perfectly easy in this perfectly magnificent house. In fact, he had a sudden, powerful conviction that here, among this unaccustomed splendor, he, the groaner and breast-beater, could find true tranquillity for the first time in his whole spiky life.

Then he was introduced to Boo. His black eyes widened with a strange mixture of awe and desire. Boo was the house; the house was Boo. Just as he found the house at once dumfounding and cozy, he saw Boo as a great, patrician, touch-me-not lady who—he was dead sure of it—had been put on earth expressly for his pleasure.

Whoa, boy. Steady, boy, he told himself firmly. First of all, you're a married man with a wonderful wife whom you love with all your black, hairy heart. Second, you are all wrong about this dame Boo. She is way out of your league, and if you make a pass at her, she will brush you off like a fly. Steady, boy. Whoa, boy.

Yet he kept returning to Boo's house on Sundays. He interspersed the visits with calls on Virgil Tatum and the various Owenses because he wanted to be sure to throw Polly off the scent—no simple matter, for Polly had a nose almost as smart as her head.

Every time he saw Boo the certainty returned that she was meant for him. He watched her closely as he told wry anecdotes of the theater and of his boyhood on the streets. He noted her big, free, open, unself-conscious laughter, and he was all the more positive that she would not say him nay. In Ira's experience beautiful women did not laugh unguardedly. It cracked the façade; it left them vulnerable. Therefore, Boo's laughter could only mean that in her heart she did not want to protect herself from Ira. She was his. He knew it, he knew it, he *knew* it; and his soul soared with the joy of it.

But when he was away from Boo, another thought would come to Ira, a thought that chilled his liver and frosted his lights. Idiot! he yelled at himself. Dumbhead! You've got a wonderful, darling, sensational, perfect wife, but you are falling in love with the princess with the golden hair. You will never have her. She doesn't even know you exist, or if she does, she thinks of you as some kind of grimy little joke-maker from the New York pavements. Dumbhead! Idiot! Dumb idiot-head!

What Ira could not know was that Boo was falling in love with him too. All her post-pubescent life she had been courted by Southern men, and they had always made her feel vaguely inadequate. Southern men, including lame Virgil, were basically Elizabethans. They fought fearlessly, copulated tirelessly, hunted skillfully, drank prodigiously. They were equally competent behind a shotgun or a desk. They shunned self-pity; they embraced strength.

Ira, on the other hand, was a woe-shouter who wore his weakness proudly. There was something little-boy about him, something that clutched the maternal strings in Boo's heart. She knew that to him she would be *necessary*. She would be more than an appendage, more than the chatelaine a Southern male would make of her.

But, of course, it was not even thinkable to reveal her feelings to Ira. He was a married man. Moreover, Boo was genuinely fond of Polly, whom she found to be a willing, cheerful coworker in all of Owens Mill's worthy projects—the hospital, the blood bank, the orphanage, the manifold fund drives. She was, besides, a witty, amusing, dear, upright woman, whose love for Ira was plain to see. No, thought Boo. Good sense, good taste, and good breeding all told her the same thing: hands off Ira.

So the tacit romance between Boo and Ira dragged on. Pain burgeoned, but no word was spoken, not on either side.

Then Polly got pregnant—doubly pregnant, grotesquely pregnant. She gave up civic virtue and stayed at home, groaning when she was not actually vomiting. Her temper, never long, got steadily shorter. Ira looked at cool, tall, slender, elegant, beautiful Boo. Then he looked at sullen, swollen Polly. Then he did some groaning himself.

When Polly went home to New York to give birth to the twins, Ira, after a fierce losing battle with himself, paid a visit, alone, at night, to Boo's house.

"Ira!" she said, startled. "What do you want?"

"I don't know," he said. Then suddenly, wildly, they were in one another's arms.

And then they were on a couch—grabbing, sobbing, sobbing, tearing, grabbing, grabbing.

"No! No!" cried Boo, pulling away.

"Yes! Yes!" cried Ira.

"I mean yes, yes," said Boo.

"But you said no, no," said Ira.

"I mean yes, yes," said Boo. "But not here. Not in this house."

"Where? Where?" said Ira.

"Come," said Boo.

"Yes! Yes!" said Ira.

He followed Boo to her car and they sped, tight-lipped and trembling, to her deserted beach house ten miles away.

There, on a bearskin rug in front of a driftwood fire, it was done. In fact, it was done several times, but always with tears, always with a sense of transgression hanging over them like a dark canopy.

"We can't do this to Polly," they kept telling each other over and over. And each time, having reached agreement, they fell once more to the pelt before the hearth.

Two nights and two days they cried and made love. Then, serious and sated, they exchanged a solemn promise. They would never see one another again. They would never write, never phone, never send a message through an intermediary. They had sinned against Polly and against God. Separation, permanent and irrevocable, would be their punishment. This they swore.

They kept their oath. This night, eighteen years later, Ira was in Hollywood, and Boo stood alone in the bedroom of her home in Owens Mill, and not once in the eighteen years had there been any sort of contact between them.

Boo turned away from her bedroom window, where she had been gazing across the countryside at the Tatum Tower. How ironic, she thought, that an innocent victim should be paying the heaviest price for her sin and Ira's. It was not she and not Ira from whom the cruelest toll was being exacted. It was their son Gabriel.

His awesome punishment was that he would never know his father. A bribed judge and a forged marriage license had given the boy legitimacy, but it would never give him the joy of clasping Ira to his bosom, of exchanging the tears and kisses that erupted so naturally from their volatile hearts.

Was Ira, too, paying a frightful price? Boo could not be sure, but she fervently hoped he was not. She wanted only happiness for him. She had never told him about Gabriel, nor would she. His all-too-fragile conscience could not bear such an affliction. Let him be peaceful. Let him rejoice in his professional success, in his marriage with good, honest Polly, in his two stalwart sons.

As for herself, she was content. Had she not, earlier this night, counted her blessings and found them abundant? Yes, she was content—not entirely, of course. She would never stop grieving for Ira, but she would grieve sweetly—indeed, grieve *lyrically*.

She moved to her little white desk. A sonnet for *The Mermaid* was stirring in her mind. She took out a sheaf of foolscap and uncapped a pen. She wrote a title at the top of the page. *"On the Blessings of Sin."* She signed her nom de plume: "by *Leda.*" She closed her eyes, thought deeply, then began:

> The pain delights, the jubilee is triste,
> A lover's moon mounts blackly in the east.

She leaned back and appraised the opening couplet. Not bad, she decided. In fact, rather good. Nice touch, that *triste*. Rich imagery, that moon rising blackly.

Yes, thought Boo, this could well be one of *Leda's* better efforts. Yes.

Chapter 9

At 4:20 of an autumn afternoon a black suit containing Harry Clendennon, president of the Star Spangled Broadcasting Network, boarded the first-class compartment of TWA Flight No. 11, nonstop Idlewild to Los Angeles.

Already aboard the plane, waiting for Clendennon, was his secretary, Haas by name, a man of thirty with pale eyebrows, thin shoulders, invisible lips, a black suit, and an attaché case lying open on his knees. Clendennon never hired women as secretaries because women, no matter how promisingly they started, always ended up behaving like women: they wanted, for instance, to leave the office before midnight, or they insisted on Sundays off, or they fell in love, or their ovaries got murky: always something. "The only kind of secretary to have," Clendennon frequently told his friends at the National Association of Broadcasters, "is a nonpracticing faggot."

As the jet reached cruising altitude, Clendennon unfastened his seat belt and turned to Haas. "All right, chickie," he said, "let's get cracking."

"Yes, sir," said Haas. Memos, correspondence, pencils, pens, and pads were neatly arranged on his attaché case. He picked up the top memo. "General Motors, Coca-Cola, and Goodyear Tires have each placed an order for that unsold minute on *Rocky Gibraltar*."

"Tell them all yes," said Clendennon. "Next?"

"A little reckless, isn't it, sir? Selling the same spot to three different sponsors?"

"That's show biz, baby. Next?"

"Mrs. Clendennon wants to know whether you'll be back from California in time for the Cotillion."

"Tell her yes. Next?"

"You know, of course," said Haas impassively, "that you won't be home in time?"

"What I know, pussycat, is that people don't like to be told no. Next?"

"I called Mr. Shapian for you again, and again he refused to accept the call. This, according to my records, is the eighth consecutive day he has refused your calls."

"Perfidious Armenian!" snarled Clendennon. "What the hell is he up to?"

"Excuse me, sir, but isn't it rather obvious? Mr. Shapian's contract is due for renewal next month. He's attempting, you might say, a war of nerves in order to get more money."

"Brilliant, ducks. Only trouble is, I've already offered him more money."

"Oh," said Haas.

"No, something else is on Ira's mind—something deep. *Real* deep. I'll tell you how deep it is: I happen to have definite information that he's been showing up at the office in a hound's-tooth jacket!"

"Shocking," said Haas politely.

"Well, never mind. I've handled Shapian before and I'll do it again. What's next?"

"Mr. Davies sent you this memo."

"Oh?" said Clendennon, sitting upright. His ruddy face went suddenly pale; a shadow of fear scurried across his hard, flat eyes. Clendennon was president of Star Spangled, but Mr. Davies was owner of the network. Mr. Davies was, in addition, a vestryman of his church, a trustee of his university, and the master of his regatta. He was an aloof, austere sort who never sent memos to his employees except when he was displeased about something, and if he was sufficiently displeased, he would aloofly, austerely have a man's head on a platter.

Clendennon cast out fear, the enemy of thought, for he needed to think. What could be irking Mr. Davies? Certainly it was not that he had gotten word of some of Clendennon's chicaneries; it was specifically to chicane that Mr. Davies had engaged Clendennon in the first place. Mr. Davies preferred to let hirelings do his throat-slitting, while he stayed clean-handed above the fray—vestryman, trustee, and master of the regatta.

No, it could only be one thing: Ira Shapian. Sure, Ira Shapian. Now Clendennon understood why Ira had been ducking his phone calls; now he knew precisely what game Ira was playing. He was, as Haas had said, conducting a war of nerves, except the war was not against Clendennon but against Mr. Davies.

For all his aloofness and austerity Mr. Davies kept an unsleeping eye on his network. Nothing, large or small, ever escaped his surveillance. He was fully aware that Ira was giving Clendennon a frost. He was further aware that Ira, the man who could *nice*, was worth his weight in rubies to the network. So foolish Ira was trying to panic Mr. Davies into believing he would not renew his contract as long as Clendennon was in charge. So feckless Ira was hoping to stampede Mr. Davies into firing Clendennon.

That's it all right, thought Clendennon, confidence flooding back to his breast. That's it, and I've got nothing to worry about. When it comes to a contest of finkery between Ira and me, why, it's just no contest. I'll handle Ira. I'll hold my job, and I'll also hold that crazy Armenian. Nobody outfinks Clendennon. No, sir! Not old Clendennon, the survivingest predator in the whole tv jungle!

"Okay, doll," said Clendennon to Haas. "Read me Mr. Davies' memo."

"Yes, sir." Haas held up a sheet of paper and read: " 'Mr. Jefferson Tatum of the Tatum Cigarette Company phoned me this morning and asked me to clear sixty minutes of prime broadcast time for a program that will emanate from Acanthus College. The topic will be the dangerous additives commonly found in food. I agreed to Mr. Tatum's request.' "

Two emotions hit Clendennon simultaneously: first there was relief that Mr. Davies still had not learned about Ira Shapian's recalcitrance; second there was annoyance that Mr. Davies should have said yes to Jefferson Tatum. "Goddammit!" Clendennon exclaimed to Haas. "How can we do a program about poisonous food additives? We've got forty million dollars a year in General Foods billings."

Haas, without a pause, continued to read from Mr. Davies' memo. " 'Yes, I know we've got forty million dollars a year in General Foods billings. I also know that the six lowest rated shows on the network are sponsored by Jefferson Tatum. You will therefore produce the program Mr. Tatum has requested. You will, of course, find somebody to present a rebuttal for the food industry during the program. Please take great pains to find a rebutter who is homesy, folksy, winsome, and trustworthy. Make sure his eyes are not shifty and that he does not perspire.' "

Clendennon grinned. No fool, Mr. Davies. "Is that the end of the memo?" he asked.

"One more line," replied Haas. He quoted: " 'P.S. Why do we still not have Ira Shapian's signature on the new contract? I should be most unhappy to lose him to another network. Men like Shapian are rather more difficult to replace than men like you. . . . Best wishes, Davies.'"

A tremor of fright rippled through Clendennon. He cursed himself for being so stupid as to believe Mr. Davies was unaware of the trouble with Shapian. . . . And yet, thought Clendennon with rising spirits, he really had no reason to panic. One way or another he would keep Ira in the fold. He had done it a dozen times in the past; he would do it again—of this he had no doubt.

"All right, sweetie," he said amiably to Haas. "What's next?"

Haas lifted a memo with a faint air of distaste. "I have been in touch with your Hollywood procurer," he said. "A lady will be at your suite between five and six on Thursday afternoon. I am told she works with patent leather boots and a can of Reddi-Whip."

"Cancel it," said Clendennon. "Too busy."

Haas regarded his employer with something almost like respect. "Yes, sir."

"Next?"

"That's all."

"Mask and pills," said Clendennon.

"Yes, sir," said Haas and handed him a black eyeshade and a vial containing one capsule each of Seconal, Miltown, Librium, and Chloral hydrate.

Clendennon swallowed the pills, tilted his chair back, slipped the mask over his eyes, and enjoyed a health-restoring nap from Cleveland to Los Angeles.

Chapter 10

Ira Shapian, wearing a hound's-tooth jacket, drove his Jaguar Mark VII into the crushed rock driveway of his half-timbered house in Bel Air. He switched off the ignition and sat wearily for a moment, his hand pressed against his forehead. He had had an even more galling day than usual at Star Spangled. A John Birching sponsor had deleted all mention of the United Nations from a documentary celebrating the founding of the United Nations, an artsy-fartsy director had shot a Western with such low-key lighting that it looked as though the wranglers were herding cattle inside a shoe, and the star of *The Day Lincoln Was Shot* had adamantly refused to grow a beard.

Only one small pleasure had accrued to Ira in the preceding twelve hours: he had, for the eighth consecutive day, declined to accept any phone calls from Clendennon. But the luster of this minor satisfaction was rapidly dimming. True, he was curdling Clendennon's liver by not taking his calls, but also true, and much more to the point, Ira knew that when the time came to sign the new contract he would sign. There was no escape now; the collar and leash were too firmly fastened. A snapping dog Ira might be, but indubitably a dog.

"Arf," said Ira mournfully and picked up a small, handsomely wrapped package on the seat beside him and got out of the car and went into the house.

"Hi," said Polly. "You look grisly."

"Thank you," said Ira. "Where's Ezra and Leo?"

"Vic Tanny's."

"Where else?" said Ira and sighed.

"Want me to fix a martini?"

"Desperately," he replied. "But first I want a kiss."

"You *do*?" Her eyes grew round with surprise.

"I do," he affirmed. "But nothing strenuous, mind you."

"This about right?" she asked and gave him a kiss that fell midway between passion and inadvertence.

"Splendid," he said. He handed her the little package he had carried in from the car. "In honor of our twenty-first wedding anniversary," he explained. "Very expensive."

She unwrapped the package. Inside lay a pair of small, flawless diamond ear-clips. "Thank you," she said courteously.

"Enough!" said Ira, raising his hand. "You know I can't stand these unseemly displays of emotion."

Polly looked him squarely in the eyes. "No, I mean it: thank you. It was thoughtful of you to remember. Trouble is, it's not what I wanted."

"So take 'em back to the jeweler and exchange 'em."

"The jeweler hasn't got what I want."

"I know I'll regret this question, but *what* do you want?"

"Well, I thought—I'm a dreamer, I guess—anyhow, I thought—no, *hoped* is the word—I hoped that tonight—I don't mean to get maudlin, Ira, but after all we *are* married twenty-one years—I hoped that tonight, as kind of a special treat, we might *talk*."

"Possibly the reason we are married twenty-one years," suggested Ira, "is that we *don't*."

"Possibly," she said without expression. "I'll fix your drink."

He followed her to the sideboard, guilt nipping softly at his vitals. He turned her around as she started working with vodka and vermouth. "Listen," he said earnestly, "what happens when we talk? You ask me not to sign the new contract. I explain why I have to. You reject my explanation. Then it's scream time."

"Is that bad?"

"Polly," he pleaded, "I'm too old. All day long I scream at the studio. Can't I have a snug harbor when I come home?"

"Yes, ancient mariner," she said. "Here's your booze."

"You *know* I can't quit."

"Like hell I do," she answered. She handed Ira his drink and poured one for herself. Mockingly she touched glasses with him. "To you, my dear. To twenty-one years, to love, to life, and to inertia."

"Sweet," said Ira, smiling tightly, his knuckles white around the stem of his glass. "Very sweet. And so beautifully timed. I give you diamond earrings, you give me a hatchet in the skull. . . . Why, Polly?"

"Because I love you, dumbbell!" she cried, abandoning civility.

"Because after all these years I love you more foolishly and more completely than ever. And I know that no matter what those people have done to you, you're still Ira Shapian. Under that heap of trauma there's still a set of large, perfectly usable balls!"

Ira unhinged his mouth to shout, then with an effort shut it. "I will give you a soft answer to turn away wrath," he said. "I think you're an absolutely marvelous woman, and I regret I'm not the man you hoped for."

"But you *are!*"

"But I'm not, and finish your drink. We have a nine o'clock reservation at Chasen's."

"Yes, dear," she said, resigned. Then a sudden thought struck her. "Wait a minute! Not Chasen's. Clendennon is in town."

Ira paled. "How do you know?"

"His secretary called from the airport a little while ago. Clendennon wants to join us for dinner. I said Chasen's, nine o'clock."

"Good thinking," he said approvingly. "Now let's see. . . . Where can we go where he won't find us?"

"How about hiring a blimp?"

"Polly, this is serious."

"Almost as serious as a five-year-old kid playing hide-and-seek. You know Clendennon is going to corner you sooner or later."

"True."

"So what do you think you're accomplishing?"

"I'll tell you exactly: I'm making Clendennon sweat. . . . But more important, I'm making Mr. Davies sweat a little bit too, and if Mr. Davies gets sweaty enough, Clendennon is out!"

"Clendennon *fired?*" said Polly incredulously. "Boy, are you playing a long shot! In fact, an *astronomically* long shot! But, okay, let's say you make it happen. Then what? Who do you think Mr. Davies will get to replace Clendennon—Albert Schweitzer?"

"Polly, I've been in the business a few years. I know Mr. Davies will go looking for a carbon copy of Clendennon. . . . But here's the point: what if, by accident, he hires a nice guy?"

"Then the network will go bankrupt, and you'll be out of work, and why am I complaining? Come on, where'll we have dinner?"

"Hey, I got an idea. Feel like eating Chink?"

"With you, pussycat? Anything!"

"I drove past a new place on the way home—not exactly Chink; Polynesian, I guess, or maybe early Dorothy Lamour. Anyhow, the sign said grand opening tonight. Let's try it."

They finished their martinis and got into the Jaguar Mark VII and drove to Beverly Hills and stopped in front of a new restaurant built of bamboo and roofed with thatch and adorned with pagan idols and girt with coconut palms and illuminated with tall torches and named, inevitably, the Muu-Muu.

The exterior decor was repeated indoors—more bamboo, thatch, idols, palms, and torches; plus war masks, spears, fan-backed chairs of rattan, and dusky waiters festooned with leis and sporting chicken bones in their hair.

The headwaiter approached, grinning hugely. "Good evening, Mr. Shapian, Mrs. Shapian. Your table is ready."

"But I haven't got a reservation," said Ira.

The waiter chuckled so hard that his chicken bones rattled. "Sahib is humorous tonight," he simpered, wagging a forefinger. "This way, please."

The Shapians shrugged and followed the waiter to a table overlooking a genuine waterfall. Seated there, smiling whitely in his black suit, was Harry Clendennon.

He leaped to his feet. "Polly honey!" he cried, kissing her cheek. "Ira baby!" he cried, wringing his hand. "Sit, sit, sit!"

"Well, well, if it ain't old Mephisto," said Polly and sat.

Ira, shaking his head, sank into a rattan chair. "Harry, how do you do it?" he asked with grudging respect.

"American know-how," said Clendennon. He turned to the waiter. "Boy, bring us three Reverend Davidsons. . . . And, boy: chop-chop!"

Giggling, the waiter rushed away. "Kids," said Clendennon to the Shapians, "let me do the ordering. I really dig this Polynesian jazz."

"Swell," said Ira.

"I head for the islands whenever I can," said Clendennon. "Wild! That sweet, scented air, that blue, blue sea, that white surf breaking on the white sand—"

"I'm getting all choked up," said Polly.

"Me too," said Ira, "but could we say aloha and turn to business?"

"By all means," said Clendennon. "Ira baby, I flew out here to tell you, friendly like, that I know your game and you're a loser. You are not going to goose Mr. Davies into firing me. He can't. Where would he find a duplicate?"

"The Cosa Nostra?" suggested Polly helpfully.

"Amusing," said Clendennon, favoring her with a smile. "Also amusing when you called me Mephisto, and that's just my point. Ira chickie, be smart: settle for the devil you know."

"I suppose I should," agreed Ira. "Still, what if your replacement turns out to be not altogether a bastard?"

"Slim chance."

"Yes, but hope springs eternal."

"Ira, I've got a little shock for you. I'm going to level with you tonight. You won't believe me, of course, but I'm going to speak the truth. Your game is not completely a bust. You *do* have Mr. Davies just a tiny bit worried. If you stall long enough on the new contract, there *is* a possibility that Mr. Davies will lower the boom on me—just a flyspeck of a possibility, but nevertheless a possibility. I'd be a whole lot happier if I had your signature right now. My happiness, of course, is not exactly what you're after, but, Ira sweetie, I've figured out a way to make *you* happier too."

"Ah!" said Polly. "Here comes the zinger."

"No, not quite yet," said Ira. "He's still got a few bars of introduction."

"You're right, Ira baby," said Clendennon. "Just a bit more—but here's our drinks."

"Three Reverend Davidsons," grinned the waiter and placed before them three hollowed-out pineapples filled with crushed ice, grenadine syrup, and a ropy admixture of rums.

"Bring us a plate of *ramaki*, boy," said Clendennon to the waiter.

"Chop-chop!" replied the waiter merrily and jogged away.

"I'm queer for this Polynesian chow," confessed Clendennon. "Drink up, troops."

"Later," said Ira. "I want to be alert while you tell the lie."

"No lies," declared Clendennon. "Plain truth. I know what's bugging you, Ira. You think you've got a big hate on for me. Well, you're wrong. Me, guys like me, we're *facts* of television. And you long ago accepted it. . . . No, buddy boy, it's not me you're teed off at; it's somebody else."

"*Now* comes the zinger," said Ira to Polly.

"I can hardly wait," she said, leaning forward.

"Yes, now comes the zinger," said Clendennon. He paused a moment for dramatic effect. "Hear me good, Ira lover. Listen to the zinger: you are not mad at me at all. Who you are mad at is a guy named Ira Shapian."

Polly watched nervously as a thoughtful frown creased Ira's forehead. "Ira," she said, plucking his sleeve, "Ira, he's getting to you."

Ira gave Polly a reassuring pat, which failed signally to reassure her. "Go on, Clendennon," he said.

"You hate yourself," Clendennon continued. "You feel filthy, violated, *used*. But most of all, you feel you've sold out a big talent for a fistful of loot. And it *was* a big talent, Ira. I remember the shows you used to make—bold, gutsy, *important* shows."

"Ira, you're buying it," said Polly sadly.

"For the moment, yes," Ira agreed. "Because for the moment, Clendennon isn't lying."

"He will," said Polly.

"He won't," said Clendennon. He whipped a document out of his breast pocket. "Here it is, all legal and binding—a brand-new contract with a brand-new wrinkle. The raise, of course. The stock options, of course. But here's the weenie: you sign this paper tonight and tomorrow you get a six-months' leave of absence to produce a show for Star Spangled. And here's the list you can choose from: you can do *Oedipus Rex*, two full hours, with Olivier and Judith Anderson; or you can sail with the first atomic sub to go under the Antarctic icecap; or you can do the Central Intelligence Agency, everything below top secret; or you can do the oral contraceptive test in Puerto Rico with full cooperation from Muñoz Marín; or you can do the NASA Space Center at Houston; or you can do the heroin traffic—Hong Kong to Sicily to New York, with actual film. All these things are locked in, pussycat. Just pick the one you want, and we'll provide full financing and all the crew, cast, and equipment you need. This is the big time, Ira baby, not like those nickel-and-dime epics you made back in the old days. . . . Well, what do you say?"

There was silence now and a total lack of motion. Ira sat wrapped in thought; Polly, eyes closed, sent out a steady beam of prayer; Clendennon was as still as an expert angler watching a trout sniff a fly.

"*Ramaki!*" announced the waiter proudly and laid a plate on the table. Clendennon dismissed him with a quick, angry gesture.

Ira spoke. "No," he said.

"No *what*, Ira baby?" asked Clendennon with a cautious smile.

"No deal," said Ira, and Polly opened her eyes and cast them gratefully heavenward.

Clendennon kept smiling. "What is it, Ira? Don't you like these projects?"

"I love these projects," answered Ira. "Who would not?"

"But?"

"But what I love even better is the possibility that I can get you fired."

"A *small* possibility. A *dim* possibility. An *infinitesimal* possibility."

"True . . . but my *only* possibility."

Without changing expression, Clendennon picked up a piece of *ramaki*. His smiling teeth lopped it in half like a guillotine. Rage boiled inside him, rage against Ira that demanded release. But he was far too shrewd to direct the wrath toward its proper target. "Waiter!" he roared.

The waiter—wide grin and lei—was instantly at his side. "Sahib?" he said pleasantly.

"You call this *ramaki?*" snarled Clendennon.

"Yes, sir," said the waiter, his grin fixed. "Very good. Specialty of the house."

"Look, boy, save that palaver for the tourists. Now take this slop back to the kitchen and bring me some *ramaki!*"

Suddenly a newcomer was at the table, a large, handsome man the color of ancient copper. He was dressed not in lei and chicken bones but in a well-cut dinner jacket. "Something wrong?" he asked in a deep, smooth voice.

Polly and Ira bounded to their feet.

"Linus!" they shouted. "Linus Calloway!"

They hurled themselves upon him, clasping his hands, slapping his back, hugging him with pure joy. And Linus replied in kind. "Polly! Ira! Ira! Polly!" he cried delightedly and enveloped them in his great, brawny arms.

Clendennon gaped. "What the hell's going on here?"

Linus' face grew instantly sober. "Excuse me," he said, releasing Polly and Ira. "Something you wanted, sir?" he said to Clendennon.

"You the manager?" asked Clendennon sharply.

"Manager and owner," replied Linus.

"Good . . . Now, about this so-called *ramaki*—"

"Oh, ignore him," said Ira, grabbing Linus again. "He's just my boss."

"What *is* all this?" asked Polly, indicating the hokey Polynesian motif. "What in the world are you up to?"

"It's a long, long story," answered Linus.

"So sit down and tell it," said Ira and pushed Linus into a fan-backed chair.

"Look—" said Clendennon.

"Butt out," said Ira.

"Linus, why didn't you tell us you were in Los Angeles?" said Polly.

"Where have you been for the last twenty years?" said Ira.

"How did you get into the restaurant business?" said Polly.

"Why haven't we heard from you?" said Ira.

"If you will forgive this intrusion—" said Clendennon.

"Eat your *ramaki*," said Polly.

"It is *not ramaki!*" said Clendennon crossly.

"Come on, Linus, start at the beginning," said Ira.

Linus laughed his deep, booming laugh. "Okay, kids, but I'll have to give it to you fast—I mean like in five minutes. This is opening night, remember, and the joint's full of customers."

"So get started already," said Polly.

"Right! Five-minute version: the adventures of Linus Calloway. Now, let's see. When's the last time we were all together?"

"New York, 1942," replied Ira. "Just before you went into the Navy."

"As a mess boy!" said Polly indignantly. "Scandalous! Making a mess boy out of a man like you just because you happen to have dark skin! Scandalous!"

"Damn right!" agreed Ira. "Well, thank God we've gotten a little more civilized since then."

"Have we?" asked Linus mildly.

"Haven't we?" asked Polly, searching his eyes. "Oh, sure, I know we've only just scratched the surface in race relations, but we have made a *little* progress. . . . Haven't we?" she repeated uncertainly.

"Look, I've given up on the *ramaki*," said Clendennon. "All I'd like to say is this: Polly and Ira, if you want to learn about Mr. Calloway in five minutes, wouldn't it be wise to postpone the symposium on the color problem till another time?"

"But Linus' life *is* the color problem," said Ira. "Anyhow, it was. Is it still?"

"It is," said Linus.

"Good!" said Polly.

"And we're with you one hundred percent," said Ira.

"But what about this restaurant?" said Polly.

"May I be moderator?" said Clendennon. "So far we have established that Mr. Calloway joined the Navy as a mess boy in 1942. Will you proceed, sir?"

"Thank you," said Linus. "Well, I was a damn good mess boy. Us folks got natural rhythm, you know, even in the kitchen. I got so good that by 1944 I was chef to an admiral at Pearl Harbor. Pretty soft gig; all I had to do was keep coming up with new Hawaiian recipes. So I made friends with the colorful natives, and by the end of the war, I could whip up one hell of a *luau*."

"With the possible exception of *ramaki*," said Clendennon. "All right, Mr. Calloway, the war is over now and you have mastered the *haute cuisine* of Micronesia. Then what?"

"I have also mastered a game called craps. I land in San Francisco with ten thousand dollars in my skivvy shirt. I open a little place just off Market Street. The Muu-Muu, I call it. I bring in a few of my kinfolk and they bring in a few of *their* kinfolk, and I teach 'em a bit of pidgin and how to braid chicken bones in their hair. The place is a smash. I expand. I open another Muu-Muu in Portland, then another in Seattle. And now, tonight, still another in Beverly Hills, and we're up to date."

"Why have you never called or written?" asked Ira.

"For a good reason," replied Linus, looking directly at Ira. "Because there's something I need from you, and you won't give it to me, and we'll both be horribly embarrassed."

"Ridiculous!" said Ira stoutly. "There's nothing in the world I wouldn't do for you. Now, come on, Linus, tell me what you need."

"A program director," said Linus.

Ira looked puzzled. "For your restaurants?"

"For my television station," replied Linus.

A tremor of nervousness shook Clendennon. "You have a television station, Mr. Calloway?"

"I'm about to open one."

"Where?"

Linus laughed. "Here comes the funny part, Mr. Clendennon. You may possibly have noticed that I am a Negro? Well, my television station is located in Birmingham."

"Oy!" said Clendennon.

"Precisely," said Linus.

Distress clouded Ira's face. "Linus, do you mind if I ask some questions?"

"Shoot."

"Where did you get the money to buy this station?"

"From my restaurants."

"And where will you get the money to operate it?"

"Same place."

"You have no grants from foundations or the government or like that?"

"No."

"Do you expect to sell any advertising?"

"Me? Black Linus sell advertising in Birmingham? Surely you jest."

"Are you aware that you won't get any network affiliation?"

"I'm aware."

"Do you know what it costs to operate a tv station?"

"I do."

"Will your income from the restaurants cover it?"

"Just barely."

"So what have you got left to buy programs with?"

"Nothing—or close to it."

"I see," said Ira and returned to gloom.

"Now me," said Polly. "Just one question, Linus, but a big one: Why?"

"Same old reason. I still believe we can do something about race relations. Only I believe it in a different way now. When you kids knew me twenty years ago, I believed it simply because I had to. But today there's a whole new face on it; there's an added ingredient —a thing called hope."

"You *are* encouraged then?" asked Polly eagerly. "I mean about the progress we've made in desegregation?"

"Not a bit. Oh, sure, there's a few places we can get into today where we couldn't get into before. But there's one place we still can't enter, and we *must*, or else the rest is meaningless. I'm talking about the Caucasian heart."

"But, Linus, what can we do about *that?* Can we pass laws? Can we legislate love?"

"No, but we can *educate* love, or, at least, the appearance of love. Every politician and clergyman on earth, working day and night, can't persuade one white man to love one Negro unless the white man wants to. But the white man can be taught that hatred—overt, active hatred, fire hoses and police dogs—that kind of thing is plain bad business. The whites need us for our big, untapped reservoir of brainpower and purchasing power; we need them because they've got the tools to open the floodgates. . . . I sure wouldn't call it love, but it'll have to do until the real thing comes along."

"And you think it will come along? I mean the real thing?"

Linus shrugged. "Someday maybe. At least there's hope. It's not a very *big* hope, I'll admit; in fact, it's pretty damn dim, but, for the first time, it's hope that can honestly be called hope. Because today we have a new way to educate people, not to love—that's too much to ask for—but to show them where their self-interest lies. Today we have in our hands the most powerful, most persuasive, most graphic, most convincing teaching device since the beginning of time. I'm talking about television!"

"Ah, now I understand," said Polly. "You're starting an educational tv station."

"Good God, no!" exclaimed Linus. "And I'll thank you never to use those words again. You say 'educational tv' and people immediately think of four guys with glasses discussing Babylonian artifacts. . . . No, Polly, I intend to give 'em shows as funny as *Beverly Hillbillies* and as scary as *Twilight Zone*, but all the time, slyly, so cute they never even notice it, I'm going to slip 'em a little learning."

"Would you mind a question from me?" asked Clendennon.

"You're my guest."

"Mr. Calloway, I agree that your approach is basically sound. But how do you expect to buy all these shows with no money?"

"Well, if I could find the right program director," said Linus, carefully not looking at Ira, "if I was lucky enough to get a man who knew how to make good, honest, entertaining shows that didn't cost a fortune, I'd be home free."

"And what would you be willing to pay such a person?" asked Clendennon.

Linus threw back his head and laughed. "Hell, man, money's no object! I could go as high as a hundred dollars a week."

Ira slid deeper into his chair, shame weighing on him like a millstone. "Do it, Ira!" cried Polly silently in her heart. "Do it! For your immortal soul—and mine—please, please, do it!" And Clendennon's face was a mask concealing triumph.

"Well, I certainly wish you all the luck in the world," said Clendennon, offering his hand to Linus.

"Thank you," said Linus, rising. "I'll take this *ramaki* back to the kitchen."

"No, no, no, no," insisted Clendennon. "I'm sorry I made such a fuss. I was all wrong. It's *fine ramaki*. That's what confused me; it's so much better than any *ramaki* I ever tasted."

"Yeah," said Linus. "Well, good night, Polly. Good night, Ira."

"Good night."

"Good night."

Linus left. "Nice fellow," said Clendennon.

"Aah, shaddup," snarled Ira. Then, turning on Polly, "And you too."

"I didn't say anthing," said Polly.

"You didn't have to. I know what you're thinking. . . . Well, forget it. You don't buy diamond earrings for a hundred dollars a week."

"Who asked for diamond earrings?"

"Who asked for two lamebrained sons?" countered Ira hotly. "Who asked for two stinking houses? Who asked for two lousy swimming pools?"

Polly stood. "I'm going home. Excuse me, Harry."

Ira jumped to his feet. He grasped Polly's hand. "I'm sorry, Polly," he said, overcome with contrition. "I was way out of line. Please forgive me."

She hesitated briefly, then nodded and resumed her seat.

"You too, Harry," said Ira to Clendennon. "Please accept my apologies. I didn't mean to make a scene."

"Don't give it a thought, Ira baby," smiled Clendennon, squeezing Ira's shoulder. "It's just like I said before, you've got a big hate on for yourself. What you need is a purification—a big project, a real challenge, something to give you back your self-respect. And it just happens I've got it for you. Here—" he shoved the contract toward Ira—"look over this list: *Oedipus Rex*, the atomic sub, Puerto Rico, NASA, CIA, the heroin traffic. Just tell me what you want."

"What I want is to see you on the street with a tin cup," said Ira.

A ball of unease began to grow in Clendennon's belly, but he clung to his composure. "All right, pussycat, forget the list. Is there anything *you* would particularly like to do?"

"Yes," answered Ira. "I would particularly like to see you on the street with a tin cup."

Clendennon's mind, fighting panic, began to function furiously. Somehow, somewhere, there had to be a project that would tempt Ira. But what? He rummaged frantically; nothing came to light. Then, finally, a thought struck him—a thin, dismal thought, but a thought.

"Listen," he said apologetically, "here's another idea, not exactly sensational, but let's see how you react."

"I hate it," said Ira.

Clendennon pressed on: "We're scheduling a sixty-minute special on the dangers in food additives. It's coming out of this college

Jefferson Tatum owns—Acanthus, it's called—which I'm told has been
turned into a first-class school."

Ira had a sudden curious sensation as of a fresh wind dispelling
a filthy yellow fog. Acanthus, he thought, his heart leaping. Acanthus. Owens Mill. Boo . . . Yes, Boo. Purification. To hold Boo again
—golden, salving, *cleansing* Boo.

"Give me your pen, Clendennon," he said, and as Polly and
Clendennon looked on, each mystified, Ira signed the contract.

Chapter 11

Virgil Tatum was seated behind his desk at Acanthus College and Jefferson Tatum was seated in a chair nearby when Ira Shapian entered the office.

Virgil rushed forward with a delighted smile. "Ira! Damn, it's good to clap eyes on you again!"

"And you," answered Ira, seizing Virgil's hand, his delight as honest as Virgil's own. "Unbelievable! Eighteen years since I've seen you, and you haven't gotten one day older!"

"Look who's talking! Why, you actually look *younger!*"

"Thank you," said Ira. "On behalf of my tailor, my masseur, and my orthodontist, thank you."

"How's that lovely Polly?" asked Virgil.

"Polly? Oh, fine, fine."

"Still gorgeous?"

"Yes, I guess so."

"Lucky pup!" said Virgil, regarding Ira with something akin to envy. "What a piece of work that Polly is! Pal, I hope you know what a rare woman you married: beauty, brains, spirit, guts, patience, kindness—in fact, everything a man dreams about!"

"Listen," said Ira, "this could be your chance. I'll be tied up for several weeks in Owens Mill. Maybe now's the time for you to fly West and try your luck with Polly."

"Don't tempt me," said Virgil. "I might forget I'm your friend."

"Hate to interrupt," said Jefferson, standing with fixed smile and extended hand, "but how do?"

"I believe you've met my father," said Virgil. "Pa, you remember Ira Shapian. He was stationed here during the war."

"Surely," said Jefferson. "You boys done a hell of a job. Not one enemy attack all the time you were in Owens Mill."

Ira grinned. "Yes, I remember you, Mr. Tatum. Virgil and I are lying to each other, but you *really* haven't changed."

"Nothing like bourbon whisky and Tatum Cigarettes to keep the roses in your cheeks," said Jefferson.

"Pa's going to show you around the campus," said Virgil. "I'm sorry I can't do it myself, but I've got a faculty meeting."

"Perfectly all right."

"But we'll meet back here at noon for lunch, okay?"

"Fine."

Virgil paused a moment. "Look, Ira, I hope you don't mind, but the whole town's been buzzing about your coming down. I asked a few of your old friends to join us for lunch."

A drum-roll of excitement started under Ira's breastbone. "Marvelous," he said with exactly the right measure of enthusiasm. "Who's coming?"

"Not many. I know how tight your schedule is. I just asked a few of the Owenses."

"Fine, fine," said Ira. Then, casually: "Will Boo be here?"

"As a matter of fact, no. I invited her, but she said she couldn't make it."

The drumming in Ira's chest slowed to dirge tempo. "Too bad," he said, keeping his tone light. "How is she?"

"Boo? There now is the one who doesn't change, except maybe to get more beautiful."

The drumming segued into bolero rhythm. "Yes, I remember," he said with an elaborately faint smile. "Nice-looking girl. It seems to me somebody—I forget who—told me she never remarried after that Navy flier got killed in the war. Can that be true?"

"It is."

"Seems impossible," said Ira.

"Seems insoluble," said Virgil.

"It's going on half past ten," said Jefferson, "and I'm thinking Mr. Shapian might maybe like to have a look at the college, seeing as how he flew all the way out here from Hollywood, California, to do a show about us on the television."

Ira and Virgil wrenched themselves back to the here and now. "Of course," said Virgil. "See you at noon, Ira."

"Right."

"Be sure to give Ira a good look around," Virgil instructed his father. "Lots of interesting new things at Acanthus."

"So I hear," said Ira. "In fact, they tell me you've passed a kind of miracle."

"That's it—a miracle!" exclaimed Jefferson. "Wait till you see our school of nutrition and public health. A real pisscutter!"

"And all our other schools," added Virgil. "Fine arts, humanities, history, economics—"

"Yes, sir," interrupted Jefferson, "we have gone and made us a real crackerjack of a college. . . . But wait, Mr. Shapian, just wait till you see the prize in the crackerjack! I mean the school of nutrition and public health. Come, sonny."

He herded Ira out of the administration building and onto an oak-shaded quadrangle. Three sides of the quadrangle were bounded by the standard structures of Academe—Gothic arches, leaded panes, red brick draped with ivy. On the fourth side there stood, anomalously, a long, low, contemporary slab of glass and aluminum. It was toward this building that Jefferson steered Ira.

"Kind of a shame Boo couldn't make it for lunch today," said Ira as they walked. "Not sick or anything?"

"No, just busy," Jefferson answered. "You remember Boo and all her fancy projects."

"Yes," said Ira, "I remember Boo and all her fancy projects."

Sweatered students carrying books, tweeded teachers carrying briefcases hurried or sauntered along the paths that crisscrossed the quadrangle. Suddenly, heading toward Ira and Jefferson, a bicycle appeared—a high, ancient, well-used bicycle of English manufacture. Hunched over the handlebars, his stumpy legs churning vigorously, was a pink, twinkly bald man with suede patches on his elbows. He braked the bike to a squealing stop. "Morning, Tatum!" he cried with a jocular toss of his head at Jefferson.

Jefferson glowered silently

The cyclist examined Ira. "And who is this swarthy gentleman with the porcelain front teeth?" he asked.

Ira waited for Jefferson to make the introduction, but the old man stood in rocklike silence. "I'm Ira Shapian," said Ira.

"Ah, yes, the television person! Heard all about you. Linden-Evarts is my name. Cultural anthropology."

"Well, well!" said Ira, impressed. "A great pleasure, sir. I've admired your work for many years."

"Thank you," said Linden-Evarts, beaming on Ira. "But it's all been finger exercises so far. The big work lies ahead." He winked at Jefferson. "Eh, Tatum?"

Jefferson made a rumbling sound.

"May I ask what you're up to?" said Ira to Linden-Evarts.

"What I am up to, young man, is far and away the most pungent enterprise going on at this yeasty new university. I, Shapian, am endeavoring to discover how this anachronism—" he pointed a thumb at Jefferson—"continues to hold the children of Ham in bondage. Has this old oak—" indicating Jefferson again—"truly bowed before the winds of change? Or is he, as I suspect, only giving a clever imitation? Negroes are in open insurrection everywhere in America, but here in Owens Mill all is serene. Why, Shapian? How does the tyrant pacify the populace? Piquant question, eh? Well, there is an answer, and I shall not rest until I know it. Good-bye, sir. Good-bye, old oak."

With a merry wave he pedaled away.

Ira looked curiously at Jefferson. "I don't mean to pry, Mr. Tatum, but you *are* still picking up the tab at Acanthus?"

"Every penny," said Jefferson, tight-lipped.

"And you're letting Linden-Evarts go ahead with his project?"

Jefferson smiled painfully. "It's what they call academic freedom," he said. Then, as the vast glass slab loomed before them, the pain in the old man's face sweetened into joy. "Here she is," he said proudly. "Five hundred feet of windows and all Thermopane. Every lab air-conditioned, triple-filtered, and irradiated. Newest, best, most expensive equipment in the whole wide world. Finest teachers, finest students, finest everything . . . Mr. Shapian, won't you come into our school of nutrition and public health?"

He swung open a huge glass door and gallantly extended his palm, inviting Ira to enter. They walked into a stark, spotless, rubber-tiled lobby, adorned only by a single bust of Asclepiades. "To your right," said Jefferson, indicating a door marked "OFFICE OF THE DIRECTOR." He knocked, and they entered.

Dr. Clara Silenko, seated at her desk in a white smock, raised her handsome head. "Good morning, Tatum," she said.

"Good morning, good morning, good morning!" chirped Jefferson. "Dr. Silenko, I'd like to make you acquainted with Mr. Ira Shapian, the famous television producer from Hollywood, California. Mr. Shapian, this here is Dr. Clara Silenko, M.D. Johns Hopkins, Ph.D. Harvard."

Dr. Silenko exchanged greetings with Ira and turned to Jefferson. "Well, Tatum, where shall we start?"

"Right here," answered Jefferson. "Tell Mr. Shapian what that is."

He pointed to a work-table beside Dr. Silenko's desk. There, held in a clamp, was a two-foot length of painted board. The paint was scaled, chipped, blistered, and, in some spots, was flaked away completely.

"That is an ordinary piece of siding," she said to Ira, "which was painted with a good grade of commercial enamel and allowed to dry thoroughly. For the last month I have been coating the board each morning with a two percent solution of polyoxyethylene mono-stearate. You can see what has happened to the paint."

"I can see," said Ira. "But what is polyoxyethylene monostearate?"

"It's an additive—specifically, an emulsifier—that is used very widely in the manufacture of cake mixes, candies, dill pickles, vita-min capsules, peanut butter, sweet rolls, doughnuts, cakes, pies, and any number of pastries."

"You hear that, Mr. Shapian?" cried Jefferson. "Did you hear that? The whole goddam country is filling its belly with paint remover!"

Ira's eyes widened in astonishment. "You mean to say the Food and Drug Administration allows this?"

"FDA!" sneered Jefferson. "Why, it's a blot, man. It's a blot and a shame and a disgrace and a puke. . . . Come on, Doctor, show Mr. Shapian some of the stuff FDA allows."

"Follow me, please," said Dr. Silenko and led them to a lab where row on row of wire cages contained colonies of white mice. Students and technicians moved among the cages, some making observations, some writing notes, some giving injections, some refilling food troughs.

Dr. Silenko stopped in front of a cage where a group of mice lay puny and listless, their tiny rib cages projecting gauntly.

"Good God!" exclaimed Ira. "What's the matter with them?"

"Cancer of the bladder," replied the doctor. "We've been feeding them beta-naphthylamine."

"Which is?"

"A dye commonly used to color butter and oleomargarine."

"And," added Jefferson, "certified by FDA! Cancer peddlers, that's all they are! Plain cancer peddlers!"

"Now, Tatum," said Dr. Silenko soothingly.

But Jefferson would not be pacified. "You said it yourself, Doc-tor," he insisted. "How many food dyes has FDA certified?"

"Seven."

"And how many of them seven can give you cancer?"

"We've proved five so far."

"Namely?"

"Yellow AB and Yellow OB—both beta-naphthylamine; you see

the results on these mice. Now observe the lesions on the mice in the next cage. These are skin cancers caused by Blue No. 1, Green No. 2, and Green No. 3—all dyes certified for use in candy, ice cream, jellies, and puddings."

Jefferson pressed on. "All right, so much for the dyes. Now let's get to that gluey stuff with the long name."

"Carboxymethyl cellulose?"

"That's the one."

"Used principally in cheeses, salad dressings, and canned fruit. Definitely carcinogenic."

"Thank you. Now the other one with the long name, the sooty one you find in bacon and ham and all kinds of smoked meats?"

"Polycyclic aromatic hydrocarbons."

"Carcinogen?"

"No question."

"Good! Would you run through a few more carcinogens, please, ma'am?"

"Well, there's paraffin, which is used to preserve apples."

"An apple a day keeps the doctor away!" snorted Jefferson. "Hah!"

"There are the pesticide residues you find in meat. Ironically, the most expensive cuts of meat, the ones marbled with fat, are the most likely to retain pesticides."

"You getting all this, Mr. Shapian?" asked Jefferson.

"What I'm getting is a little sick," replied Ira.

"And who would not?" said the old man righteously. "The nerve of them little pantywaists in Washington, every one of 'em on the public tit. . . . Oh, excuse me, ma'am."

"You're excused," said Dr. Silenko.

Jefferson resumed: "The nerve of 'em, I say, the ungodly gall of them little clock-punchers to accuse cigarettes of giving people cancer when *they're* the real cancer merchants in this country!"

"Aha!" said Ira quietly, for suddenly a truth came clear to him. All the way from Hollywood to Owens Mill, in those rare moments when he was not thinking of Boo, he had speculated on Jefferson Tatum's motives: Why had a rough old buzzard like Jefferson spent millions to make a first-class university out of Acanthus? Why was he spending another bundle of money to buy sixty minutes of prime television time for a public service show? Now, in a flash, Ira saw and understood the whole plot.

Foxy old grandpa, thought Ira admiringly. Shrewd old gut fighter! But, thought Ira, there were *rules* in this fight. If old Tatum was under the impression he was going to have everything his way, he had better be disabused of the notion, and quickly. Equal time for both sides was a cardinal law of television, and unless Jefferson was prepared to agree, Ira intended to kill the program here and now.

"Mr. Tatum," said Ira with a careful smile, "these are very interesting things I'm learning from you and Dr. Silenko."

"Oh, there's lots more, sonny. Not just cancer, but heart trouble and breakbone fever and the dry heaves and any other misery you might name. We are getting poisoned to death, and worse every year. Every year new poisons, new additives, new chemicals—tons and tons—more, always more. And that's what you're gonna show people on the television, ain't you, Mr. Shapian?"

"Oh, yes, that's what I'm going to show people on the television. But you understand, of course, there will also be a rebuttal, that I mean to present both sides of the argument?"

"Wouldn't have it any other way," said Jefferson piously.

"And whoever rebuts," continued Ira, "is likely to have some pretty sharp questions. In fact, I can think of one right now."

"Go ahead, sonny. Ask the pretty lady doctor. My money's on her."

"All right, Dr. Silenko. It's an obvious question. If it's true that Americans are eating all these poisons, why are we living so much longer than we used to live, say, fifty years ago?"

"I will give you an obvious answer to your obvious question," said Dr. Silenko. "Today, because of better sanitation, better housing, better doctors, better hospitals, better surgery, better medication, we are keeping people alive who wouldn't have stood a chance fifty years ago."

"Is that bad?"

"Is it good? Sure, life is good, if by 'life' you mean health and vigor. But America has become a nation of invalids. Let me cite figures. Nearly one-half our population—and I include babies—are suffering from some sort of chronic disease. In the United States at last report there were a total of 88,959,534 *registered cases* of chronic illness. Some more figures: in the seven years from June, 1947, to June, 1955, 4,321,000 young men were called up by their draft boards; out of that number, 2,248,000—*fifty-two percent*—were rejected as unfit. That is an increase of eleven percent over World War II, an increase of *twenty-one* percent over World War I.

. . . The signs are written large, Mr. Shapian: America is getting
sicker by the day."

"And you blame it all on food?"

"Most of it. The body is a machine designed to be fueled by certain natural nutrients, not by chemicals. Add chemicals, and the
machine simply won't function as it should. Oh, yes, you can be
kept alive, but how? By adding more chemicals, that's how. More
work for the kidneys, the liver, the gut. More years and less health.
I don't know about you, sir, but I call it a poor bargain."

"That's telling him, missy!" crowed Jefferson. "Come on, let's go
look at them mice you injected with sodium nitrite."

Dr. Silenko shook her head. "Too late, Tatum. They only lasted
thirty-five minutes."

"No kidding?" said Jefferson, a sunny grin lighting his face. He
turned to Ira. "You like hot dogs, Mr. Shapian?"

"Hot dogs? Sure. Why?"

"Sodium nitrite is what gives 'em that pretty pink color," he said
jovially. "Okay, kids, let's go over to Dr. Levine's lab. Dr. Levine's
our water expert."

"One moment," said Ira. "The thought really isn't terribly appeal-
ing to me, but it's time for lunch."

And, indeed, the campus bell tower was chiming noon.

"Hell!" complained the old man. "Just when it was getting interesting."

"Thank you, Dr. Silenko," said Ira. "I'll try hard not to get under-
foot, but I'm afraid you're going to have me around for a while."

"I look forward to it," she said. "Good-bye, Shapian. Good-bye,
Tatum."

"Fine woman," said Jefferson to Ira as they walked back across
the quadrangle. "But no action."

"Tough," said Ira politely.

"And speaking of that," Jefferson continued, "should you crave a
little nookie while you're in town, just let me know."

"You're very kind," said Ira.

"Proud to help out. I like you, Mr. Shapian. Fact is, I like practically all you Jew fellers."

"Not that it makes any difference," said Ira, "but I'm an Armenian."

"You're right," said Jefferson. "It don't make any difference."

They walked through the arch of the administration building and
into Virgil's office. An elderly Negro in a mess jacket was setting a
table for lunch at one end of the large room. Virgil was seated at his

desk; across from him sat William Ransom Owens and, carrying the inevitable briefcase, Robert E. Lee Owens.

The Owenses bounded to their feet and exchanged hearty greetings with Ira.

"Mr. Shapian," said William Ransom, twitching with eagerness, "I've been thinking that possibly I might be of some slight help with the background music for your television show. What I had in mind were authentic regional airs—'Black Is the Color of My True Love's Hair,' 'Bile Dem Cabbage Down,' things of that sort—all symphonically arranged, of course. Done, you might say, in the manner of Dvořák's 'New World.'"

"Sit down and shut up," said Jefferson.

Ira placed a gentle hand on William Ransom's shoulder. "Thank you, William Ransom," he said. "It sounds just right. I'll put you in touch with my music director when he arrives."

"You *will?*" cried William Ransom, clapping his hands.

"I will," Ira promised.

"And I," said Lee, approaching Ira with his briefcase, "want to assure you sir, that my department is prepared to make all its data available to you. I have here, for instance—" He started to unzip the briefcase.

"You close that thing before I tear it up for dog leashes," said Jefferson.

"Thank you, Lee," said Ira. "My script writers will call on you as soon as they get here."

"Thank you, sir," said Lee and stuck out his tongue at Jefferson— as soon as Jefferson's back was turned.

"Excuse me," said Virgil, a small frown of bewilderment on his brow. He walked across the room to the Negro waiter. "I think you've made a mistake, Charles," he said. "You're setting six places, and there's only five for lunch."

"No, Mr. Virgil, there's going to be one extra," replied the waiter.

"Oh? Who?"

"I hope you don't mind," said Boo, entering the office. "I found out I could make it after all, so I phoned Charles."

"Delighted," said Virgil. "Boo, you remember Ira Shapian, of course."

"Of course," she said.

"Of course," said Ira. *Of course*, said his swelling heart, his rushing blood, his brimming black eyes.

He took her outstretched hand.

Chapter 12

A thin, frosty moon hung over the pounding waters, and inside the beach house Boo said to Ira, "This is wrong."

"Don't you think I know?" he cried. "Don't you think I'm crumbling inside?"

"Oh, my poor Ira!" she whispered and laid a tender hand upon him.

"My poor Boo, my poor Boo!" He took her hand in both of his, pulled it to his mouth, kissed each knuckle fiercely. "My poor Boo!" he repeated. "To love so much, to be so alone for so long, for so long!"

She looked at him closely in the light of the dancing driftwood flames. "My poor Ira!" she said, her voice trembling with anguish. "You are crying!"

"For you," he replied. "For your beauty. For your gallantry."

"Ira, Ira, Ira!" She kissed his salty eyes and pulled his head to her bosom.

"I love you, Boo. I *want* you."

"And I you!"

"Now!"

"Yes, yes, now!"

He raised his head. His mouth found hers, clung, probed.

"Ira, Ira, Ira!"

"Yes, yes!"

"No!"

"No?"

"This is wrong."

"Oh, wrong," he agreed. "Oh, *deeply* wrong!"

"We can't do this to Polly."

"You're right, Boo. We can't. We mustn't."

"I love you, Ira—achingly and forever."

"Me too, Boo."

"I love you tempestuously and in my marrow."

"Yes," said Ira. "Yes."

"There are no words for how I love you. There is only song."

"Song," said Ira. "Yes."

"You are my dream, my essence."

"Kiss me," said Ira.

"Oh, Ira."

Again they kissed, their lips prehensile with desire. His hand held her nape, stroked the golden tendrils of her hair, found the zipper in the back of her dress.

"There's a hook on the top," she said.

"I can't seem to work it."

"Here, I'll show you." But as she started to reach, resolution abruptly returned. She sprang away from Ira—all the way to the other end of the long sofa before the fieldstone fireplace.

"What can we be thinking of?" she cried.

"You're right, you're right," said Ira, hanging his head in shame.

"It was madness to come out to the beach house."

"Insanity."

"We must go now."

"Yes."

"We have been strong for eighteen years. Let us not weaken now."

"When I think how strong you've been," said Ira, "I want to cry."

"But you're not going to, are you?" she said with anxiety.

"No," he said, biting his lip.

She rose. "Come."

He got up, grasped her hand tightly. Together they walked out the front door of the beach house and into the sudden glare of a pair of headlights speeding up the driveway.

Boo and Ira stood frozen. A small, homemade sports car screeched to a halt, the headlights full on them. Gabriel Owens Fuller got out of the car slowly. He approached his mother, his head tilted with puzzlement. "Ma, what are you doing out here this time of night?"

Boo tried desperately to still her breathing. "Hello, dear," she said, achieving a small smile. "Gabriel, I'd like you to meet—"

"Ira Shapian," said Gabriel before Boo could finish. "It *is* Ira Shapian, isn't it?"

Black Armenian eyes searched black Armenian eyes. *Oh, my God!* thought Ira, for he knew immediately and with perfect certainty that he was looking at his son. *Oh, my God in heaven!* he thought.

And Boo, seeing the truth strike Ira like a hammer blow, seeing him reel with the force of it, looked quickly at Gabriel to find out whether he had been visited by the same staggering realization. But Gabriel was grinning; in fact, Gabriel was chuckling.

"Sure, it's Ira Shapian," he continued. "Right, Mr. Shapian?"

Ira nodded dumbly.

Gabriel laughed now, peal on merry peal.

"What's so funny, dear?" asked Boo, controlling the flutter in her voice.

"Ma, do you remember the time we were talking about that old photo of Mr. Shapian? Remember I told you about the crazy feeling I had, that I kept seeing Mr. Shapian's eyes all the time? Well, I was right! Every time I passed a mirror, I saw those eyes. Look, Ma —they're exactly like mine!"

"Yes, they are rather alike," said Boo.

"*Exactly* alike!" declared Gabriel. "And that explains what happened. First I saw Mr. Shapian's eyes in the photo; then, whenever I looked in a mirror, I saw the afterimage. A common case of *déjà vu*, that's all it was."

"Yes, that's all it was."

"Oh, boy, what a relief to get that mystery cleared up! If there's anything I hate, it's something I don't understand."

"You see, dear, how simple things are?"

"Yeah," said Gabriel. "So what are you doing out here in the middle of the night with Mr. Shapian?"

"Well—" said Boo.

"Wait!" exclaimed Gabriel. "That's simple too. You're just showing him some of the places he knew when he was stationed here. A sentimental journey, sort of."

"That's it," said Boo eagerly. "That is precisely it."

"Gee, Ma, I hope I didn't scare you, pulling in the driveway like this," said Gabriel apologetically. "I was out testing my new fuel injection system and I saw lights in the beach house."

"Perfectly all right, dear."

"Well, I'll be on my way now," said Gabriel.

"As a matter of fact, we were just leaving ourselves," said Boo.

"As a matter of fact," said Ira, suddenly finding his voice, "I'd like to stay and have a drink, if you don't mind, Boo."

She gave him a curious glance. "Of course," she said.

"It's certainly been a great pleasure meeting you, my boy," said Ira and shook his natural son by the hand.

"Thank you, sir," said Gabriel. "Good night, Ma."

He vaulted into his car and roared away. Ira took Boo firmly by the elbow and steered her back into the beach house.

"Ira, I don't understand. We had just agreed to go back to Owens Mill."

"No," he said. His voice was gentle, his face was soft with love, but his no was definite.

"Ira—"

"Sit," he said quietly and drew her down beside him on the sofa. "Sit and be truthful with me."

"Ira, listen—"

"He's mine, isn't he? Gabriel is mine. You never married that Navy flier. It was all a fix to give the boy a name."

Boo's eyes were downcast, her voice scarcely audible. "Yes."

"Gabriel is my son," said Ira slowly, overcome with the force of it. "My son," he repeated and suddenly leaped to his feet. "I must go to him!" he cried.

"No, Ira, no!" She clutched his arm fiercely.

"But he's my son! My flesh! My blood!"

"Ira, think! You can never tell him, don't you see?"

Ira struggled, then went slack. "I see," he said sadly. "Yes, of course. I can never let him know. My flesh, my blood, can never know."

"Poor Ira!"

"And what about poor Boo? For eighteen years you've kept this secret bravely, telling nobody, not even me."

"I'm sorry, Ira."

"*Sorry?*" It was a shout. "You say you're *sorry?* For what, Boo? Do you know what any other woman would have done in your circumstances?"

"I don't know. I only did what I had to."

"Observe, Boo. I am on my knees." He was.

"I don't want you on your knees," she insisted, tugging at his shoulders.

He knelt firmly. "I spend my life in a world where honor is dead and purity is an obscene joke. I grovel with the pack. I wear their stench. . . . Now in the presence of such cleanliness, I must kneel."

"Arise, my love," she said, still tugging.

He still knelt. "I worship you, Boo."

She fell to her knees beside him. "I love you, Ira."

"I called you gallant before. Now I know just how gallant you are, how *noble* you are!"

"It is you who are noble, good and gentle and tender and sweetly vulnerable."

"Kiss me, Boo."

"But how can we do this to Polly?"

"We can because we must. There may be retribution ahead; I don't know. All I know is that I can't let go of such great beauty, now that I truly know the greatness of it. Boo, kiss me. Hold me. Be *one* with me."

"Yes! Oh, yes, yes, yes!"

Wildly they embraced, wildness begetting wildness.

"You are like the murmur of wings in my heart," said Boo. "You are the morning."

"How do you work this hook on top of your zipper?" said Ira.

Chapter 13

When a man passes the age of forty, the incursions of time are too evident to be denied. The joints stiffen, the wind dwindles, the belly skids, the psyche churns turgidly, and the crankcase needs oil. There are, however, certain measures a man can employ to stem the melancholy tide: he can take up calisthenics and massage; he can eat moderately and sleep immoderately; he can go on frequent vacations; he can interest himself in hobbies; he can enroll in adult education classes. . . . Or, most efficacious of all, he can fall in love.

Ira Shapian, in the weeks following his reunion with Boo, became as young as Romeo and as unlikely. Often and loud he cried the tonic words "I love you!" and as the phrase came rushing from his lips and sweetly reverberated in his ears, his heart would soar and his every corpuscle would shimmer.

And there were words from Boo too, protestations so rhapsodic that Ira's toes would curl and his respiration loiter. "My beloved," she would say, "you are a cello become tympani; a flute swollen to sounding brass." Or, in another idiom, "My dear one, you are a river at flood, a mist-bound crystal cataract."

Ira listened, stroking, the while, Boo's tawny flanks before the driftwood fire, or looking into her tranquil eyes grown stormy with desire, or nuzzling her throat, or running a palm along the high, graceful arch of her foot, and as he listened and felt, the erosions of time were magically repaired, and winged youth was his.

Guilt came later. Returning to his room at the Stonewall Jackson Hotel after each tryst with Boo, Ira always felt an irresistible compulsion to phone Polly in California. His hands trembled on the telephone, but his voice was steady—steady and breezy and amiably matter-of-fact. He asked Polly about her health, about the house and the twins. When Polly recounted the boys' latest achievements in mindlessness, he replied with indulgent laughter. Then, seeking to hear Polly laugh, he told her how things were going in Owens Mill, inventing anecdotes when there were none to report.

And all the time the fox of guilt slashed at his liver. How rotten I am, he thought, how stinkingly corrupt, to summon up such glibness—such purulent, slimy glibness!

Only once in each conversation did the glibness desert him. When, at the end of their talk, he said, "Well, good night, Polly," and she answered, "I love you, Ira," a cold, iron silence would seize him. Struggle as he did, he could find no words. "Did you hear me?" she would ask at last. "I just told you I loved you." Still fighting for an answer, he would listen to Polly's patient, regular breathing and finally the tiny sigh just before she hung up the telephone.

Then Ira would castigate himself in earnest, threshing and wallowing in his guilt, grinding his face in the muck of it. But eventually—sometimes late, sometimes soon—a radiance would appear, a tall, slender, ethereal princess, with hair of pale gold, and she would shine such tender, healing eyes on Ira that all his sins were taken away, and he would lay down his raven head and sleep, a flickering smile of peace playing on his lips.

Boo, like Ira, felt rapture and felt guilt, but she also felt despair —her own private blend. In Boo's set of values, despair was the inseparable companion of romance, and, in fact, not an unpleasant companion. Her despair was the nonvirulent kind that only the rich can afford: wan, wistful, poignant, Brontë-ish. It was a dulcet unfulfillment that did not drive one to insert one's head in one's oven, but rather to pick up the poet's pen. Never had *Leda's* lyrics been more freighted with emotion than during those first weeks after Ira's return. A quatrain, selected at random from *The Mermaid*, will illustrate:

> The sea has turned to fire. The flame is salt.
> My wounds implore the smold'ring balm to enter.
> I would not if I could command a halt.
> Burn, salt! Burn, sea! Let pain remain my center!

Secretly and happily Boo wrote her verses and, on those nights when it could be managed discreetly, took Ira to her house on the beach and there made clawing love or serene love, or some of each, or the two commingled. Nobody in Owens Mill had the slightest suspicion of Boo's energetic new bed-life, for she stayed as active as ever, possibly more so, as clubwoman, civic leader, mother to Gabriel, and manager of her estate.

And Ira, younger than springtime, moved into an office at Acanthus College and started working rapidly, accurately, and without fatigue on the huge task of preparing a television documentary about the hazards of eating.

On Ira's first day in his office at Acanthus College, Jefferson Tatum came calling. "Just thought I'd drop by and see you got everything you need," said the old man.

"You're very kind," said Ira. "Yes, I'm in fine shape, thank you."

"About them phones on your desk," said Jefferson. "The black one's a regular phone, and the white one is direct to Clendennon in New York."

"Yes, my secretary explained."

"Very efficient girl, your Miss Whittaker," said Jefferson. "Takes 120 words a minute and got the hottest britches in Owens Mill."

"I'll bear it in mind."

"She'll slap your hand a couple of times at first, but that's only for show. You just keep grabbing, hear?"

"I hear."

"Well, I know you're busy, so I'll mosey on. Anything you want, call me."

"Thank you."

"On the black phone."

"Yes."

"Well, I'll be going now."

"Good-bye."

"Oh, one more thing." Jefferson removed a pamphlet from his pocket and laid it on Ira's desk. "You might glance at this when you get time. It's last month's bulletin of the Food and Drug Administration. . . . Mind you, it ain't nothing we wrote here at Acanthus. It's FDA's own official monthly report to the American people."

"Thanks, I'll read it later."

"You do that. And be sure not to miss them items I checked with a red pencil. This one, for instance." Jefferson pointed to a story on the first page of the bulletin. The headline said:

FDA CHIEF ASKS NEW RECRUITING DRIVE; INSPECTORS SERIOUSLY UNDER STRENGTH

"See that, sonny?" said Jefferson, poking the item with his forefinger. "The man says they're *seriously* short of food inspectors. Not *me* says it; *him,* the boss of FDA. There it is in black and white in the official authorized bulletin of FDA. See?"

"I see," said Ira.

"Now take a look at this," said Jefferson. He flipped the bulletin open and pointed at another story marked with a large red check. The headline said:

SUMMARY OF SEIZURE ACTIONS

Jefferson read aloud. " 'During October, FDA seizures of filthy and spoiled foods totaled 1,816,994 pounds—a figure somewhat below the normal monthly average. Largest seizures, as usual, were of wheat contaminated with rodent droppings—1,216,290 pounds last month.' "

"What?" exclaimed Ira.

"Read it yourself," said Jefferson, pushing the bulletin in front of Ira. "There it is, plain as day, official and authorized, written, published, and distributed by the Food and Drug Administration of the Government of the United States."

Ira looked, saw that the story was precisely as the old man had quoted it, shook his head with incredulity. "But this is terrible!" he said.

"It is a cataclysm," said Jefferson. "It is a visitation and a curse. Think about it, sonny. The boss of FDA says his staff of inspectors is way under strength. But even so, last month, undermanned as they are, FDA still managed to grab over a million pounds of contaminated wheat. Now think hard, sonny. Think how many million pounds they *didn't* grab. Think if they was up to full strength how many million *more* pounds of wheat they'd find that was shot full of mouse turds."

"Pleasant thought," winced Ira.

"Well, I'll leave you to your work now," said Jefferson. He paused at the door and smiled sweetly. "Just one last word of advice: stay away from raisin bread."

With a benign wave he made his departure.

In the days that followed, Ira paid numerous visits to the school of nutrition and public health, asked hundreds of questions, made hundreds of notes, held frequent meetings with the script writers and the production people whom the network had sent down to Owens Mill, prepared a rough preliminary version of the television show, enjoyed felicitous excesses with Boo before the fire or outdoors on the beach when the weather was fine, made guilt-ridden phone calls to Polly in Bel Air, slept briefly but deeply each night, lost six pounds from his middle and gained a luster of eye, a briskness of step that he had not known in a decade.

To preserve his new-won euphoria Ira scrupulously avoided using the white telephone which connected him directly to Clendennon in New York. But one day necessity forced him to pick up the white phone.

"Ira chickie!" cried Clendennon. "How are you, doll buggy?"

"Oh, shut up," said Ira. "I've got two questions for you. Number One: is there any chance of getting an air date a few days later than December 18th?"

"Baby, you know better than that," replied Clendennon. "I don't have to tell you how hard it is to clear sixty minutes of prime broadcast time."

"So it's December 18th for sure?"

"For sure," said Clendennon firmly. "So when do you want to start taping the show? December 11th? Twelfth? Thirteenth? Fourteenth? Pick your date, baby."

"No," said Ira.

"I beg your pardon?" said Clendennon, an edge of nervousness in his tone.

"The point is, I can't tape this show. There's not enough time. I'll have to go on the air live."

Clendennon's nervousness increased. "Why, Ira? Do you need more writers? More crew? More anything?"

"No, Clendennon. It's not me. I could be ready in plenty of time to tape. The trouble is, Dr Silenko has a batch of experiments in progress that can't possibly be finished before air date."

"Couldn't they be speeded up?"

"*People* you can speed up; hamsters, no."

"I don't like it, baby. Too many things can go wrong with live shows."

"Relax, Clendennon. I was making live television when you were still selling mechanical dogs. . . . Now let's get to my second question: have you found someone yet who will do the rebuttal for the food industry?"

"I have," answered Clendennon, and there was no trace of unease in his voice now. He oozed confidence. "I have found an excellent man."

"He better be excellent if he's going to tangle with Dr. Silenko,"

Ira warned. "He better be *better* than excellent, because if he's not, forty million dollars' worth of General Foods billings are down the drain and you are just another unemployed person in a black suit."

"I am touched by your concern for my job, Ira ducks—truly, deeply touched."

"Yeah, yeah, yeah. So who did you find?"

"A simple man. A modest, kindly, New England, Anglo-Saxon, Protestant man. A man who looks like a Norman Rockwell painting even as he sits on the board of the Lahey Clinic, the Rockefeller Foundation, the Payne-Whitney Medical Center, the Surgeon General's Panel on Smoking, the Space Medicine Advisory Committee, the Salk Institute. A man who seemed homespun even as he stood in white tie and tails receiving the Nobel Prize in Medicine."

There was authentic awe in Ira's voice. "Did you *really* get Andrew McAndrews?"

"I knew you'd be pleased."

"Pleased, hell. I am ecstatic. When are you sending him down?"

Clendennon hesitated an instant before answering. "Well, the fact is, Ira baby, I'm not *sending* Dr. McAndrews. I am personally accompanying him. After all, a man of such eminence deserves every courtesy, don't you think?"

"What I think is you're scared stiff to let me do a live show, so you've just decided to come down here to keep your hand on the switch."

"Now, Ira, that's plain silly."

"It really is," agreed Ira. "Come to Owens Mill if you like, look over my shoulder, breathe down my neck, tap my phone, steam open my mail, but, Clendennon, be smart: leave your paws off my show. I've got all the pieces now—Silenko on one side, Andrew McAndrews on the other, a powder keg in the middle, and the air full of sparks. Put 'em all together, they spell Emmy."

"Emmy?" said Clendennon, and Ira could see his beady eyes widen with cupidity. "You seriously think so?"

"Good-bye, pussycat," said Ira and hung up the white telephone.

One afternoon, following a politely insistent invitation from Virgil Tatum, Ira agreed to accompany him on a visit to those departments of Acanthus not connected with food research—the arts, the humanities, the learned disciplines—and after the tour Virgil drove Ira home to the Stonewall Jackson Hotel.

"I hope you weren't bored," said Virgil as he drove.

"Enjoyed it thoroughly," replied Ira.

"Good. I've been thinking you ought to get out of the food labs and take a more rounded look at the campus. Could be helpful to your tv show."

"Oh? How?"

"I know, of course, your subject is food poisons, but it seems to me —and I'm speaking strictly as a layman—that you might possibly add a little scope to the program if you covered the whole of Acanthus."

"Uh-huh," said Ira. "Also, you wouldn't be entirely broken-hearted if the world found out you've turned Acanthus into the best university south of Harvard. Right, Virgil?"

"Right," grinned Virgil. "And up yours."

Ira grinned back. "All right, prexy. I'll hand you a few posies. You've got 'em coming."

"Thanks."

"Forget it."

"Hey, Ira, would you like to have dinner tonight with Boo and me?"

Ira jerked upright. This night, as it happened, he had a seaside rendezvous with Boo. "Gee, I'm sorry, Virgil," he said, speaking carefully, "but I'm booked."

Virgil sighed. "Yeah, Boo told me the same thing when I asked her. She's got one of those damn committee things tonight. But I thought if I called her back and said you were coming, she might change her mind. She's pretty impressed with you, you know."

"No, I don't know."

"It's a fact. Truth is, I'm pretty impressed myself. You're a pretty impressive fellow, Ira. You'd have to be to catch a great woman like Polly and keep her all these years."

"Yeah," said Ira tonelessly.

"I'm not sure exactly what you've got," Virgil continued. "Something volatile, I expect. Something mercurial and unpredictable that's pure catnip to women. No female can tolerate the sight of an undomesticated man, as I'm sure you know."

"Really?"

"Maybe that's why I've been striking out with Boo for twenty years. Too tame, too square. Sometimes I think I ought to buy a beret or something."

"Forgive the question," said Ira, "but after twenty years, have you ever considered giving up on Boo?"

"Daily."

"But?"

"Love," said Virgil solemnly, "is very mysterious."

"Amen," said Ira, also solemnly, as the car pulled up to the Stone-wall Jackson Hotel.

As Virgil suggested, Ira thereafter spent more time poking about the whole of Acanthus, and he was properly impressed with what he saw. But his primary focus remained on the school of nutrition and public health. Daily he came, observed, and recorded. He never got entirely hardened to the sight of expiring rodents, but it was, as it happened, a cage full of healthy mice rather than a cage full of sick ones that brought Ira closest to the edge of trembling.

"Shapian," said Dr. Silenko as he entered the lab one morning, "how would you like to see a genuine dilemma?"

"Why not?" said Ira.

"Look here," said she, indicating two cages of mice on a lab table. In one cage the mice were pathetically moribund; in the other they were sleek and agile, their eyes bright with health.

"We have been dosing the mice in both cages with AB Yellow, which, you will recall, is a dye commonly used in butter," continued Dr. Silenko. "One cage of mice has been getting very large doses; the other cage has been getting very small doses. Now, Shapian, which is which?"

"Okay, I'll play straight for you. The sick mice have been getting the big doses—and I'm wrong, right?"

"You're wrong, right," nodded the doctor. "The sick mice—very sick, indeed; they are dying of cancer—have been getting the *little* doses, and the healthy mice the *big* ones."

Ira looked mystified. "I don't understand."

"You don't understand, and neither, obviously, does the Food and Drug Administration. But the explanation is perfectly simple. Shapian, look at that shelf behind you. See the tall blue bottle? That's a quart of ink. Now what do you think would happen if you gulped down that whole quart of ink?"

"I'd throw up," said Ira, who was, in fact, feeling on the queasy side.

"Either that or you'd have violent diarrhea. One way or another, you'd expel the ink. . . . Now to the next question: what would happen if you drank only one drop of that ink?"

"I don't know. Nothing, I suppose."

"Exactly, and there is the simple answer to the dilemma. The body has natural defenses against *large* doses of poison. When, however, the dose is *small* enough, the body's defenses are not aroused; the poison is allowed to enter."

"You mean it just lays there *forever?*" asked Ira nervously.

"Of course not. Small doses of poison taken infrequently—there's the key word, Shapian: *infrequently*—will be evacuated. But small doses of poison, taken day after day, year after year, doses which FDA, in its wisdom, chooses to call *permissible*, will in time overtax the liver and kidneys. The poison will not be evacuated, not entirely. A residue will accumulate in the fatty tissues until sooner or later—" she pointed at the cage of wretched, dying mice— "this kind of thing will inevitably happen. Let FDA talk about permissible doses. I say when it comes to poison—" her voice shook with indignation—"no dose whatsoever is permissible!"

"Bravo!" cried a small man with a large red beard who had just entered the lab.

"Hello, Levine," she said sheepishly.

"Excuse me, Joan of Arc," said Levine. "I hate to bother you when you're making a speech, but I need another centrifuge."

"I'll send one over," said Dr. Silenko. "Oh, Levine, this is Ira Shapian, the television man."

"I know it's Ira Shapian the television man and good-bye," said Levine.

Ira caught Levine's elbow before he could make an exit. "Excuse me, sir. I've been meaning to pay you a visit. You, I understand, are the one who thinks water is so dangerous."

"For washing, no," said Levine. "For drinking, you got to be crazy."

"Could you be more specific, sir?"

"I could be specific for six, eight months if you got the time," answered Levine. "But even if *you* got the time, I ain't. So what do you want to know, mister? Pollution? Chlorination? Purification? Storage? Fluoridation? What?"

"Well, let's start with fluoridation."

"All right, come to my lab," said Levine. "Silenko, the centrifuge, you'll remember?"

"I'll remember," she said. "Good-bye, Shapian."

"Good-bye, Dr. Silenko," called Ira and raced to overtake Levine, who was already speeding down the corridor.

"What do you have against fluoridation?" asked Ira, catching Levine as he entered his own laboratory.

"You got a notebook?"

"Yes, sir," said Ira, taking out pad and pencil.

"Write fast. I'm a busy man," said Levine. "Objection No. 1: dental. Objection No. 2: hydraulic. Objection No. 3: legal. Objection No. 4: medical. Objection No. 5: economic . . . Got it?"

"Got it."

"Okay. No. 1: dental. About cavities I wouldn't even argue. You tell me fluorine prevents cavities, I'll say fine, fluorine prevents cavities."

"Well then?"

"Look at this." Levine reached in a drawer, took out several eight-by-ten color photographs, and spread them for Ira to examine. "In the South Atlantic there's an island called Tristan da Cunha. The water on this island is not artificially fluoridated. It contains, in its natural state, two ppm—that means *parts per million*—of fluorine. Now here you'll see some photographs of the happy, smiling natives of Tristan da Cunha. Nice-looking fellas, yeah?"

"My God!" gasped Ira. "What's wrong with their teeth?"

"Mottled," said Levine. "Here's one with brown and white stripes, here's one with polka dots, and how do you like this fashionable her-ringbone?"

"Okay, Doctor, I admit it's scary, but on the other hand, there aren't too many of us living in Tristan da Cunha."

"Don't be a wise guy. You'll find teeth exactly like this in parts of Texas, in parts of England, in parts of Pennsylvania, in any place in the world where there's too much fluorine in the water."

"But how much is too much?" asked Ira. "As I understand it, the American Dental Association has set a strict limit."

"The American Dental Association should be locked up, the whole bunch," replied Levine. "Sure, they put a limit: one ppm. And maybe one ppm wouldn't hurt you. But how can you be sure you're only getting one ppm? Let's take my Objection No. 2: hydraulic." Levine dipped into another drawer and ripped out a sheaf of papers. "I got here reports of water commissioners from New York City, from Pittsburgh, from the State of Wisconsin, from Morristown, New Jersey, from twenty other places. All of them say the same thing: *incrustation*. You keep pouring fluorine into a water supply, the valves develop such a crust that nobody knows from day to day how much fluorine is getting in or staying out."

"And no way to control incrustation?"

"Sure. Pour more chemicals in the water to dissolve the fluorine. What's the difference if they dissolve your guts in the bargain?"

Ira's pencil was flying over his pad. "All right. Now Objection No. 3: legal."

"Listen," said Levine. "If there should happen, God forbid, a plague in this country, then the government got a right to go in and vaccinate everybody. No argument. But cavities is not a plague, and the government positively got no right to invade your body with fluorine. Anybody wants fluorine, let 'em buy it in the drugstore. The rest of us stand on the Fourteenth Amendment."

"Good point," allowed Ira.

"And here's another—Objection No. 4: medical. Now, I'm not one of them nuts who says fluorine causes everything from cancer to clap. Just the same, we know fluorine is a poison; four and a half grams will kill you, no question. Also, we know fluorine got a definite action on the skeletal structure. If it works on the teeth, it works on the bones, that's for sure. How it works, we're still trying to find out. Probably bad, but, like I say, we're still trying to find out. So, mister, answer me this: until we find out, what kind of craziness to go dumping fluorine in the water?"

"Yes," said Ira, "another good point."

"And if you ain't convinced yet, let me give you the clincher. Objection No. 5: economic. Do you know that out of every $10,000 we spend to fluoridate our water, $9,975 goes for flushing toilets, sprinkling the lawn, washing clothes, and like that? Only twenty-five dollars out of every ten thousand is for drinking! I rest my case."

"Quite a case."

"Thank you. So now will you go away and let me work before them dentists put us all in the hospital?"

Making his rounds one day, Ira dropped in on Linden-Evarts at the cultural anthropology department. He found him presiding over a small seminar composed entirely of Negro students: three young men seated on one side of the table, three coeds on the other, Linden-Evarts at the head.

"Ah, Shapian, come in, come in," beckoned Linden-Evarts. "Students, this is Ira Shapian, a television lackey. Shapian, I'd like you to meet Lucy Swift, Mary Groves, and Helen McDermott on this side of the table; and on the other side Jim King, Ed Riley, and Phil Tolliver."

"Hi, kids," said Ira with a friendly smile. "Professor, please forgive my busting in on your class, but I'm trying to cover as much as I can of Acanthus in the tv show. I was thinking maybe I'd find something here I could put on television."

"You won't," said Linden-Evarts positively. "And I'll tell you why. Two reasons: first, because I am not the kind of man who is invited to make television appearances. It is, in fact, generally agreed that I have the personality of a pissant."

"Oh, I wouldn't say that," Ira demurred politely.

"Yes, you would," said the professor.

"On second thought," said Ira, "you're right. I would."

"That's better," said Linden-Evarts. "Now add to my obnoxious manner the subject under discussion here, and it becomes quite obvious that the work being done in this department is no fit matter for the pap machine called television."

"Do you mind if I listen awhile and judge for myself?" asked Ira.

Linden-Evarts shrugged. "As you like," he said and indicated an empty chair at the foot of the table.

Ira sat. The professor addressed his seminar. "Now then, class, let us continue. I was saying before Shapian interrupted that I am chairman of the board of trustees of the William Lloyd Garrison Foundation. In a few weeks we will be picking the recipient of our annual Community Relations Award. Among the leading candidates is Jefferson Tatum." He turned to one of the students. "Phil, how would you vote on old Tatum?"

"I would vote a big loud no!" said Phil vehemently. "Mr. Tatum doesn't care anything about Negroes. He is nothing but a tokenist—a *shrewd* tokenist, I grant you, but a tokenist. His only concern is to keep his town nice and quiet and tractable."

Linden-Evarts quickly surveyed the other students. "Do you all feel the same?"

Everyone nodded.

"Your position has merit," allowed the professor. "Tatum is, without question, a tokenist. Still, how can one ignore all he has given to Acanthus College and the town of Owens Mill?"

"Now you've said it!" cried Jim, slamming both fists down on the table. "Mr. Tatum *gives*. Whatever Negroes have achieved in this college and in this town has been the result of Mr. Tatum's bounty. . . . Well, we don't want it that way. We don't want things *given* to us. We don't want to depend on any man's generosity. We have *rights*, legal and moral, and all we ask is what the laws of God and man say we're entitled to!"

There were shouts of assent from all the undergrads.

"Bravely spoken," said Linden-Evarts with a tolerant smile. "All right then, let me propose another candidate for the Garrison Award. How about Governor Wallace of Alabama?"

The students looked bewildered, as did Ira.

"Why not?" continued Linden-Evarts. "Has any man's conduct done more to unite the Negro community in America? Isn't that worthy of recognition?"

"Look, Professor," said Lucy, "I thought this was a serious discussion."

"Oh, I'm serious all right," Linden-Evarts assured her. "However, I see you are not persuaded by my reasoning. Very well, we'll scratch Governor Wallace along with Jefferson Tatum. I will try another name on you: Senator Mansfield of Montana."

The students paused, pondered, exchanged looks of general approbation. "He's a good man," said Mary, summing up for her colleagues.

"He's a *fine* man," said Linden-Evarts. "He's a decent man, an intelligent man, an enlightened man. His heart is in the right place. The only trouble is, he is not even remotely in the running for the Garrison Award."

"Why not?" asked Helen.

"Why should he be?" countered Linden-Evarts. "How difficult is it to be an equalitarian when you are the Senator from Montana, a place where, if you look diligently, you will find perhaps fifty Negro families in the entire state? No, students, forget about Mansfield and Hubert Humphrey and McGee of Wyoming. The Garrison Award is not for people who have so little to lose."

"I don't follow your thinking, Professor," said Ed.

"No, none of you does. And the reason you don't is that you are all cursed with the principal affliction of youth: you are not terribly bright."

"Sir," said Mary, "I would like to say I resent that."

Linden-Evarts chuckled. "That's your problem, my dear. I do not retreat from my statement: you are no more intelligent than any other members of your generation. Surely, you cannot believe that a black skin is an automatic guarantee of wisdom?"

"Now I resent *that!*" declared Ed.

"Resent and be damned," said Linden-Evarts cheerfully. "You are young and therefore foolish. If not, why would you be wasting time on these countless, aimless protest marches, these ridiculous prostrations on highways and bridges?"

"I see," said Lucy bitterly. "What you're saying is for us to put the handkerchiefs back on our heads and keep turning the other cheek."

"I am saying no such thing," denied Linden-Evarts. "I believe you should holler when you're hurt, fight when you're abused. Go to court for even the slightest infraction of your civil rights. Boycott bus lines, restaurants, stores, and factories that are segregated in any way whatever. But, in the name of common sense, will you stop these ridiculous, random, disorganized marches and demonstrations? For your own good, use the time instead to do a little calm, patient planning."

"*Calm! Patient!*" Jim spat the words out like two foul things. "You talk about calm and patient when one hundred years after the Emancipation Proclamation we're still being treated like animals!"

"Anybody here taking American history?" asked the professor.

They nodded.

"Then you know that long before the Emancipation Proclamation there was in this country a political group called the Know-Nothing Party. Their platform was charmingly simple: keep all Catholics out of public office. And from 1830 to 1856 the Know-Nothings held the balance of power in the federal Congress and the state legislatures. Yet in 1961 John F. Kennedy, rest his soul, moved into the White House."

"*White* House, yes," said Phil indignantly. "Sure, we finally got a Catholic President, but he was *white*, and don't you forget it. How long, do you suppose, before we get a black President?"

"I don't know, but we surely will." Linden-Evarts' tone was serenely confident.

The students hooted.

Linden-Evarts smiled faintly, sadly. "This will astound you, but I know exactly how you feel. Fact is, I wouldn't have much respect for you if you felt different. Kids are full of ideals, and patience isn't one of them. You want everything to happen *right now*. Well, it's a crying shame, but that's not the way the world moves. *Little* steps, my starry-eyed young friends, that's the cadence. Tiny steps. Sometimes imperceptible steps. But *forward* steps: there's the encouraging thing."

"You mean forward steps like in Birmingham?" asked Helen mockingly.

"I am acquainted with Birmingham," answered Linden-Evarts

without heat. "And I know about Chicago and Harlem too. But I also know that the armed forces are desegregated today. I know there are black men making policy on Capitol Hill and in the Executive Branch. I know the Supreme Court has said that separate can never be equal. I know we have an FEPC, a civil rights division in the Justice Department, and a whole battery of presidential powers to stop discrimination."

Mary scoffed. "And what good are all these things?"

"More good than Malcolm X," replied Linden-Evarts quietly. "More good than Adam Powell and all the other fishers in troubled waters. What too many of you lose sight of, my dusky countrymen, is that when the smoke clears—and it finally will—you are going to have to live alongside your white neighbors. We are Americans, every single one of us, and America is, first and foremost, a melting pot. It did not get that way because the pot welcomed every new ingredient—quite the contrary—but because the pot understood, sooner or later, that it could make a richer stew if it took in some exotic arrivals like Irishmen and Italians and Greeks and Jews. You Negroes have not been invited into the pot yet, but I would remind you of something: there is no lid on the pot and there never was. With patience, courage, and steady, intelligent pressure, you too will be asked to jump in someday. In fact, though you'll deny it hotly, it's already beginning to happen."

Now the conversation was loud, disorganized, and passionate. Linden-Evarts leaned back and grinned at Ira. "Well, Shapian, how much of this stuff can you use on television?"

"Are you kidding?" replied Ira. "If I put a discussion like this on the air, within minutes I would be picketed by the NAACP, the Urban League, the White Citizens Council, the Civil Liberties Union, the Democratic Party, the Republican Party, CORE, SNICK, the Ku Klux Klan, the Americans for Democratic Action, and possibly the Miss Rheingold Pageant."

"Good-bye, Shapian," said Linden-Evarts. "Come back if you should have a sudden attack of courage."

"Courage? *Me?*" sighed Ira, departing. "Hah!"

Some nights later Ira rented a car and drove out to Boo's beach house, where he made love to her before the driftwood fire. He found the lovemaking curiously unsatisfactory—well, perhaps not unsatisfactory, but certainly less than rapturous. If coition could be rated on a scale of 1 to 10, this particular encounter would be marked about 6—6.5 at the outside.

For an Ira-Boo match this represented a very low score. In previous meets Ira had chalked up many a 10 and never lower than a 9. But this night a troubled mind had dulled the edge of ecstasy. A host of specters hung over him: the rapidly approaching date of the telecast, the parting with Boo, the return to Hollywood, the dismalness beyond.

Silently he put on his clothes and sat and lit a cigarette and stared into the driftwood flames.

For a long time Boo watched him intently, then said, "I love it when you're moody, darling. Your eyes are like a storm—a beautiful, black, flashing storm."

Ira patted her knee absently.

"Brood, my dark angel, brood," said Boo. "And should you want to talk, I'm here."

Ira nodded.

Twenty mute minutes passed.

He turned to her and seemed about to speak.

"Yes, love?" she said gently.

He shook his head in despair. "I don't know where to start."

"I hesitate to intrude, but I think I can help," she offered.

"Please."

"You're thinking it's only three more weeks until you do your television show."

"Yes."

"And then you must leave me."

"I love you, Boo!" he cried and plunged his face into her breast.

"And I love you, Ira," she answered, stroking his hair. "And that is the thought that must sustain us—not the parting, but the love. Not the separation, but these wonderful, golden, unexpected days we have had together."

"I am not comforted," said Ira.

"Poor darling," said Boo.

He rose. "Let's put on some sweaters and walk on the beach."

"Yes, dear."

Silently, hand in hand, they walked along the shore. A cold wind tumbled off the sea. The angry tide pursued but never caught their feet. Ira pondered.

Boo is right, he thought. I am sad because the time to say good-bye is almost here. I am sad because this flawless interlude is ending.

The nights with Boo have been bliss. The days of honest work at an honest trade have made me feel like a man again, like a mover and shaker, and not just a tentacle of Clendennon. In three weeks all of this will be taken from me, and I am sad.

But that is not all of my sadness. I grieve as much for what is approaching as I do for what is receding. After ineffable rapture with Boo, I am returning to strained civility with Polly. After the truth and toil of making a television show, I am returning to sit behind a desk and *nice* for a living. I am leaving glory for ashes, verity for tinsel, a mountaintop for a bog.

Ira turned and looked at Boo's face, at the handsome, patrician lines jutting cleanly into the wind. Oh, God! he thought, if only I could hold her strength and beauty forever! She would renew me; she would rekindle the flame long doused by the combination of Hollywood and Clendennon and lovelessness and deals and defaults and trumpery. I would use my talents fearlessly again. I would make tough, uncompromising television shows, shows that goaded and illuminated, shows about important topics like poverty and disease and corruption and the most urgent of all problems, race relations. I would, by God, go to work for Linus Calloway in Birmingham! Yes! I would wrench myself from the gold-baited trap of commercial television and take that job with Linus. I would fight for the right. I would!

A short, bitter laugh spurted from Ira's lips.

"What, my darling?" asked Boo.

"I was having a dream," said Ira. "A lovely, impossible dream."

"Are you sure it's impossible?" she said.

"I'm sure," he replied. Then he paused. *Was* it impossible? "Sit," he said and pulled Boo down beside him on a rock.

He cerebrated furiously. What obstacles stood between him and the dream?

Well, first there was Polly. But she was not, in truth, an obstacle. All Ira had to say was "I want a divorce," and she would promptly reply, "You got it." Polly, bless her spunky soul and body, was never one to stay where she was not wanted.

Okay, so much for Polly. Next obstacle: the Star Spangled Broadcasting Network. A *real* obstacle, this one. You can't say "I want a divorce" to a network, especially after you've just signed a new contract. For the next seven years Ira belonged to Star Spangled, unless, of course, Star Spangled decided to fire him for some reason.

Ira's eyes glowed with inspiration, for suddenly he knew a reason why Star Spangled would fire him—a beautifully simple reason, a simply beautiful reason. In three weeks he was going to do the Acanthus telecast live, on the spot, precisely as it happened. If, during the show, he could slip in a few words so rapidly that nobody would have time to cut him off the air—and he knew precisely the words and the place to insert them—then not only would Ira get fired from Star Spangled, but he would be totally and forever unemployable in any area of commercial television anywhere!

And, thought Ira with a chuckle, it would not only be himself who was stoned out of commercial tv. The ultimate responsibility for the Acanthus telecast rested on Clendennon; thus if Ira pulled down the temple, Clendennon would be buried in the rubble right alongside him! Ah, what a heart-warming prospect! What a darling consummation!

"Why are you smiling, Ira?" asked Boo.

"Shh," said Ira.

"Yes, dear," said Boo.

Ira resumed thinking. Two obstacles down—Polly and Star Spangled—and one more to go. And this was the steepest of all: where to work after he had outlawed himself from commercial television. Sure, he could take the job with Linus Calloway, but what about the salary, five thousand paltry dollars a year? How in God's name could he get along on such short money? There would be alimony for Polly. There would be the twins to support. There would be Boo as his new wife.

A fresh idea came to Ira, an ignoble, loathsome idea which he rejected as soon as it arrived. But it would not stay rejected. It returned and kept returning until at last Ira spoke. "Boo," he said, "how much money have you got?"

"I don't know," she said honestly. "Scads, I'm sure." Then, suddenly concerned, she grasped Ira's hand. "Why, darling? Do you need some?"

"No. Oh, no."

"You're sure?" she said, searching his eyes. "Please tell me if you do. You're welcome to all I have."

"Hmm," said Ira, rubbing his chin.

"There's a checkbook in the beach house. Shall we go in?"

"Boo, I've got something very important to ask you and you must be absolutely honest. Would you still love me if I accepted money from you? I don't mean just once or twice. I mean regularly and systematically for the rest of our lives."

She looked at him with unfeigned bewilderment. "I don't understand, Ira. Of course I'd still love you. What's money got to do with love? If I have something you want or need, then my greatest joy is to give it to you. Don't you know that?"

"Kiss me, Boo, and then I've got one more thing to ask."

She gave him her lips, then withdrew to await the query. "Yes, dear?"

"We've never talked about the race problem, Boo. I'd like to know where you stand."

Her brows knit. "You really *are* full of riddles tonight. Race problem, you say? *What* race problem, Ira? There's only one race, the human race, and God grant we all recognize it soon."

"Kiss me again, and this time good."

She kissed him good.

"Thank you," he said. "Let's go."

She rose with him. "Don't you have any more questions?"

"No."

"Then may I ask one?"

"Of course."

"What, exactly, is going through your mind?"

"I can't tell you. I just can't!" he exclaimed in anguish.

"All right, dear."

"But I must!" he cried, abruptly giving way. "If I don't talk, I'll break into pieces, little jagged pieces!"

"Poor, tormented dark angel!"

"Listen, Boo," he said, grasping both her hands. "What I'm about to say, it's not an offer, you understand. Not a proposal. Not a commitment."

"Speak, my love."

He spoke. Wildly, gushingly, he undammed his thoughts about divorcing Polly, burning his bridges in commercial television, taking a job with Linus, living on Boo's money.

She gasped. Even in the scant moonlight he could see her face go pale.

"No, no, Boo!" he said hurriedly. "No, no! Don't be frightened. I'm not proposing. I'm just thinking out loud, is all."

"Ira, I love you."

"And I love you," he replied loudly. "I love you, love you, love you!" He poured kisses randomly on her face and shoulders.

"Ira, please let me finish."

"Sorry."

"I love you," she repeated. "But we can't do this to Polly."

"You're right."

"We *can't.*"

"I know," he said. Then: "Why not?"

"You know why, Ira."

"Yes, I know."

"We must be brave."

"Brave!" he said bitterly. "Heaven within our reach, and we must bravely turn away!"

"We must."

"Boo, I don't know if I want to go on without you," he said quietly.

She looked deep and long into his eyes. "Think some more about it, darling. Think it through calmly, slowly. Then we will talk again."

"You mean you *would* marry me?" he asked, half-hopeful, half-fearful.

"I don't know. I honestly don't know. Perhaps if you can find it in your heart to hurt Polly, I might be strong enough to go along with you."

"I see," said Ira. "Terrible mean thing to do to a good woman like Polly, of course."

"Unspeakable."

"But you'd go along, you say?"

"I don't know," Boo answered. "You must think it through first."

"Good idea. I'll think it through."

"I love you, Ira."

"I'll think real hard," he assured her. "Real, real hard . . . And," he added, "I love you too."

They exchanged a soft good night kiss, got into their separate cars, and drove to Owens Mill. As he drove, Ira tried hard to sort out this night's developments, but the din of his pounding heart made thought impossible. Whether his heart pounded with joy or fright, he could not tell. But pound it did, and his extremities were clammy, and his face was feverish, and his mouth was dry.

He parked the car in the Stonewall Jackson garage, walked into the hotel lobby, and stopped at the desk for his room key. "Oh, Mr. Shapian, here's a message for you," said the room clerk, handing him a telephone slip. "Urgent, it says."

Ira looked at the slip. It was a phone call from Polly, the first she had made to him in all the weeks he had been in Owens Mill. "UR-GENT" said the operator's notation, and the word was underlined three times.

There was no confusion now in Ira's mind as to whether his heart pounded with joy or with fear. It was pure, raging fear, irrational fear, a wild, demented certainty that somehow Polly had been leaning over his shoulder tonight and listening to every word.

Ira did not wait for the elevator but ran up the four flights of stairs to his room. He snatched the phone off the hook and stammered his home number to the operator.

"Hello," said Polly in Bel Air.

"What's wrong? What's wrong?" he yelled. "What's wrong?"

"Ira, are you loaded or what? Who says anything's wrong?"

"The phone message. Urgent, it says. Urgent. Urgent. Urgent!"

"Will you calm down, you nutsy Armenian? I told them to write 'urgent' because I wanted to be sure you'd call back tonight."

"Why? Huh? Why?"

"Oh, brother, you *are* in terrible shape! It's a good thing I'm coming out there tomorrow."

Ira's voice fell to a hoarse whisper. "You're *what?*"

"That's why I wanted to be sure you'd call tonight. My plane gets into Owens Mill at ten A.M."

"But how can you come out here?"

"Well, Ira, it's not simple, but here's how you do it. You take a taxi to the Los Angeles airport, see? Then you get on a big, shiny airplane. Then you fasten your seat belt. Then you—"

"Polly, cut the clowning. How can you leave the twins home alone? You know how they are."

"Boy, do I know how they are!" said Polly with feeling. "But," she added cheerfully, "it's not my problem any more, or yours either."

"Polly, listen to me. I'm not yelling now, right? I'm calm, right? What are you trying to tell me?"

"Just this: our boys were inducted into the Marine Corps this morning."

"*Huh?*"

"A very colorful ceremony. Too bad you had to miss it."

"Marine Corps? What Marine Corps?"

"The *United States* Marine Corps," said Polly. "Our kids are now the responsibility of the government, which, if you ask me, is only fair. We've been paying taxes for a lot of years; it's time we got something in return."

"Polly, what kind of gag is this? Those kids can't join the Marines without their parents' signatures. *Both* parents."

"Oh, honey," said Polly gaily, "I learned how to forge your name *years* ago."

"My God," said Ira.

"Well, I'll see you at ten tomorrow morning. Good night, old husband."

Ira listened to the click at the other end of the line. Then slowly, very slowly, he hung up the telephone.

Chapter 14

At twenty minutes past eleven the following morning, Polly and Ira Shapian were in Ira's suite at the Stonewall Jackson Hotel. Polly was unpacking the bags she had brought from California; Ira stood with his back to her, staring silently out the window.

As Polly hung dresses in the closet and stashed lingerie in drawers, she paused occasionally to look at her husband. But he did not look back; his eyes remained stonily on the window. After several minutes, she muttered a brief expletive, flung a panty-girdle into a corner, and said, "Listen, Ira, I really didn't expect you to leap with joy when I got here, but do you have to look so *stricken?*"

Ira turned. "I'm sorry, Polly," he said, attempting a smile. "It's just that I've got things on my mind."

She gave his arm a light, tentative touch. "You're miffed because I let the twins join the Marines without asking you. That's it, isn't it?"

"No, Polly, not at all. Honest."

"Yes, that's it. And I apologize. It was a brassy, bitchy thing for me to do. . . . But I had to, don't you see?" Her grip tightened on his arm. "Those kids need to be shaped up—and fast. So who's going to do it? Soft old Dad? Spongy old Mom? No, Ira, this is a job for an iron-assed drill instructor with a heart to match. . . . And, believe me, the job will get done. Those kids have great stuff inside of them, in spite of our best efforts to lard it over. It's there, and the Marines will find it, I promise you!"

Ira patted his wife's hand. "I know, I know. You did the right thing, and I'm not a bit sore."

"So why are you walking around with a face like a basset hound?"

"I'm sorry."

"Don't be sorry. Smile. Your wife is here. If you can't smile, spit. Do *something!*"

"Polly, it's only that I'm working day and night on the tv show,

and suddenly you arrive in this hick town, and I don't have time
to entertain you, and I'm afraid you'll get bored into a coma."

"Rest easy, chum. I don't expect you to entertain me, and I don't
intend to be bored. I've got friends in Owens Mill too, remember?
In fact, I sent a note to Virgil Tatum a couple of days ago to let
him know I'd be here."

"Virgil? Good, good."

"I also wrote Boo."

"*Boo?*" he said. He was feeling, actually *feeling*, the blood drain
from his head.

"Yes, Boo. You remember. We knew her during the war. Southern
belle type—portico, thoroughbred horses, eighteenth-century furniture, high cheekbones—everything ante-bellum except the legs.
Haven't you seen her since you've been here?"

"The phone is ringing," said Ira gratefully and snatched it up.
"Hello," he said. "Oh, hi, Virgil . . . look, I didn't even know about
it myself till last night. . . . Yes, she's right here. Just a minute."

"Virgil!" said Polly joyfully into the phone. "How are you?"

"Never mind the small talk," said Virgil. "Just one question: are
you still beautiful?"

"Oh, yes," answered Polly. "Withered and wrinkled also, but
beautiful, definitely."

"That's all I wanted to know," said Virgil. "Now, in reply to your
note inquiring whether we might have lunch sometime, let me state
that we are going to have lunch every single day, starting today. In
addition, on every evening when your greasy-grind husband finds
himself occupied with his television show, we are going to have
dinner. And after dinner—well, my dear, who knows? Perhaps we
can provide one another with a little Southern comfort."

"You are a dirty old man," said Polly.

"You're thinking of my father," he answered. "However, I'm trying. . . . Now what time shall I pick you up for lunch?"

"One hour."

"I'll be there."

"You see?" said Polly to Ira as she hung up the telephone. "I'm
going to be royally entertained while I'm here, so you tend to your
business and don't worry about me languishing alone in a hotel
room."

"Fine fellow, Virgil," said Ira.

"A lamb," agreed Polly, "which is precisely his trouble. A little less
lamb and a little more *toro*, he would have it well and truly made."

"Poor Virgil. All right, Polly, I better get over to the factory."

"Listen," she said, touching him again, lightly, almost shyly, "I'm not pressuring, you understand, but I didn't really come flying out here to parley with the natives. So if you can spare some time from your job—"

"I'll do my best."

"Will you have your secretary phone the hotel about five and let me know how it looks for tonight?"

"Sure."

"Oh, wait a minute. I might not be here. If she doesn't reach me at the hotel, tell her to try Boo's house."

"Boo?" said Ira and felt his blood plummet again.

"I thought I'd call and invite myself over for tea this afternoon. . . . Ira, what's wrong?"

"Nothing, nothing. Got to run!"

Run he did—down the stairs, out of the hotel, across the street, into a drugstore, into a phone booth. Rapidly he dialed Boo's number.

"Boo, listen—"

"I know, dear. I just now opened Polly's letter."

"She's going to call you in a few minutes. She wants to come for tea this afternoon."

"I shall invite her."

"You *shall?*"

"Ira, it is fated. Last night we had a vexing riddle to fathom. Now it is answered for us."

"Could you be a little less oblique?"

"Don't you understand? We can't see each other again. Not ever."

"Oh," said Ira. "Now I understand. . . . Except one thing: *why* can't we see each other again?"

"A sign has been given us, my darling. Acknowledge it, and praise what was."

"Oblique again! Goddammit, will you talk plain? . . . Sorry, Boo."

"It's all right, dark angel. My heart breaks with yours. But we must do what we must."

"So you're going to have Polly to tea?"

"Yes."

"Boo, you're crazy! What will happen if Polly sees Gabriel? She's got an eye like a chicken-hawk, that wife of mine. She'll figure it out in two seconds."

"Oh, dear!" said Boo.

"So if you're going to have Polly to tea—and obviously you are—"

"I must, don't you see?"

"No, I don't. But never mind. Just listen. When Polly is in your house, make damn sure Gabriel is away—*far* away."

"I can't send him out, Ira. The boy has a heavy cold."

"All right, then, lock him in his room. Lock him *tight!* And keep him there!"

"Yes, dear."

"You sure you've got to have Polly to tea?"

"Ira, sweet, blind Ira, a higher power has provided us with an answer."

"Oh, Jesus Christ!"

"Perhaps," said Boo softly.

"Boo, listen—"

"Good-bye, Ira. Good-bye, dear soul and flesh. Good-bye."

For an hour Polly and Boo had been sitting in Boo's eighteenth-century drawing room drinking Lapsang souchong out of Sèvres cups, nibbling delicately at ladylike cookies arranged on a Dresden plate. The conversation had been steady and easy. They covered the old days, the new days, the days in between. They touched on life and art and domestic matters. The talk flowed placidly, with an occasional ripple of pleasant laughter.

Yet, to Polly's chicken-hawk eye and Doberman ear, it was clear that beneath Boo's composure there lay a tightly controlled, but unmistakable, stratum of hysteria. What I think, Polly told herself sagely and silently, is that this lady is underscrewed. I know the feeling.

But not a blink, not a twitch, not the tiniest shrillness perturbed the serenity of the hour. Like a mill-run it trickled gently by, until, all of a sudden, an apparition filled the doorway: a gangly young man with wrinkled pajamas, a floppy robe, tangled hair of shining black, smoldering dark eyes, and a nose grotesquely red and rheumy.

"Hey, Ma," said Gabriel indignantly, "what's the idea of locking me in my bedroom?"

"What *ever* can you be talking about?" replied Boo, tittering nervously, trying to interpose her body between Gabriel and Polly without actually making a standing broad-jump. "I didn't lock you in your bedroom."

"You did too," Gabriel insisted. "I heard you turn the key."

"Nonsense, dear, you were dreaming," said Boo. "How'd you get out?"

"Any fool who can't pick a simple lock—"

"We'll talk about it later," said Boo, taking a firm hold on his arm. "Back in bed with you now. You know what the doctor said."

Gabriel stood rooted, staring at Polly. "Who's this lady? I think I know her."

Polly stared back. She did not *think* she knew Gabriel; she *knew* she knew him. One look into those burning, black, Armenian eyes, and she was sure beyond the doubting of it. *Ira's son,* she said to herself, and there was a hollowness in her belly and a banging under her breastbone, and her color mounted, and there was a tightness in her throat, and her lips clung together as though sealed.

Her head swiveled slowly from Gabriel to Boo, and there she saw a blush as deep as her own, an aimless flexing and unflexing of fingers.

"This is Mrs. Shapian, Gabriel," said Boo hollowly.

"Yeah!" he cried with a broad smile. "Sure, that's who it is—Ira Shapian's wife. She was in the picture you used to have by your bed."

"Does anybody smell something burning in the kitchen?" said Boo, desperately avoiding Polly's stare. "I'm *sure* there's something burning in the kitchen!" she cried and fled from the room.

"Mrs. Shapian?" said Gabriel.

Polly turned her face back to him.

"Excuse me, Mrs. Shapian," he said, "but you're spilling your tea in your lap."

"Oh, thank God!" said Polly. "I was afraid it was something else."

Gabriel looked at her curiously for a moment, then laughed loud and deep. "That was funny, what you just said," he told her.

"Yeah," said Polly.

"You're kind of a funny lady," continued Gabriel.

"Thanks."

"Good-looking, too," he said. "I don't mean you're pretty or glamorous or like that, but you've got *character* in your face."

"Uh-huh," said Polly.

"Are you smart?"

"No," said Polly.

"Aw, come on. Don't be modest. I'll bet anything you've got a sensational I.Q."

"Young man," said Polly, rising, "I am without question the stupid-
est woman you will ever meet. Now, if you'd be kind enough to say
good-bye to your mother—"

"Wait, wait, wait!" Gabriel spread his arms and barred her way.
"There's something I want to ask you."

"Yes?"

"Actually, there's something I want to *tell* you."

"Yes?"

"Do you have any idea what my I.Q. is?"

"No."

"Well, I'm a little embarrassed to give you the actual figure. Let
me put it this way: in the entire history of intelligence measure-
ment—and I include Europe as well as America—there have only
been two scores higher than mine."

"I am very happy for you," said Polly.

Gabriel frowned. "Now why do you suppose I went and told you
that?" he asked, honestly puzzled.

"I don't know, Gabriel. Why don't you go back to bed and figure
it out? I have to call a cab."

"A cab?" he cried. "I won't hear of it! I'll drive you home."

"You'll do no such thing," said Boo, returning to the room. She was
composed now, or nearly so. A small spot of crimson remained high
on each cheek, but her limbs were still and her voice was firm. "Gabriel, you will march right to bed and stay there. I will drive Mrs.
Shapian home."

"No, no, I'll get a cab," said Polly.

"You will *not*," said Gabriel vehemently to Polly, and to Boo he
said, "Honest, Ma, I feel fine now. No fever or anything. I'll take
Mrs. Shapian home."

"Gabriel, no!" said Boo.

But he was already rushing from the room. "I'll be dressed in a
minute, Mrs. Shapian," he called as he disappeared.

"Strong-minded boy," said Polly.

"Yes," said Boo.

"How old? About eighteen?"

"That's right. Eighteen."

"Uh-huh," said Polly. "Is there a cigarette in that box?"

"Polly, stop turning your head away. Look at me."

"What for?"

"We have to talk—honestly, openly, woman-to-woman."

"Who says so?"

"Will you *look* at me?" cried Boo. "I know you know about Gabriel. You knew the minute you saw him."

"So?"

"So what do we do now? Pretend there is no Gabriel? Pretend I never did you this great, unforgivable wrong?"

"That is *exactly* what we do," declared Polly, facing Boo squarely. "I don't know whether there's a statute of limitations on adultery, but if there isn't, there should be. Gabriel happened eighteen years ago. I sure as hell don't intend to start making waves at this late date."

"You mean you are able to forgive me?"

"I mean it doesn't signify any more."

"And what about Ira? Can you forgive him too?"

Wrath suddenly kindled Polly's eyes. "Ira is *my* business!" she spat.

"You're quite right," said Boo contritely. "I'm sorry."

"Me too," said Polly, all anger gone. "Excuse me for snapping at you. But it's a plain fact: Ira *is* my business. I have been, God help me, in the Ira business for more than twenty years. It's not what you'd call a *fun* business, but, on the other hand, it's the only business I know, and I don't propose to close up shop now on account of something Ira did back in his impetuous youth."

"You are a woman of great wisdom," said Boo sincerely.

"I am a woman—period. Sure, I can be big about what happened eighteen years ago. But if I should find out that you and Ira are still shacking up—well, I don't know exactly what I'd do. Nothing out of a Noel Coward comedy, I promise you."

"Are you saying you suspect that Ira and I are still lovers?"

"I suspect *nothing*, and that's one of the reasons I've stayed married. I simply take it as an article of faith that Ira is true to me. I know now he had a fling with you, but he came home, didn't he? And possibly he's taken an occasional jump on one of those eager young starlets who infest Hollywood. I doubt it, but maybe he did. So what? What's it got to do with *me?* All I need to know is that Ira comes home. He always has; I believe he always will."

"I see. What you don't know won't hurt you."

"That's one way to put it. Here's another: marriage is a very fragile structure, and the foundation stone is called *trust*. Chip away at the foundation, and the whole thing comes tumbling down."

"In your opinion, then, a wife should see no evil."

"As long as she possibly can—yes. There is, of course, a breaking point. It's no good holding a husband at the cost of your own self-respect."

"You truly are wise, Polly," said Boo with admiration. "I suppose it's not possible for us to see one another again?"

"You suppose right, Boo. So good-bye, and thanks for the tea, and tell the kid with the runny nose I'm ready to go home."

"I'm here," said Gabriel, appearing fully dressed in the doorway. "Is that how you think of me, Mrs. Shapian, as a kid with a runny nose?"

"I'm sorry, Gabriel," said Polly. "I meant no offense."

He nodded. "My car's right in front," he said.

Polly went outdoors with him, got into a low-slung, handmade sports car. For a time Gabriel drove in silence. Then, sadly, he said, "But that *is* your image of me, isn't it? Just a kid with a runny nose."

Polly groaned. Her back was already overloaded with bundles of traumas; what she particularly did not need at this moment was to take on the added burden of an adolescent's funk. "Gabriel," she said patiently, "you're a very nice boy and I'm sure in the fullness of time your nose will stop running."

"*Boy,*" he said bitterly. "You call me *boy.* You call me *kid.* Never mind that I've got the third highest I.Q. in all history. To you I'm just a *boy,* a *kid!*"

"Gabriel, why should it matter what I think of you?"

"Why should it *matter?*" he shouted wildly. "Are you blind? Can't you see?"

"See what?"

"It happened the minute I met you. One look and I knew—I *knew!* Oh, God, how happy I was! Do you know that I've been trying to find a mate for years and years? And for years and years I've been striking out. I kept thinking there was something missing in me. 'Face it,' I told myself. 'When a man has an intellect like yours, he's bound to be deficient in other areas. Face it: you are an emotional inadequate.' . . . Only I never quite believed it. I couldn't stop feeling that when the right person came along, this dormant thing inside me would all of a sudden blaze into life. And I was right! I saw you and—*wham!*—it happened! There and then! *Wham! Zowie! Varoom!*"

"Gabriel," said Polly, enunciating slowly and carefully, trying to contain a horror that sprouted and spread, "tell me you're not telling me what you seem to be telling me."

"But I am! Sure, it sounds crazy, but it's true. It happened the second we met; it's happening right now. All I have to do is look at you, and I get this weird, tight, constricted feeling in my gut."

"Maybe your pants are buttoned to your vest," said Polly.

"You are very funny," he said somberly.

"So laugh."

"You are very funny," he continued. "You are very witty and intelligent, and you are not too bad-looking, and for the first time in my life I feel I have found a woman with whom I can communicate on every level—cerebral, social, and sexual."

"Stop the car!" yelled Polly. "Stop the car this minute, you nasty, snot-nosed kid!"

"Polly, listen to me!" he wailed and jammed the accelerator pedal to the floor.

"What do you mean, *Polly?* I am Mrs. Shapian, and don't you forget it!" The car was careening at eighty miles an hour, but Polly's voice, honed by outrage, cut the wind like a knife. "Slow down! Slow down immediately, do you hear me?"

"Yes, ma'am," he said, biting his lip. He slowed to thirty miles an hour.

"Now pull over to the curb," Polly ordered.

"Please, Mrs. Shapian," he begged, "don't get out. It's not the way you think it is."

"It better not be!" said Polly with a shudder. Good God! Cradle-robbing was infamous enough, but this was cradle-robbing *cum* incest! Exactly how incest applied to this situation, she was too distraught to reason out—probably not at all, if one were to get technical, but this was not the time, nor had Polly the inclination, to explore dialectics.

"Stop the car and let me out," she said. "Now."

"Mrs. Shapian," said Gabriel humbly. "Mrs. Shapian, please, ma'am, let me talk for just a couple of minutes. I'll drive slow and I won't talk more than two minutes, I promise. Then, if you still want me to stop the car, on my honor, I will."

Looking at the guilelessness of Gabriel's face, at his liquid, vulnerable, dark eyes, Polly suddenly got the crazy feeling that it was one of her own twin sons beseeching her, and, as it always happened with her own boys, she could not find it in herself to say no. "Oh, all right," she told Gabriel. "You've got two minutes. And drive slowly."

"Thank you, Mrs. Shapian."

"You now have one minute and fifty seconds."

"Mrs. Shapian, I know you are a fine, decent woman who is old enough to be my mother, and I know you are married to a fine, decent man who is old enough to be my father—"

Polly caught her breath sharply.

"And," continued Gabriel, "I'm sure you love Mr. Shapian and he loves you, and I surely don't mean to suggest that you and I should have what they call an affair."

"Hallelujah!" said Polly, dabbing her forehead.

"Even if you were to stop loving Mr. Shapian for some reason, or if if he were to stop loving you for some reason, I would not insult you by suggesting that you and I should have what they call an affair."

"Good, good, good," said Polly.

"I would, however, ask you to marry me if you stopped loving Mr. Shapian or he stopped loving you."

"That tears it," said Polly. "Stop the car."

"Please, ma'am, I still have almost a minute. I would, as I say, ask you to marry me, which may sound strange to you—"

"Oh, wondrous strange," said Polly.

"Not really," he replied. "Not when you consider my I.Q. Many people have been called geniuses in the course of history, and although there is much disagreement about who was and who was not, two men are accepted by almost everybody—Shakespeare and John Stuart Mill. Both these men, Mrs. Shapian, married women older than themselves. Don't you find that interesting?"

"Not very," said Polly, "and your time is up."

"Not quite. I just want to say this in conclusion. I don't have any real hope that you will stop loving Mr. Shapian or vice versa, so I regard it as highly unlikely that you and I will ever be married. As for what they call an affair, that, of course, is out. So, Mrs. Shapian, though I love you deeply and forever—"

"Oh, hush!" said Polly crossly.

"It is true. Deeply and forever. But I ask only this: will you please be my friend?"

A sharp answer came to Polly's lips but faded abruptly as she saw the plea in Gabriel's eyes. "You are a very difficult boy," she said helplessly.

He nodded. "I know. The I.Q. of a superman; the social grace of a clod. You are the first woman who has ever wakened my heart."

"Damn you, Gabriel," said Polly as she felt the tears start down her cheeks.

"Shall I pull over to the curb?"

Polly resolutely blinked back her tears. "No, drive me to the Stonewall Jackson Hotel—slowly. And shut up while I talk."

"You're not mad any more?"

"Eyes front. Mouth closed. Ears open," said Polly sternly. "Gabriel, I cannot be your friend. To give you the simplest reason, I'll only be in Owens Mill three weeks and then I go back to Hollywood."

"I've thought of that," said Gabriel. "No problem. I can transfer to Cal Tech. In fact, they begged me to come out there after I published my paper on miniaturization. Do you know, Mrs. Shapian, that I can make a parabolic microphone that will fit on the head of a pin?"

"I am delighted to hear it. Truly delighted," said Polly. "Because that solves everything. You stay home and make those cute, teensy microphones and keep your mother company and go to Acanthus College and someday soon—I guarantee it—you will meet a fine, intelligent girl your own age and get married and live happily ever after."

A crooked, mirthless smile appeared on Gabriel's face. "You were crying before, Mrs. Shapian, and for a minute I thought maybe you cared about me a little bit. But I'm wrong; I see that now. To you I'm just the kid with the runny nose."

"In a minute you might be the kid with the *bloody* nose," said Polly with a rush of annoyance. "Doesn't that mighty I.Q. of yours work anywhere except on miniature microphones?"

"Doesn't look like it."

"It sure doesn't. Gabriel, the answer is no. N-O. No, we cannot be friends—not in Owens Mill, not in California, not anywhere, not ever. Do you hear?"

"I hear, but I can't believe you would be so cruel to me."

"Here, thank God, is the Stonewall Jackson Hotel. Stop the car. Thank you for the ride. Good-bye. Forever."

"Mrs. Shapian," said Gabriel as she stepped out of the car, "I will die if I don't see you again."

Polly looked hard at him, clenched her teeth, whirled on her heel, and strode into the lobby. "Any messages?" she asked the desk clerk.

"No, ma'am," he answered. "But Mr. Shapian is upstairs in the suite. He got here about ten minutes ago."

Aha! thought Polly. So he knows I've met Gabriel and the cat is out of the bag. So, like a naughty kid who's earned a spanking, Ira has come home early to get it over with fast. . . . Well, sorry, old man, I will not put a hairbrush to your swarthy bottom. You keep your guilt; I intend to keep my husband.

"Will you please send up a bottle of vodka and a bottle of vermouth?" said Polly to the desk clerk.

"Mr. Shapian already ordered it," said the clerk.

"Splendid," smiled Polly, and still smiling went upstairs and entered the suite. "Hello, darling," she said airily and brushed Ira's cheek with her lips. "Have a good day?"

"Fine," said Ira, watching her closely. "How about you?"

"Oh, most enjoyable," she said, widening her smile. "Does this old parched nose detect martinis in that pitcher?"

"Want one?" asked Ira, his wary eyes steady on Polly.

"Love it."

He poured a drink, handed it to her, and resumed his watchful waiting.

She sipped her drink. "Mmm, good," she pronounced. "Well, it sure was pleasant to see Virgil again. He doesn't change much, does he?"

"Not much. Does Boo, do you think?"

"No," said Polly, looking innocently at Ira. "Boo is Boo—beautiful, patrician, gracious."

"What did you think of Boo's son?" asked Ira. His eyes were locked with Polly's now—a duel of inscrutability.

"Gabriel? Nice boy. Very intelligent. Courteous, too. He drove me home."

"So you got a good look at him."

Polly shrugged. "I guess so."

"Notice anything special?"

"Only that he's a bright kid," she said casually. "Well, Ira, what do you want to do tonight?"

"I will tell you exactly," replied Ira, for, indeed, he knew exactly. When a man has just been stabbed with the sneakiest weapon in the entire arsenal of female cutlery—to wit: forgiveness—there is only one possible course of action open to him. "What I want to do tonight," said Ira, "is to get slowly, carefully, thoroughly, painstakingly, scientifically, systematically, and heroically drunk."

"I'm with you, sweetheart," said Polly and handed him her glass for a refill.

Chapter 15

Polly and Ira woke the next morning with hangovers that made death seem like a month in the country. Thereafter, out of regard for their livers and eyeballs, they reduced their alcohol intake to submorbid levels. But drink they did. Each day Ira went to the campus and worked hard on the television show, while Polly lunched with Virgil. Sometimes there were just the two of them, sometimes they were joined by the better talkers on the Acanthus faculty—most often Dr. Silenko and Linden-Evarts. Then, each night, Polly and Ira met in their suite and ingested martinis until they could commune sociably, if not amorously.

Thus passed twenty days. Ira worked prodigiously, lushed amply, dwelt in a state of truce with his wife, and achingly refrained from phoning or visiting Boo. Labor plus vodka combined to keep his life tolerable—miserable, to be sure, but *tolerably* miserable.

At 9 A.M., December 18th, the day the Acanthus telecast was to go on the air, Clendennon arrived in Owens Mill with Dr. Andrew McAndrews. From the airport they went to the campus and located Ira in the impromptu tv studio he had caused to be built in the Acanthus gymnasium.

Lined up against all four walls of the gym, somewhat like the booths in a church bazaar, were the sets. In the center of the floor stood a jungle of cameras, microphones, lights, and sound equipment. A large, shiny van—in fact, a converted house trailer—was parked alongside one wall. This was the control booth. Along the front ran a window; inside were three small tv sets—monitors, as they are called—and a console studded with dials and switches. From this console the technical director and his staff would regulate the shooting and transmission of the show. Behind the console were two rows of easy chairs where important personages from the sponsor, the network, and the agency could sit in comfort and watch the show on the monitors. And everywhere in the gym technicians were building, painting, adjusting, testing, yelling, and running to Ira with their problems.

Ira was adjusting a heated dispute between his cameraman and his engineer when Clendennon, carefully leading Dr. McAndrews through a thicket of equipment, came into view. "Excuse me, Ira," he said apologetically. "May I interrupt you?"

Ira, preoccupied with his warring technicians, looked at Clendennon and almost failed to recognize him. "Oh, it's you," he said. "Yeah. Wait a couple of minutes. I've got to get this settled."

"Of course," murmured Clendennon and stepped back while Ira handed down his judgment and sent the cameraman and engineer, both unsatisfied but at least docile, back to their jobs. Then Ira turned to Clendennon.

"How good to see you again, Ira," said Clendennon with a pleasant smile and a correct, unfulsome handshake. Ira shot him a curious glance. No chickie-baby? No doll buggy? No parade of teeth? No effusive palpation of shoulder and nape? Why the disguise? wondered Ira.

"This," continued Clendennon in a tone respectful yet unservile, "is Dr. Andrew McAndrews."

Ira looked at the newcomer and understood at once the reason for Clendennon's false-face. McAndrews was definitely the wrong type to chickie-baby. It was not that the old doctor lacked humor; laugh lines were deeply etched around his mouth and the twinkle of wit stood plainly in his eyes. But even more plain was his authority. It was clear at first sight that here was a man patient, polite, even courtly; but what he knew, he knew, and he would not suffer fools.

"I can't tell you, Doctor, how pleased I am to have you on this program," said Ira. He offered McAndrews his hand and received, in return, five strong, clean fingers that could, with equal assurance, build a stone fence or suture a bile duct.

"The pleasure is all mine," said McAndrews, and on his lips the tired old phrase seemed new and true.

"Now, sir, your opponent tonight is Dr. Clara Silenko—a formidable woman, as I'm sure you found out when the two of you were on the Surgeon General's panel."

McAndrews chuckled. "I found it out long before the Surgeon General's panel," he replied. "It happens that Clara was once my student. In fact, she's the brightest student I've ever had."

"Well!" said Ira, pleased. "I didn't realize."

"Oh, yes, I've known Clara for thirty years. First-class doctor. Excellent researcher. Too bad she's a nut."

"Nut?" said Ira, eyebrows rising.

"It's a medical term meaning nut," explained McAndrews.

"I've heard the term," said Ira. "I just never thought to apply it to Dr. Silenko."

"Mr. Shapian, dedication is an essential part of any scientist's makeup. But when dedication becomes fanaticism, scientist becomes nut."

"Well, she *does* get a little passionate," admitted Ira. "But, on the other hand, she seems to have the facts to back up her opinions."

"There's more than one way to look at a fact," said McAndrews. "Where will I find Clara?"

"I'll take you over," Ira offered.

"No, no," said McAndrews, observing the tangle of men and machines around Ira. "You've got enough to do right here—more than enough, it looks like. Do you actually expect to make a show out of all this pandemonium?"

"One hopes," said Ira.

"Incredible!" said the doctor, impressed. "Well, I'll get out of your way. Tell me where to find Clara."

"Out that door and across the quadrangle. The big, modern building with all the glass. You can't miss it."

McAndrews nodded. "I'll catch up with you gentlemen later," he said and walked away with long, erect strides.

When McAndrews was safely out of sight, Clendennon flung off his cloak of austerity. "Well, chickie-baby," he cried, rubbing Ira's neck with gleeful vigor, "what do you think of my Dr. McAndrews?"

"I think you picked a winner," said Ira. "I also think you're choking me."

Clendennon's hand slid from Ira's neck to Ira's back, where it delivered an assortment of frisky pinches and pummels. "You bet your sweet Nielsen I picked a winner!" he crowed. "I don't care how tough your Silenko is; my boy will chew her up like gum."

"Fine," said Ira. "Now stop massaging me before you get to the prostate."

"Sorry, doll buggy," said Clendennon, removing his hand. "It's just that I get all excited when I think of the Emmy we're going to carry home. But I'm thinking way beyond this show. I'm thinking of the next seven years. Big years, Ira baby, big projects, big deals, big

scores. You and I, Ira doll. You and I together, pussycat, for seven
fat years!"

There suddenly descended upon Ira a sadness as black and sti-
fling as the hood which is slipped over the head of a hangman's
victim. He, too, saw the seven years ahead—the finagling, the lying,
the crud. In just a few hours the Acanthus telecast would go on the
air, and Ira's sun-dance would be ended; his subscription to manhood would expire.

"Clendennon, would you excuse me, please?" said Ira. "I've been
looking at you for almost ten minutes. That's all I can stand at one
time."

Clendennon gave an understanding nod. "That's the way I affect
most people. In fact, some cop out within *five* minutes."

"I'm going to my office and hide now," said Ira. "Please do one
thing for me: get your snooping over with as fast as you can and
leave my stage. I must get back here and go to work."

"Sure, chickie-baby."

Ira left the gym, lurched across campus, entered his office, and sat
at his desk, staring silently at the white telephone and the black
telephone, and seeing neither. He did not curse Clendennon. How
could he? Clendennon was not the villain of the piece. The villain,
the rogue and peasant slave, was no one but Ira—spineless, gutless
Ira, former male.

Oh, Boo! he thought with a surge of wistfulness. Boo, where are
you? Where is your purity so pure, your strength so strong, that for
a moment it nearly brought back my own? Are you forever out of
reach, Boo? Am I to sink helplessly into the mire, so defeated I cannot even try once more to grasp the hand that would save me?

"No!" shouted Ira aloud and brought both fists down on his desk
with such furious determination that the telephones jumped twenty-
four inches straight up. Ira seized the black phone in mid-air. He
dialed Boo's number. Nostrils flaring, he listened to the ringing at
the other end of the line.

"Hello," said Boo.

"Listen, I'm not supposed to call you, I know that," cried Ira, the
words cascading from his mouth, "I know that, I know it, but I've
got to, do you understand? I must!"

"As a matter of fact, Ira, I had just made up my mind to call you,"
said Boo.

"Do you understand, Boo?" cried Ira, not hearing her. "I've got to
talk to you. *Got* to! Please, please don't hang up!"

"I won't, Ira."

"Remember those things I said last time I saw you—about leaving Polly and quitting my job and working for Linus Calloway? Do you remember?"

"Of course."

"Well, Boo, I know that if I don't do it now—*right* now—I never will. I know that without you by my side I—" Ira paused; some words of Boo's, delayed in transmission, had suddenly arrived. "What did you say, Boo?" he asked.

"When, dear?"

"Just a minute ago. Did you say you were about to call *me?*"

"Yes, dear."

"Boo, I'm so happy! I am so very, very—" He paused again. Elation was abruptly stilled. "*Why*, Boo?" he asked cautiously.

"Why was I going to call you?"

"Yes, Boo."

"I have to see you, Ira. As soon as possible. I'm going out to the beach house this evening at six o'clock to talk to a man who's building a new jetty. I'll surely finish with him in a half-hour or so. Could you meet me out there at seven o'clock?"

"How can I, Boo? At eight o'clock I'm doing the telecast from Acanthus."

"That's right, I forgot," she said. "All right then, how about this: I'll wait at the beach house and you can meet me there when you finish the telecast. Okay?"

"But you'll miss the program. You don't have a tv set at the beach."

"I know, Ira, and I'm terribly sorry. But this is more important. Please, *please*, my darling, I *have to* see you tonight!"

Elation came galloping back to Ira. "Yes, yes, tonight!" he cried. "Tonight! Yes!"

"At the beach house."

"Yes, my darling. Yes, my good, sweet—" Elation made another quick retreat. "What do you mean, you 'have to' see me?" he said warily. "Do you mean it's like an *emotional* need? For example, when two lovers are kept apart for a length of time, there is a certain psychic compulsion to be reunited. Is that what you had in mind?"

"Ira, I can't talk any more. There are people in the house."

"Wait, wait, wait!" he insisted. "I just want to clarify this one point. It boils down to those words 'have to.' Could you possibly be a little less ambiguous?"

"Ira, good-bye. Please?"

"Listen—"

"The beach house. Tonight. All right?"

"Fine. Now, Boo, what I'm getting at—"

Boo's phone clicked dead.

Ira hung up his telephone. He sat and tried to be two men, one of them magically empowered to look into the soul of the other. These questions he asked himself:

Why after deciding he had to call Boo—why after receiving the joyful tidings that she too had to call him—why after such a happy return of resolution and hope did he now feel panic slithering around his innards?

Was he so totally degutted that courage had no place to cling to?

Was he doomed forever to burrow like a blind, defenseless thing in the safe, dark muck?

Was that all that remained of Ira Shapian?

Calmly, without haste, again and again, Ira asked himself these questions. But no answers were vouchsafed to him. The fruitless interrogation was interrupted by a buzzing of the phone on Ira's desk.

"Yes?"

It was the assistant director calling from the stage. "Ira, listen, I've got a big problem."

"You too?" said Ira wryly. "What a coincidence."

"Could you get over to the stage right away?"

"That depends," answered Ira. "Is Clendennon still there?"

"Just left."

"I'll be right over."

Ira started across the quadrangle to the gym. He had no doubts he would solve whatever problem awaited him on the stage. As for the deeper, knottier tangle that fouled his life, he had doubts aplenty even though the solution lay in his grasp. He had only to make one simple, quick decision tonight, and his course would be forever altered. But would he find the strength to make the decision? Or would this night be still another torment of agonized vacillation?

He did not know; he plainly did not know.

Chapter 16

Meanwhile back at the Stonewall Jackson Hotel, Polly was waking slowly from a refreshing night's sleep. She stretched her bones, made four yawns—two long, two short—and looked at the bedside clock. She was pleased to note it was only a few minutes after ten, which meant she could unhurriedly bathe, breakfast, dress, and perform a little sorcery on her face and hair before Virgil arrived to take her to lunch at 12:30.

Room service in this Southern hostelry being not only magnolia-gracious but also honeysuckle-slow, Polly had learned that if she ordered breakfast before she got in the tub, she had time for a leisurely soak while awaiting the waiter. "This is Room 411," she said into the phone, "I would like one small orange juice, one large coffee, and two slices of whole wheat toast, no butter. And will you please send up the latest magazines, omitting, if you can, *Modern Romances* and *Official Detective?*"

She poured a tub of hot water then, added fragrant unguents, and settled in with a sigh remarkably voluptuous for one who was not a voluptuary. And Polly was surely not; it was pure pragmatism that dictated this bath. Since Ira provided her with no satisfaction at all, she seized, pragmatically, such other comforts as were available— like long sleeps and extended yawns and vodka martinis and daily lunches with Virgil and occasional conversations with Acanthus luminaries like Linden-Evarts and Dr. Silenko, and, as now, dreamy, unhasty immersions in perfumed baths.

She was, therefore, considerably annoyed when she heard a knocking on the door of the suite less than ten minutes after she had arranged herself comfortably in the tub. Why on this morning, she thought testily, should room service suddenly get so rapid? "Coming! Coming!" she shouted as the knocking continued. Muttering and dripping, she got out of the tub, flung on a terry-cloth robe, and made a trail of wet footprints from the bath through the sitting room.

She stepped backward as she opened the door, concealing herself behind it. "Good morning, Swifty," she said. "You must be new here. Will you put the tray on the coffee table, please?"

But it was not a tray-bearing waiter who entered the suite; it was young Gabriel, eyes frantic and knuckles cracking like pistol shots.

Polly's jaw fell in stark disbelief. "You've got to be kidding," she whispered.

"Please, Mrs. Shapian," he begged. "I won't stay long."

"You most certainly won't. You will leave. Now."

"Please close the door."

"Go!" said Polly, pointing one finger, using the other hand to clutch her robe together.

"You're standing in a draft."

"Out! Out!"

Two chambermaids, pushing a cart of linens down the corridor, paused and observed the scene with frank curiosity.

Polly swung the door shut. "Gabriel, listen," she said, talking quietly, dipping deep into her reservoir of patience, "I speak to you as a woman old enough to be your mother. The last thing I want is to be unkind. I realize you're going through some kind of hell and, believe it or not, I'm sympathetic. . . . However, you simply *must* stay away from me. This situation is ridiculous. It's ludicrous. It's— it's—it's *obscene!*"

"Excuse me, ma'am, but you're wrong. It is tragic and beautiful, is what it is."

"It is *over*, is what it is. Are you going peacefully, or do I call the house dick?"

"I am going peacefully, if you'll just let me say what I came to say."

Polly walked weakly to the chair farthest from Gabriel and sank down. "All right," she sighed. "Talk, but keep your distance."

"Mrs. Shapian!" exclaimed Gabriel, profoundly shocked. "Is that what you think I came here to do—*molest* you?"

"How do I know what you're going to do? I never met anybody like you in my whole life."

"Nobody has," he said desolately. "I'll tell you something weird: half the time I don't even believe I exist."

"That would help explain a lot of things," said Polly.

"But I do exist," he assured her. "And there's the tragedy. I exist, and so do you, and as long as you exist, somehow, come what may, I've got to be near you."

Polly pulled her robe more tightly around her. "Okay, Gabriel, you said what you came to say, and I listened, just like I promised. Now you're leaving, just like *you* promised. True?"

"But I didn't finish what I came to say."

"Sorry. Proceed, please. *Rapidly*, please."

"Yes, ma'am . . . You know that big, white Spanish-style house next to yours in Bel Air?"

"I know it well," she answered nervously. "How do *you* know it?"

"This real estate man out in California sent me a picture of it."

"Why?"

"I bought it," answered Gabriel.

Polly tamped down a shriek. "What do you mean, you bought it? That house is worth 150 thousand dollars, and you are an eighteen-year-old boy."

"Actually," he said, "I paid 175 thousand. But that's okay because I got a million dollars from my trust fund on my last birthday. I get five more millions when I'm twenty-one."

"I feel like my sanity is running out my ears," Polly announced solemnly.

"I know it's bad taste to talk about how rich you are," he went on. "I only mentioned it so you won't worry that I can't take care of you if we get married—I mean, in case you ever want to leave Mr. Shapian."

"Gabriel, pay close attention. I *never* want to leave Mr. Shapian."

"No? Then how come you're spending so much time with Virgil Tatum?"

Anger propelled Polly to her feet. "Have you been *following* me?"

He blushed incandescent red. "I'm sorry," he said in a tiny voice.

"That is the filthiest, sneakiest thing I ever heard of!" she declared. "Have you no shame?"

"Yes, ma'am," he replied earnestly. "I am miserably, loathsomely ashamed. . . . Aren't you?"

"*Me?* For what?"

"For spending so much time with Virgil," he answered. "Obviously you wouldn't be chasing Virgil if you still loved Mr. Shapian."

Polly clenched her fists tight, seeking control. She was not entirely successful. "Young man," she said, "I want to show you what you're doing to me. It's ten-fifteen in the morning, and I have not had my breakfast yet. However, watch!" She walked rapidly to the sideboard, uncorked a bottle of vodka, lifted it to her lips, tilted it back, and did not stop swallowing until at least four ounces had disappeared. "You see, Gabriel?" she said, wiping her mouth with the back of her hand. "You see what you are doing to a respectable American housewife?"

"It grieves me something terrible, Mrs. Shapian," he said sincerely. "It hurts me real bad to see you in such terrible shape. I swear I'd give anything if I knew how to stay away from you. But I don't, and that's flat. So I guess you better get used to the notion."

He lifted his arm in a small, despairing gesture of farewell and left the suite.

Polly looked at the bottle of vodka she was still holding. Her hand started to raise it to her mouth, but her other, wiser hand came shooting out, snatched the bottle and returned it to the sideboard.

Calm, she said to herself and sat down slowly in a chair beside the desk. Calm, calm, calm, calm. Think green thoughts. Think of sylvan glades and bosky dells. Forget you are soaking wet, and pursued by a demented boy, and married to a squashed Armenian. Calm, calm, she told herself, and soon she grew still—except for one hand: the wicked, vodka-wanting hand. It lunged out and grabbed the telephone on the desk. "Where the hell is my breakfast?" she yelled.

"On the way, ma'am," stammered a terrified voice, and, indeed, the waiter was knocking on the door within two minutes.

He brought in a tray. Coffee, juice, and toast were neatly arrayed on one end; on the other end was a stack of magazines.

"Who the hell ordered magazines?" yelled Polly.

"You did, ma'am," replied the waiter timidly.

"I'm sorry I can't stop yelling," yelled Polly, "but something's gone wrong. I just can't stop. Wait! Don't leave yet. I want to give you a tip, a great big one, on account of the yelling."

"Oh, that's all right, ma'am," said the waiter and tried to sidle away.

But she found a purse on the desk, snatched out a five-dollar bill, and handed it to him before he could make his exit. "Here you are," she said. "Listen. How do I sound? My voice, I mean. Am I still yelling?"

"No, ma'am," answered the waiter, nearly as relieved as Polly. "Sounds normal. *Real* normal."

"Glory be!" she breathed.

"And thank you for the tip. I surely do appreciate it."

He left and Polly sat down to her breakfast. Slowly, inhaling deeply between each sip, she finished her orange juice. She poured a cup of coffee, picked up a slice of toast, opened a copy of *Time* magazine, and began, with forced deliberateness, to read and eat. After a few minutes she decided that *Time*'s accounts of calamities in Uganda, Indonesia, Bolivia, and Washington, D.C., were less than an ideal tranquilizer. She laid *Time* aside and took the next magazine off the stack.

It was a publication unfamiliar to Polly. The paper was heavy and expensive, the edge of the pages were deckled, the type was hand set, and on the plain beige cover, in tastefully modest letters, was the legend:

THE MERMAID
The Literary Quarterly of Owens Mill

Polly opened the cover. A short poem, surrounded by wide margins, was printed on the first page. "O, Speckled Love!" was the title of the poem. Underneath was the author's name: "by Leda."

Polly read "O, Speckled Love!" by Leda. Then she blinked and read it again, her lips moving slowly as her eyes scanned the lines:

> *Sand between the lovers' toes*
> *Recalls, like thorns, the flawless rose.*
> *Gritty crunching in the shoes*
> *Recollects, rejoices, rues*
> *Untamed blood that starts the hearts*
> *Till sand adheres to yearning parts.*
> *Rasping flesh in grasping hand:*
> *Abrasive love—pervasive sand.*
> *Sorrow learns what bliss can teach*
> *On the fierce and tender beach.*

Polly closed her jaw and the magazine. "It is my considered opinion," she said gravely to herself, "that 'O, Speckled Love!' is beyond any doubt the worst poem ever written in the history of the entire world. Leda, whoever the poor woman is, must be returned with all possible dispatch to her sandbox."

Polly stood, left her breakfast tray, and went back to the tub. Her best hope of recovery, she decided, lay with hydrotherapy. She added hot water and fresh bath oil, removed her robe, slipped into the fragrant liquid, folded her arms on her breast, and wooed peace.

By and by it arrived, and brought with it a smile. And soon the smile ripened into a giggle—a nonsynthetic, nonhysterical giggle of pure, billowing amusement. "Sand between the lovers' toes"? thought Polly. Come *on!*

Healing laughter bubbled out of her. She rose from the bath, toweled, put on underthings, and sat at the vanity to apply her face —no easy chore because couplets from "O, Speckled Love!" kept coming back to fling her into long, jiggling guffaws. But, with good humor, she wiped the mascara from her ears and the lipstick from her nose and restored them to their assigned positions. Then, between giggles, she did some cunning things with her hair and went to select a dress.

The rack in the closet was hung half with Ira's clothes, half with Polly's. "Love, O love, O speckled love!" she sang hilariously as she riffled through her wardrobe. She settled on a two-piece Don Loper of wool as blue as her eyes. The result, as revealed in the full-length mirror on the closet door, was eminently satisfactory.

What shoes? Polly asked herself and immediately had to sit down while a new fit of laughter rolled in. "Gritty crunching in the shoes," thought Polly, slapping her thighs. Oh, Leda honey, I don't know who you are, but this I do know: you are fruitier than a nutcake!

She waited for the last, tickling twitch of laughter and returned to the shoe-rack which stood tilted on the floor of the closet. The rack held eight pairs of Polly's shoes, all in a line, and beside them were three pairs of Ira's. Her eye ran quickly along the row of pumps and chose Pair No. 8—black suede. As she reached down for the shoes, her hand brushed against the pair of Ira's which were directly adjacent. A sudden frown creased Polly's brow; she froze in jackknife position. Not a muscle moved, except for the fingertips resting on Ira's shoes. Delicately, probingly, they stroked the leather.

These shoes feel strange, thought Polly. These shoes feel—what is the word I want? *Gritty* is the word I want. *Gritty!*

Now she flew into motion. She lifted Ira's shoes and held them to the light. A film of sand was clearly visible. She shook the shoes beside her ear and heard the soft, scuffling rustle of sand. She turned the shoes upside down and watched the pale, scattered grains come trickling out.

Carefully she returned Ira's shoes to their place on the rack. She picked up her black suede pumps, put them on, and walked without expression into the sitting room. She opened the copy of *The Mermaid* and reread Leda's poem. She closed the magazine, went to the sideboard, filled a highball glass with vodka, sat down, and took a first slow sip.

Why am I not screaming? she asked herself. The answer came readily: I am not screaming because screaming is the opposite of action, and I must act. I must act or I will crumble. After this final outrage in a morning of outrages—in half a lifetime of outrages—I must *do* something.

But do *what?* And to *whom?* Shall I summon Gabriel, put him over my knee, and spank him? Shall I go find Boo and snatch her bald-headed? Shall I wait for Ira to come home and give him a thousand kicks with my little pointy shoes?

All three prospects had a certain fleeting appeal, but Polly knew that none of them touched on the heart of the matter. The heart of the matter, she thought, making slow but steady progress toward the bottom of her glass of vodka, the heart of the matter is simply this: I have been ignominiously cuckolded. To be cuckolded is, of course, always ignominious, but in this case the ignominy is total, for I have been cuckolded by two fools.

A new thought jarred Polly. Could I be the *third* fool? she wondered. Well, let's see. About Boo I am not now nor have I ever been a fool. It's true I found her moderately attractive in the past—after all, she does have a warm, generous soul—but I knew from the very beginning her patrician brow had never been troubled by an idea. And she gets no smarter; witness "O, Speckled Love!"

And Ira? Have I been a fool about him? Was I stupid to go on believing that his quick, tough, valiant intelligence remained intact? Buried, yes, but intact—still whole, still capable of returning to full, fiery life, and, most important, still wise enough to realize that he is married to one hell of a dame?

This I counted on—Ira's intelligence. This I trusted. Sure, I've seen him do a million foolish things, but I've never lost faith that someday the big, bright beacon in his skull would light up and show him the truth: that he loves me, always has, always will, and properly so, because I am a woman well worth loving.

But could I be wrong? She walked over to pour another drink. Am I really the woman I think I am? If so, why is my husband still banging Boo? This time I can't dismiss it as a youthful indiscretion. It is not eighteen years ago; it is today, and Ira has had plenty of time to learn who I am and what I am. Maybe he sees something I don't. Maybe he's discovered there's nothing left of me—nothing, anyhow, that would interest a man.

"Mirror, mirror, on the wall," said Polly to the looking glass over the sideboard. "Is any woman left at all?"

That's what I have to know, she thought, pouring vodka. Am I a woman or the empty shell of a woman? If I'm a woman, I'll hold that Armenian if I have to nail him to the floor. If I'm not, the best thing I can do for both of us is to let go, and the sooner, the better.

But how do I find out whether I'm a woman? Who on earth can let me know?

The telephone rang. "Yes?"

"Mr. Virgil Tatum is waiting in the lobby," said the desk clerk.

Chapter 17

Virgil smiled delightedly as he watched Polly step out of the elevator doors and into the lobby. "You, my dear," he said, "should always wear blue."

"How interesting. Yesterday you told me I should always wear red."

"Actually," he said, affecting a leer, "what you should always wear is the least possible."

Polly sniffed. "Big talk."

"Big hurry," said Virgil. "Let's make tracks, you pretty blue thing. I've got a deans' meeting at two."

He took Polly's arm, but she seemed disinclined to move. "What happens if you miss the deans' meeting?"

"Chaos. You know the place wouldn't last twenty minutes without me."

"Seriously, Virgil. What if you didn't show up?"

He stepped back and gave her a close scrutiny. "Your dress is lovely. Your face is lovely. Your eyes are strange. . . . Polly, is anything wrong?"

"Of course not. Come, you mustn't miss your meeting."

Now it was Virgil who stood immobile. "To hell with the meeting. We're going someplace quiet, and you will tell Uncle Virgil what's clouding those beautiful eyes."

"You are *not* my uncle," she said irritably.

"I am your friend." He made it a plain statement of fact. "Whatever is wrong, I want to help."

She touched his hand. "Sorry I growled."

"There's a new restaurant called Le Coq d'Or. It's so damn chic nobody goes there. We'll have plenty of privacy."

He offered her his arm. She held it tightly as they walked out of the lobby. She had bolted another glass of vodka just before leaving the suite, and though her mind was alert and her diction was crisp,

165

her feet seemed to belong to somebody else. However, with Virgil's assistance, she made it to his car without even a hint of a stagger.

They got into the car. All of a sudden, before he could pull away from the curb, she started to speak, insistently, rapidly, determinedly, as if to get everything said before a failure of nerve or a return of good sense should silence her. "Virgil, when Ira and I were stationed here during the war, there was a place out on Route 12 called Big Eddie's. It's still there; I know because I passed it on my way in from the airport. It's a tacky, roadhouse kind of joint. You know."

"Yes," he said, regarding her narrowly. "I know Big Eddie's."

"Well, I don't. I mean I've never actually been there. It was off limits for troops during the war. Private dining rooms and stuff like that. You know."

"And that's where you want to go for lunch?"

"Does it still have private dining rooms?"

"Yes."

"Let's go."

"All right. I should point out, though, that the food is inedible, the kitchen is filthy, and the proprietor is a degenerate. Still want to go?"

She nodded.

"Care to tell me why?"

"After we get there."

"How much have you had to drink this morning?" he asked, gently, inoffensively.

"Quite a lot," she replied. "Can we go?"

"We can," he said and swung his car into traffic.

A moment later a small, homemade sports car, with young Gabriel at the wheel, pulled out of an alley. Skillfully driving a half-block behind Virgil, allowing other cars to intervene lest his quarry become suspicious, Gabriel continued his surveillance.

It took Virgil fifteen minutes to reach Big Eddie's. Polly did not speak. She switched on the car radio and listened, unhearing, to a concert of hillbilly music. Virgil gave her a sidelong glance from time to time, but he too was silent.

He parked in front of a one-story building covered on all sides with asphalt roofing shingles, half of them hanging awry. There was one window in front of the building, and none anywhere else. A riot of neon signs flickered behind the flyspecks in the window. One sign, in yellow, proclaimed MILLER'S HIGH LIFE. BUDWEISER was in red, SCHLITZ in brown, PABST in blue, and BALLANTINE in green. Centered among the brewers' emblems was a sign in colorless neon script; the tubing had long since burned out. BIG EDDIE's, it said.

Virgil got out, helped Polly from the car, escorted her cautiously around the potholes that dotted the parking area, and ushered her into the roadhouse. Inside the door, barely discernible in the dimness, was a barroom. Six booths, covered in gamy oilcloth, stood against one wall. Another wall accommodated a long bar on which were carved a profusion of graffiti—names and nicknames, initials twined in hearts, Appalachian ribaldries, and genitalia of a size no man has yet seen. The other two walls were blank except for pine doors, each bearing a crudely painted number. The doors were marked 1 to 10; these were the entrances to the private dining rooms.

No customers were in the barroom; only Big Eddie. Gross and unshaven he stood behind the bar. In his mouth was a twisted stogie; in his hand was the newspaper of the White Citizens Council. He looked up, knew instantly who Virgil Tatum was, but his colorless eyes betrayed not the slightest sign of recognition. If old Virgil felt like tearing off a piece, why, that wasn't nobody's business but old Virgil's, was it?

"Howdy," said Big Eddie, neither politely nor impolitely.

"Howdy," answered Virgil. "Can we get some lunch?"

"Surely," said Big Eddie. "Room No. 6 is nice and clean."

"Thank you," said Virgil.

"Let me know when you're ready to eat. We got rabbit with turnip greens, or there's canned salmon."

"We'll let you know," said Virgil.

"Can you make a vodka martini?" said Polly to Big Eddie.

"Well, yes, ma'am," he replied. "But not too good."

"I see," she said. "All right then, will you just give us a bottle of vodka and some ice?"

"No, ma'am, I don't believe I can."

"No vodka?"

"Oh, plenty of vodka. Thing is, though, the ice is spoiled."

"The *ice* is spoiled?"

"Settin' too long, maybe. Don't get much call for it around here."

"Just a bottle of vodka, okay?" said Virgil.

"Yes, sir," said Big Eddie. He handed Virgil a bottle of vodka, two glasses, and a key attached to a tag marked No. 6.

Room No. 6 was, as Big Eddie had represented, clean, and there its attractions ended. It was a cell about six feet wide and eight feet

long. The furnishings consisted of one breakfast-sized table of
chrome and red plastic, two chairs of the same, and a studio couch
draped with a corduroy throw.

Virgil pulled out a chair for Polly and sat in the other one. Using
his breast pocket handkerchief, he wiped the drinking glasses,
opened the vodka, and poured two generous shots. He raised his
glass to Polly. "Well, my dear, what would you like, the rabbit or
the canned salmon?"

"Please!" she said, shuddering. She tossed off her drink and handed
the glass back to Virgil.

He made no move to fill it. "Maybe you better talk while you still
can. What's this all about?"

"How old are you, Virgil? Can't you add it up?"

"Oh, yes, I can add it up. That is, I *could* add it up, only there's
one part of it that just plain won't figure. I mean *you*. You are Polly
Shapian. What is Polly Shapian doing in a place like this?"

"Damn it!" she said hotly. "Where else could I take you? Everybody in the hotel knows me. Everybody in the *county* knows you.
Where, except in a joint like this, could we do what we're going to
do?"

"I see. . . . All right, next question. *Why* are we going to do what
we're going to do?"

"Can I have my drink?"

He poured two fingers of vodka and handed it to her.

"Virgil, you've been making a lot of sexy banter with me. Is that
all it is—banter?"

"In the circumstances, what else could it be?"

"Don't you think of me as a woman?" she asked, panic in her eyes.
"Don't you find me *desirable?*"

Virgil stood. "Finish your drink, Polly, and let's get out of here. I
don't know what's tormenting you, but whatever it is, you're not
going to fix it on that couch over there."

"Wait!" she cried. She jumped to her feet. Her fingers raced down
the buttons of her jacket. She yanked off the jacket, dropped it on
the floor, reached for the hooks in the back of her bra.

"Stop it!" said Virgil, his voice hard, his brow black with anger.
"Stop it. I get the idea."

Polly removed her hand from the fasteners of her bra. Bleakly
she looked up at Virgil. "And you're not interested, are you?"

"I'm not interested in being part of this crazy, drunken game
you're playing."

"That's not what I mean. You're not interested in *me*. You don't find me attractive or desirable. You don't even look on me as a woman. That's a simple fact, isn't it?"

"Polly, put down that booze and listen to me carefully and re-member what you hear, because I am going to tell you some things that are mighty nice and altogether true. For the past twenty—" He paused suddenly; it seemed to him he had just heard a soft, thudding sound on the outside wall of the room. "What was that?" he asked.

"What was what?"

"I thought I heard something hit the outside of the wall over there. Didn't you hear it?"

"No."

"Sure?"

"Positive," she said. "I'm afraid you're a little jumpy, Virgil. Sorry. My fault."

"Funny," said Virgil. "I could swear I heard a sound on that wall. Not very loud, but I could swear I heard it. . . . Well, I guess I was wrong."

But Virgil was not wrong. The sound he had heard was an arrow softly imbedding itself in the asphalt shingles outside their room, and the hand that had drawn the bow that had shot the arrow was young Gabriel's.

Gabriel, successfully avoiding detection, had followed Virgil's car all the way to Big Eddie's. When Virgil had taken Polly inside, Gabriel had parked his sports car in a thicket near the roadhouse. Using field glasses, he had spied through the window of Big Eddie's and seen Virgil and Polly go into Room No. 6. Then he had removed from his car a bow, an arrow, and a carrying case roughly the size of a small valise. Keeping to the woods, he had circled Big Eddie's until he calculated he was directly opposite Room No. 6.

Then he had opened his carrying case. Inside was an excellent, battery-powered tape recorder. A long, fine wire was attached to the recorder. Gabriel had taken one end of the wire and fastened it securely to the head of his arrow. It was a hollowed-out arrowhead, containing an ultrasensitive miniature microphone handcrafted by Gabriel himself. He had slipped the arrow into the bow and, from a distance of fifty yards, had taken careful aim.

The arrow had flown true. It stuck now in the wall of Room No. 6, the microphone picking up everything that was said inside. The long, fine wire ran from the arrowhead to the tape recorder. Gabriel squatted, pushed the "RECORD" button, started the reels spinning, slipped on a pair of earphones and listened. This is what he heard:

VIRGIL: Where was I?

POLLY: You were about to tell me something nice.

VIRGIL: Oh, yes . . . Polly, you ask whether I think of you as a woman, whether I find you desirable. Yes. Yes to both questions. I have thought of you as a woman and I have found you desirable since I first laid eyes on you twenty years ago. I am now a middle-aged gentleman and the president of a university, and, you will agree, it is hardly fitting for a man of my age and attainments to indulge in sex fantasies. However, I still recall, as though it were yesterday, an afternoon during the war when we all went out to the beach. . . . In fact, I recall it so vividly that I'm going to shut up right now.

POLLY: Come on, Virgil, that's not fair. You started something. Now finish it.

VIRGIL: I better not.

POLLY: If you've got any kind words for me, please, I beg you, don't hold back. Never in my life have I needed so desperately to hear some kind words.

VIRGIL: Well, these are pretty *sexy* words.

POLLY: What kind of kind words could be kinder?

VIRGIL: Well, if you insist—

POLLY: I do. . . . All right, it was wartime and we were all at the beach one afternoon. Go on, and don't skip anything.

VIRGIL: There were a lot of us out there that day—Ira, Boo, several of the Owenses—but it's only you I remember. You were wearing a white two-piece bathing suit with tiny blue fleur-de-lis printed on it. I remember every detail. I can still see your breasts when you came out of the water—the thrust of them, the round perfection of them. Your halter had slipped a bit while you were swimming, and I saw your nipples, how the cold water had made them rise like two happy, eager things, ready for fun and play.

POLLY: Twenty years have passed, Virgil.

VIRGIL: The years have been kind. I look now at your breasts and I see the same vitality. I see more. I see tenderness, womanliness, passion come to full maturity.

POLLY: You startle me. I'm not sure I know what to say.

VIRGIL: Say nothing. Listen. I want to tell you about your legs now. They're beautiful, Polly, not just because they're so faultlessly proportioned, but because they *dare*, they *venture*. I have thought of those brave legs around me, arching and striving. I have wished to be embraced by such courage. . . . May I continue?

POLLY: For God's love, yes!

VIRGIL: Your buttocks.

POLLY: You like them?

VIRGIL: You have, without question, the most defiant behind in North America. Did you ever get a look at your backside while you were engaged in an argument?

POLLY: A little difficult, isn't it? I mean, have you ever seen *yours?*

VIRGIL: Good point . . . But I have seen *yours*. Many times. Do you know that your butt absolutely *bristles?* It leaps with conviction. It launches you!

POLLY: Like a rocket, you mean?

VIRGIL: Like a comet! Dear Polly, you in bed are the combination poets dream about—those eager breasts, those feisty legs, that brazen ass. . . . Oh, excuse me.

POLLY: Not at all, not at all!

VIRGIL: And I haven't even mentioned your face, the gorgeous honesty of it. And those creamy shoulders and supple arms. And the deft hands, the strong, nimble fingers that know where to touch a man. . . .

This much Gabriel, breathing hard, heard. Then he heard this: "Gabriel," came a voice like thunder, "what the hell do you think you're doing here?"

The boy leaped up in terror, tangling his feet in the wire, kicking it loose from the tape recorder, making the spools stop turning. Looming over him was the fearful scowl of Jefferson Tatum. And behind Jefferson stood two broad-beamed women in their mid-forties, each with the same slack, placid, inbred face—Esther and Millie McCabe, the pushovers from packaging.

"Oh, hi, Uncle Jefferson," stammered Gabriel. "I was just leaving."

"Wait a minute! Isn't that one of them tape recorders?"

"Leaving. That's what I was doing—leaving." Gabriel ducked under the old man's arm, snatched up his tape recorder and started away.

"Why are you hanging around a place like this? Don't you know what kind of place this is? Wait till I tell your mother!" yelled Jefferson, but Gabriel was already gunning his sports car out of the woods.

"Crazy, mixed-up kid!" muttered Jefferson, darkly. Then, remembering the McCabe twins, he gallantly offered an arm to each. "Shall we go in, ladies?" he said with a debonair toss of his head.

"Sure, mister," they said and started walking with him toward Big Eddie's.

And meanwhile in Room No. 6 Polly was asking hopefully, "Is there more, Virgil? Have you finished or is there more? Huh? Huh?"

"I guess that just about covers it," he replied.

"Not quite. There's one last thing I have to know. And please, please, Virgil," she entreated, "be honest. These pretty words you've been saying—are they true? Really and truly true?"

"On my oath as a Southern gentleman," he said solemnly.

"Then why have you never let me know? I don't mean you had to make a pass at me. Why didn't you somehow let me know?"

"I've just answered that," he said with a wry smile. "The Southern gentleman syndrome. I'm afraid I've got it bad. Another man's wife is strictly out of bounds."

"I'll accept that," she said. "But I don't think it's the whole answer."

"You mean Boo?"

"Yes."

"A most curious thing is happening here," said Virgil. "You're the one who's supposed to be drunk, but it's me who's spilling my innermost secrets. Well, okay, I might as well finish the job. . . . Yes, I love Boo. I have loved her more than twenty long, unrequited years. In fact, I love her right this minute, and, frankly, looking ahead, I see no relief in sight. All the same—please try to understand this—I am not a masochist, and I'm thoroughly tired of playing on the losing side. Polly, I tell you plainly that if you were not married and if you would have me, I'd leap at the chance. And don't get any wrong ideas: I wouldn't be taking you as a consolation prize. You, my beauty, are clearly, definitely, and spectacularly a *first prize*. You are bingo. You are the laurel wreath, the winner's circle, and the Medal of Honor, and any man lucky enough to have you should drop to his knees and give thanks several hundred times a day."

"Virgil, that funny look you see on my face is the happiest smile I have smiled since I don't know when. Would you mind if I kissed you?"

"I'd be proud, only first you must put the top of your dress back on. I may be a Southern gentleman, but let's not push it too far."

He held up the jacket she had thrown on the floor. She slipped into it, fastened the buttons, and gave Virgil an honest kiss on the mouth.

"Now then," said Virgil, "shall we order the rabbit or finish the vodka?"

"Neither," she said. "You've got a deans' meeting, and as for me, I don't want food, and I don't need liquor. Take me back to the hotel. I am going to stand naked in front of a mirror all afternoon."

Laughing, arm in arm, they walked out of Room No. 6—just as Jefferson was entering the bar with the McCabe twins.

Jefferson stared at his son, stared at Polly, stared back at his son. The old man's eyes popped with admiration bordering on awe. "Why, you *dog!*" he said proudly to Virgil. "You peter-pussing hound!"

"Howdy, stranger," replied Virgil, deadpan, to Jefferson. He tossed a ten-dollar bill on the bar and, looking neither right nor left, escorted Polly outdoors.

Chapter 18

Gabriel drove rapidly but not recklessly away from Big Eddie's; he did not want to endanger the precious cargo he carried in his sports car—the reel of tape with which he would dissolve the marriage of Polly and Ira Shapian, thus making Polly free to become his wife.

His hunch, Gabriel told himself with grim satisfaction as he speeded toward Acanthus College, had not been wrong: Polly was out of love with Ira. That is why she had been spending so much time with Virgil: her feeling for Ira was dead. Only habit and inertia kept the union together; love was gone. Gabriel had proof of it now —this spool of tape, this incontrovertible recording, testimony beyond refuting.

But Gabriel took no pleasure in what he had to do next—play the tape for Ira Shapian. It was a devastating blow to inflict on a man so sensitive. And yet, thought Gabriel, he must be cruel only to be kind. Certainly Mr. Shapian deserved better than a wife who had stopped loving him. When the initial shock had passed, he would probably thank Gabriel.

And even if he did not, even if he hated Gabriel ever afterward, the fact would remain that a mockery of a marriage had been terminated. As long as Polly and Ira stayed together, neither had a chance for happiness. Once asunder, the prospects for both were immeasurably brighter. Mr. Shapian, in spite of his advanced years, was still a colorful figure and surely he would somewhere, sometime, find a woman who would love him truly. As for Polly, she already had Gabriel.

Yes, thought Gabriel as he drove through the gate of Acanthus, he was doing the right thing, the only thing, the *human* thing.

Carrying the tape, he went looking for Ira and found him in the gymnasium which had been converted into a television studio. Ira was directing a camera rehearsal. To Gabriel's inexperienced eyes, it seemed like an outbreak in a violent ward. Technicians screamed, cursed, dashed, spun, and jittered. Only Ira was undisturbed. Calmly, softly, steadily, he issued orders.

"Move No. 3 in closer, Mr. Harris," said Ira.

"I'm getting effing mike shadow," cried the operator of Camera No. 3.

"Raise your boom, Mr. Santini," said Ira to the sound man.

"It's on the effing ceiling right now!" yelled the sound man.

"Dolly him back, Mr. Cohen," said Ira to the laborer who pushed the boom carriage.

"He'll knock over my effing brute!" roared the electrician who held a huge arc light behind the boom.

"All right, Mr. Cohen, crab," said Ira to the boom pusher. The man crimped the wheels, moved the boom backward at such an angle that he missed the arc light by a clean inch. "Now, move No. 3, Mr. Harris," said Ira, and the camera rolled closer. "Still got mike shadow?" asked Ira.

"No," admitted the camera operator.

"Mark it, Mr. Dooley," said Ira, and a laborer slapped ribbons of adhesive tape on the floor to indicate the precise spots where the camera and microphone must stop rolling.

"Next setup, Mr. Schultz?" said Ira to the script clerk.

The script clerk consulted his notebook and said, "Lab No. 4. Cameras 1, 2, and 6. Two booms."

An overlapping chorus of howls erupted immediately.

"That's the smallest effing set on the stage," said the cameraman. "I can't get three effing machines in there."

"Where the hell am I gonna put two effing booms?" asked the sound man.

"How do I get lights into this effing mishmash?" demanded the electrician.

"Kill Camera 2, Mr. Harris," said Ira placidly to the cameraman. "Mr. Santini, use one boom and two lavaliere mikes," was his soft answer to the sound man. "Stick obies on the cameras, Mr. Keefe," he said in an unruffled voice to the electrician. "All right, gentlemen, let's move to Set No. 4."

Ira, followed by the technical director, the script clerk, and the assistant director, started toward Set No. 4, a replica of one of Dr. Silenko's laboratories. Meanwhile crewmen fixed tiny, bright spotlights to the bottoms of the cameras and got ready to wheel equipment into position.

Max Shulman

Gabriel chose this moment of relative quiet to seize Ira. "Hi, Mr. Shapian," he said.

"Hello, Gabriel," said Ira. "Good-bye, Gabriel."

"Please, sir," insisted Gabriel, touching Ira's sleeve, "I have to talk to you."

"*Talk?*" Ira regarded the boy in popeyed disbelief. "Are you crazy or what? I've got to get this mess on the air in less than four hours and you want to sit and *talk?*"

"Just a couple of minutes," said Gabriel supplicatingly, earnestly, urgently. "That's all I want, two minutes. I promise you, sir, they'll be the two most important minutes of your entire life."

Ira looked and was impressed. "All right. Talk."

"Privately."

"Now, listen, son—"

"Please?"

Ira met Gabriel's eyes—passionate, black plagiarisms of his own. How could he refuse his very flesh and blood? And, moreover, this very night Ira was going to Boo's beach house where—who could tell?—he might at last reach the decision that would make him Gabriel's legal as well as actual father.

"Back in two minutes," said Ira to his assistants. "Come on," he said to Gabriel and led him across the quadrangle to his office. "What is it, boy? And fast."

"Have you got a tape recorder?"

Ira pointed to a machine on a table beside his desk. Gabriel put on the spool of tape he was carrying, threaded it, switched on the recorder and sat.

The machine talked and Ira listened. For ninety seconds the tape unreeled and Ira, quite still, listened. With each passing second his face grew more blank. He did not pale; he did not redden. It was as though all his powers of feeling, thought, and motion had suddenly, quietly ceased.

"Shall I play it again?" asked Gabriel.

"No," said Ira. His voice was steady, but not much like his.

Gabriel peered at him curiously. "Sir, did you understand what you just heard?"

"Yes."

"That was Mrs. Shapian speaking. The man was Virgil Tatum."

"Yes."

"I think you are in shock, sir," said Gabriel.

"Maybe."

"Can I get you some water?"

"No."

"Look, sir, if you want to cry or scream or anything, please feel free."

"Thank you."

"Would you care to hit me? I mean *hard.*"

"No, thank you."

"I've got it coming, Mr. Shapian. That was a lousy, sneaky thing I did—following your wife, making that tape. That was the lowest thing I ever did in my life, and I want you to know I'll never stop being ashamed of it. Never!"

"Fine."

"And I knew you'd get all shook up when I played you the tape —not *this* shook up, maybe, but shook up. . . . Still, what's right is right. Who is more entitled to this information than you?"

"What?"

"I'm saying, sir, that I didn't have any choice. I had to play the tape for you because the next move is yours."

"Move?"

"Are you sure you don't want any water, Mr. Shapian?"

"Yes."

"Can I feel your pulse?"

"No."

"I wish you'd let me because there's no other way I can tell how bad off you are. I mean just looking at you, your color is okay and you're not shaking or anything. Give me your pulse, please, sir?"

"No."

"I'm watching the vein in your neck, which is also a pulse. It seems to be beating normally, so I'm going to assume you're not in dangerous trauma, even though you just had this terrible shock. Believe me, sir, I wish I could wait a few days to tell you what I'm about to tell you now, because I'm well aware this is the wrong time and place for conversation, especially since your attention-span is so short and the things I have to say are real deep and philosophical. But consider this: chances are you'll never let me anywhere near you for the rest of your life, so I've got to speak right away, even if the circumstances aren't what you'd call ideal. . . . Sir, I hope someday you'll forgive me for what I've done, but that's not important. What's important is that you should forgive Mrs. Shapian. Remember, sir, the nature of love is still a mystery after all these thousands and thousands of years. Nobody can explain why love hits you; nobody can explain why love dies. What's the profit in trying to find out? It's not a science; there are no rules. Mrs. Shapian loved you, and then she stopped. Why ask why? It happened, that's all. Don't blame her; don't blame yourself. Just keep this in mind: life goes on, and you are still a fairly vigorous man and there is every reason to hope that you will find another wife, maybe even a permanent one, after you divorce Mrs. Shapian."

"I—" said Ira.

"Yes?" said Gabriel, leaning forward. "You what?"

"I have just come to a decision," said Ira.

"Yes?" said Gabriel.

"The most important decision of my life," said Ira.

"Yes," said Gabriel.

"After I do what I am going to do tonight, I will never again be able to work in commercial television," said Ira.

"Yes?" said Gabriel.

"Like Samson, I am going to tear down the temple," said Ira.

"Sir, I don't quite understand," said Gabriel. "Could we get back to the tape recording?"

"Go home, Gabriel," said Ira. "I am needed onstage."

He rose resolutely to his feet and dashed out of the office.

Chapter 19

The clock on the wall of the gymnasium showed twenty-five seconds before eight P.M.—air time for the Acanthus telecast. Ira Shapian sat on a swivel-topped stool in a simple little set with Camera No. 1 focused on him and a microphone boom hanging over his head. In this set Ira would open the show when the clock's second hand reached air time.

The catatonia which had gripped Ira upon hearing Gabriel's tape recording some hours earlier had lifted, but only in patches. He had returned to the stage after the session with Gabriel, made all preparations, improvised, invented, soothed raw nerves, repaired bruised egos, and, without sweat, accomplished prodigies of work.

To the mob of people onstage—the crew, the sponsor's minions, the ad agency men, Clendennon, the various participants in the telecast—Ira had seemed the very model of an unflappable professional. But deep inside his soul squatted a numbness, a chill, undislodgeable blankness that was not pain but simple *unbeing*.

There was no hysteria. He could speak rationally, listen intelligently, move purposefully, and act decisively; what he could *not* do was bring himself to think about his fateful decision to use tonight's telecast as the means to bar himself forever from commercial television. He knew precisely how he would conduct this evening's program; he even knew, to the last detail, how he would accomplish his ostracism from commercial tv. But whenever he attempted to think of the consequences of this irrevocable act, he could summon up only nothingness. Not panic and not elation, just nothingness. His mind flatly refused to function. It was as though a door had slammed shut, blocking out all awareness.

The second hand on the wall clock approached the figure 10. Ira's practiced glance made a rapid circuit of the stage: everything in order. The sets were lit; cameras and booms were on their marks; performers were stationed where they belonged. Clendennon sat in the control booth, and along with him, safely out of the way, sat a gathering of important personages.

A small red light beneath the lens of Camera No. 1 flashed red; simultaneously, the assistant director cued Ira with an outthrust forefinger.

"Good evening, ladies and gentlemen," said Ira, speaking directly into the camera. "Tonight, live from the campus of Acanthus College, we are going to take a very hard look at a very controversial question: have we Americans gotten to be the biggest, strongest, healthiest people on earth because of the food we eat—and many say we have; or are we slowly, bit by bit, day by day, digging our graves with our knives and forks—and many say we are. . . . My name is Ira Shapian. In exactly sixty seconds we will begin our investigation."

At this point the first commercial took over the screen. Muscular young men and busty young women cavorted strenuously on a seashore, all the time smiling strenuously, all the time strenuously singing the Tatum Cigarette jingle. During these jolly antics, Camera No. 2 rolled silently into place about five feet to the side of Camera No. 1. As the commercial ended, Camera No. 1 flashed red and Ira was cued to resume.

"A lot of people," said Ira to Camera No. 1, "will wonder why we picked Acanthus College to conduct an inquiry as complex as the one we are carrying on tonight. You don't automatically think of Acanthus when you think of scholarship; at least, you didn't in previous years. There used to be another word, not *scholarship*, that came more quickly to mind when Acanthus was mentioned. The man sitting across from me knows more about it than anybody."

The red light switched on beneath the lens of Camera No. 2. Seated on a stool near Ira was a large, wide, lugubrious, slack-jawed man, wearing a collar one size too big and blinking porcinely into the camera.

"Your name, sir?" said Ira.

"Nineteen Meyers. Edward Plenart Meyers, actually, but they used to call me Nineteen on account of that was my collar size. No more though. I doubt if my neck is even eighteen now. Everything's gone to hell."

"I understand football has been dropped at Acanthus."

"And a good thing. You see them specimens walking around campus? They couldn't beat a deef and dumb school."

"How was it when you were coach, Mr. Meyers?"

A nostalgic smile lifted the corners of Nineteen's pendulous lips. "I had *material,* friend. Wasn't a kid in the whole school couldn't lift five hundred pounds. Fact is, some of 'em *weighed* pretty near that. You know, mister, we never lost one single game all the time I was coaching?"

"I do. I also know the Association of American Universities said Acanthus scored the lowest average student I.Q. in all history."

"Can't have everything," shrugged Nineteen.

"Also the lowest average *faculty* I.Q.," added Ira.

"They was good old guys," said Nineteen loyally.

"But gone now?"

"Teachers gone, students gone—all gone. New bunch now—mess of students with arms like twigs, passel of bald-head profs with vests."

"Who rank—again I quote the Association of American Universities—among the first five in the nation, both in student and faculty intelligence. As an old Acanthus man, Mr. Meyers, don't you take any pride at all in the fantastic intellectual jump that's been made here?"

"Some," admitted Nineteen. "Seems like every college you can name has got a hard-on for education lately. Well, if that's the way it is, I suppose you might's well be on top of the dunghill like we are. . . . Sure, I'm proud of Acanthus—except on them afternoons in October and November when I can still hear them big old boys slamming off-tackle—thud! crunch! bang!—six yards, eight yards, sometimes all the way! And them silly, happy kids standing in the end zone just flinging the ball up in the air with pure joy while the stretchers came out to pick up the defensive linemen. . . . Call me sentimental, but I got to be honest: I miss it!"

Nineteen took out a bandanna and blew his nose loudly.

"Off-tackle plays were kind of your specialty, weren't they?" asked Ira.

"Had to be," replied Nineteen. "My boys couldn't remember hardly nothing else."

"Thank you, Mr. Meyers, for a colorful picture of Acanthus as it used to be. We switch you now to a round table discussion between Virgil Tatum, president of the college, and some of the new department heads."

"Do I have to watch?" said Nineteen.

"Not if you don't want to."

"I sure-God don't."

"Good-bye, Mr. Meyers. Take it, Virgil Tatum."

Three new cameras went to work in another set, a grouping that consisted of a low oval table and a dozen comfortable swivel chairs. Virgil Tatum sat at the head of the table. Around him, all drinking coffee, most puffing pipes, were the heads of the various departments. (The only department head absent was Linden-Evarts of cultural anthropology.) Virgil moderated the conversation with easy firmness. He let each man trot out his erudition, but briefly and without abstruseness. He leavened the talk with wit; he scotched obscure words and precious phrases immediately they were uttered.

Ira stood and admired Virgil's skill for several seconds. Then suddenly Ira could not stay. The sight of Virgil abruptly, without warning, released a flood of murderous rage—a compulsion, almost maniacal, to run, howling, onto the set and strangle, on camera, with all America watching, the man who had made him a cuckold.

With a huge effort of will, Ira tore himself away from the set. He would figure out what to do about Virgil later; right now there was more pressing business. He walked to the control booth, ramming down his temper with each step. Calmly he opened the door and entered.

A double row of easy chairs was in the rear of the booth. Here sat important personages—Clendennon, Robert E. Lee Owens, William Ransom Owens, Dr. Andrew McAndrews, brass from the ad agency —comfortably viewing the show on the monitors above the control panel. But the most important of all the personages present, Jefferson Tatum, was not sitting, not viewing comfortably. He was on his feet, pacing and purpling the air with profanity. He descended on Ira like a Mongol horseman.

"Goddammit, Shapian, I'm paying a jillion dollars for a show about food poisons. Who gave you license to do all this crap about art, science, and the learned disciplines—whatever the hell *they* are!"

"Now, now, Mr. Tatum," said Clendennon, smiling whitely.

"Shut up, you New York pimp!" snarled Jefferson.

"Pimp?" said Ira, tilting his head thoughtfully toward Clendennon. "No, Tatum, I don't believe *pimp* has quite got it. To my way of thinking, he looks more like the leading man in a stag movie."

"Jokes!" yelled Jefferson, outraged to the point of disbelief. "Jokes! I'm going bankrupt and he tells jokes! Shapian, you shitepoke, when you going to start doing what I'm paying for?"

"Depends on how soon you start being polite," answered Ira, staring hard at the old man.

Clendennon quaked. Jefferson gathered himself for a major explosion, then saw the steeliness in Ira's eyes and quieted at once. "Yes, sir," he said meekly.

"I'm giving Virgil ninety seconds more," said Ira. "Then comes a commercial. After that Dr. Silenko goes on."

"Thank you, sir," said Jefferson. "That sounds real nice."

"Dr. McAndrews?" called Ira.

"Yes, young man," answered McAndrews from the rear row.

"When Dr. Silenko finishes, there will be another commercial, then a station break, and then another commercial. I'll come fetch you while all that is going on."

"Excellent."

Ira left and walked quickly to Dr. Silenko's set. There stood three tables, each bearing cages of lab animals and racks of equipment. Dr. Silenko, handsome in a crisp smock and her tv makeup, was at the center table. Flanking her, at the other tables, were several colleagues. Cameras covered the set from three different angles.

"Good evening, Doctor," said Ira. "Fine makeup job they did on you."

"Oh, splendid," she said. "I'm wearing enough arsenic on each cheek to destroy a middle-sized city."

"It'll wash," Ira assured her. "Did you get all your experiments completed?"

"Just barely. In fact, the final report arrived less than a minute ago. And it's a beauty! Listen, Shapian, you couldn't by chance give me a few extra seconds tonight, could you?"

"Sorry."

"No, of course not," she said bitterly. "After all, the poison industry deserves equal time to rebut. That's the American way, isn't it?"

"Please, Doctor," said Ira, "you're on in a few seconds. I haven't bothered you with rehearsals because I know how frantic things have been at the labs. So now, very quickly, let me tell you how it goes. When I cue you to go on the air, feel free to say whatever you like. If you want to move, the cameras will follow you. When I hold up one finger, it means you've got one minute left. When I cross fingers like this, it means you've got a half-minute. When I do this—" he made a throat-cutting gesture—"you're off the air. Got it?"

"Got it."

"Dr. McAndrews will follow you with his rebuttal. Then comes a commercial. Then, to finish the show, I want you and McAndrews face-to-face while I ask a couple of questions. Clear?"

"Perfectly."

The assistant director whispered in Ira's ear. Ira nodded.

"I'll introduce you in just five seconds," he said to Dr. Silenko. "You take it from there."

The camera nearest Ira blinked red and the assistant cued him to start. "This," said Ira into the camera, "is a program about the possible dangers in the food we eat. So far we haven't mentioned food because first we wanted you to know the people who teach at this college are out of the very top drawer in the academic world. We're not asking you to accept opinions from any second-raters. The Acanthus faculty would do credit to any university anywhere, and I want particularly to include Dr. Clara Silenko, M.D. and Ph.D. She is director of Acanthus's School of Nutrition and Public Health. Her professional reputation is immense; her opinions about the American food industry are violent. Dr. Silenko, you're on."

"Thank you," she said. Her manner was crisp and level, not so much fervent as positive beyond the possibility of refutation. "I'm here to tell you flatly—and I propose to prove it—that the American food industry, mad for profits, and the federal government, afflicted with incompetence, laziness, venality, and insufficient funds —possibly all four—are engaged in a giant conspiracy to poison you and your neighbors. . . . A large accusation? Well, let's see. Dr. Nylet, step over here please."

A thin, bespectacled, balding man of forty, dressed in a white smock, joined Dr. Silenko. "Yes, ma'am?"

"Dr. Nylet is a member of my staff," explained Dr. Silenko. "What did you do before you came to work here?"

"Well, first I spent two years at Northwestern getting a Ph.D. in biochemistry. Before that I was an inspector with FDA."

"Tell us what FDA is."

"The Food and Drug Administration. A federal agency, part of the Department of Health, Education, and Welfare."

"Its duties?"

"To inspect all foods and drugs used by the public and reject those that are dangerous to health."

"Admirable. Now, Dr. Nylet, how did you happen to go to work for FDA?"

"Well, actually, I wasn't a *doctor* then. I had a B.S. in chemistry, and my grades weren't good enough for a scholarship, and I didn't have enough cash to go ahead on my own. I needed a job real bad, and, to be honest, there wasn't anyone much interested in a foul ball like me—except FDA. Man, how they wooed me! You'd of thought I was Robert Oppenheimer or somebody! Well, anyhow, with nobody else bidding, I finally joined FDA as a food inspector for $4,525 a year."

"After you became a member of FDA," asked Dr. Silenko, "how often, on the average, did you inspect a typical food processing plant?"

"You're talking about an ordinary company with a good record? Not somebody who was always in trouble with the law?"

"Yes. A standard, reputable food processor, a firm whose label people automatically trusted. How often did you inspect such a plant?"

"On the average," said Nylet, "I'd drop in for a day about once every two years."

"And you'd open a few cases at random, and unless you actually found the food stinking with ptomaine or crawling with vermin, you'd give them a clean bill and stay away for another two years?"

"Look, Doctor," said Nylet pleadingly, "I didn't like it any better than you, but there just wasn't time to do any more. Most of my days were spent in the FDA labs checking the thousands of new food additives that the processors kept sending in for approval."

"Ah, yes, approval. Under the law, no additive can be used without FDA approval. What tests, Dr. Nylet, determined whether you granted or withheld approval?"

"Well, we'd try the stuff on lab animals, and if they didn't die, we passed it."

"So," said Dr. Silenko, "the criterion was, in fact, that the new additive did not have to be beneficial to humans; it had only to be non-poisonous to rats."

"Correct," said Dr. Nylet. "And I wish you wouldn't glare at me. I *did* quit FDA, you know. I *did* go back to school and wait on table for two years until I learned some chemistry. I *did* end up smart enough to get a job with you."

"Sorry, Doctor," she said contritely. "I am filled with admiration for your courage and your talent, and I'm proud to have you aboard."

"Thank you," he said, mollified.

"You're welcome. Let's talk a bit more about food additives. Every day, you say, a flood of applications would come in from food com-

panies asking FDA to approve some new additives. Had any research been done on the additives before FDA received them?"

"Oh, yes. We always got long reports on each additive from some
independent lab."

"And who paid for these long reports?"

"The food companies."

"Very reassuring . . . Don't pout, Dr. Nylet. I am *not* glaring at
you. I am simply wondering whether FDA accepted these outside
reports or whether you ran some tests of your own."

"Well, we ran *some* tests, but, of course, we didn't have too many
people and, more important, we didn't have too much time."

"*How* much time?"

"The law says we have to complete our tests in 180 days or else
the product is automatically approved for market."

"This is the law passed by Congress and signed on September 6,
1958, by President Eisenhower with the full concurrence of the Food
and Drug Administration?"

"Yes, ma'am."

"In the brief period of 180 days, what kind of tests can you run?"

"Just experiments to find out how poisonous the stuff is."

"No tests for cancer?"

"Oh, come now, Dr. Silenko. You know cancer tests usually take
years. FDA doesn't have the staff or the money or the equipment,
and besides, the law says 180 days is all you get."

"One final question, Dr. Nylet. Since you left FDA, have you kept
in touch with any of your friends? Have you heard of any recent laws
or regulations that would protect the American consumer more ef-
fectively?"

"Yes, ma'am, I have kept in touch, and no, ma'am, there have been
no new laws or regulations whatsoever."

"Thank you, Dr. Nylet . . . Will the cameras please follow me to
the table on my right?"

With the cameras in accurate pursuit, Dr. Silenko moved to the
next table, where a pair of identical jars with large, uncapped
mouths lay side by side. One jar was partially filled with coarse dark
flour; the other jar was completely filled with snowy white flour,
so completely filled that some of it was spilling out of the open
mouth.

"The largest single item of foodstuff sold in America," said Dr.
Silenko, "is white bread. In order to make white bread white—I
speak now of common commercial-grade white bread, not of French,

Italian, or other crusty breads—the flour must first be chemically emulsified, oxidized, hydrogenated, neutralized, stabilized, and, most significant, bleached with chlorine dioxide. I have just this evening completed an experiment, and I would like to show you the results. Several weeks ago I laid these two jars down in a room in my laboratory. The jars were not covered. One jar was filled with ordinary bleached white flour. The other jar filled with unprocessed natural whole wheat flour. Please observe."

She took a scoop, dipped into the jar of white flour. The camera moved in close as she sifted the flour slowly through her hand. Not a bug, not a dropping, not a speck of filth, marked the whiteness of the flour.

"Now," said Dr. Silenko, "let me apologize in advance to the squeamish, but watch this."

She took a scoopful of the dark flour and sifted it slowly through her fingers. The flour was riddled with roaches, beetles, ants, and vermin.

"Not an appetizing demonstration, but a revealing one. The bugs had precisely the same access to the bleached flour as to the whole wheat flour. They ignored the white flour and concentrated totally on the whole wheat. Why? Because, my friends, in order to prepare the kind of flour that makes our ordinary daily bread you first have to strip away all the nourishment. It pains me to say it, but sometimes bugs have more sense than people."

In the control booth Jefferson Tatum, watching Dr. Silenko on the monitors, cackled gleefully, slapped his knee, and turned with a smirk to Dr. Andrew McAndrews. "How do you like them apples, Doc?" he crowed triumphantly.

McAndrews, unruffled, smiled. "Very old apples, Mr. Tatum. Very old and very *expected*."

Clendennon tried to keep the anxiety out of his voice. "She's making quite a case, Dr. McAndrews. Not that I'm worried or anything, because I feel *sure* you've got all the answers."

"Bullshit!" said Jefferson Tatum.

"Well put," agreed McAndrews. "Mr. Tatum is correct: I *don't* have all the answers. And that's what keeps me ahead of the game: I know what I *don't* know."

"But you *do* know more than Dr. Silenko?" asked Clendenon nervously.

"Rest easy," said McAndrews soothingly to Clendennon.

"Yeah, rest easy," echoed Jefferson. "And hush up. I want to hear what the pretty lady doctor's saying now."

All fell silent and watched the monitors. Dr. Silenko had moved to another table and was showing cages of mice dying of bladder cancer induced by butter coloring. As though to television born, she kept the tempo of her presentation rapid and crackling. While the prop men switched exhibits, she moved from table to table, demonstrating the horrendous results of additives, pesticides, antibiotics, and hormones. Occasionally she turned away from her exhibits, sat on a stool, faced the camera, and delivered a statement that trembled with tightly capped passion. Other times she was light and dry. Once, for three fulminating minutes, she relinquished the camera to Dr. Levine, who attacked water as nobody had attacked it since Noah.

Ira Shapian stayed in the background until it was time to give the doctor the one-minute signal. With an imperceptible nod, she acknowledged Ira's sign. She started her peroration—unhurried, unfrantic. Nor did she become overhasty when Ira flashed her the half-minute warning. When he made the throat-cutting gesture, indicating she was off the air, her argument was completed, her points were well and forcefully made, each one.

"Thank you, Doctor," said Ira. "Fine job. Now I'm going to get Dr. McAndrews to do his rebuttal. He'll work in that set over there, the one with the drape. Would you be good enough to stand close by? As soon as McAndrews is finished, I want to put the two of you together for a quick interview."

"Right," said Dr. Silenko.

Ira rushed to the control booth. "Sonny," said Jefferson, fervently grasping Ira's hand, "I want to tell you—"

"Tell me later," said Ira, yanking loose. "Dr. McAndrews, come with me please."

He escorted McAndrews to a set containing a drape and three stools. "Want a lectern?" asked Ira. "Got notes?"

"No notes," replied McAndrews.

"Fine. You sit on this stool. I'll sit on that one. There's a station break on now. Then comes a commercial, and then I'll introduce you. When you've finished your rebuttal, there's another commercial. After that, I'm going to wind up the show by putting Dr. Silenko beside you and pitching a question or two."

"Good . . . And may I say, Mr. Shapian, I'll never know how you managed to turn this chaos into such a smooth operation."

"It's called television, Doctor, but thanks."

Ira felt a tugging at his sleeve. "Excuse me, Ira," said Clendennon, his face wild, his eyes burning with tightly held excitement. "I know you're on after the next commercial, but could I see you for just a few seconds?"

"This better be damn important," said Ira, following Clendenon to a quiet corner.

"Honey lover, would I bug you at a time like this if it wasn't?"

"So?"

"Take a look at McAndrews sitting there."

"So?"

"See how his eyes dart around? See how he soaks up everything? See how *fascinated* he is?"

"So?"

"He's been like that all day. Ira baby, my radar tells me—and it's never wrong—that this distinguished Nobel Prize winner, this kindly, craggy, reassuring, heart-warming, gentle—"

"The point, Clendennon! For God's love, the point!"

"Don't you see it, Ira baby? This eminent physician, loaded with years and honors, is stage-struck! He is hooked by show business! And look how great he looks in makeup!"

"Aha! Now I dig. We do a new hospital series. We find some surly kid with hairy arms to play the intern, and hire McAndrews to play the wise old chief of surgery."

"We will send Ben Casey and Kildare to the showers!" cried Clendennon. "This man makes Sam Jaffe and Ray Massey look like a pair of cutpurses!"

"Clendennon, you've done it again!"

"So you'll con him into it, huh, Ira baby?"

"Depend on it."

"It's you and me, kiddie," said Clendennon, embracing Ira, "all the way to the top!"

"To the top!" echoed Ira. "Now be a doll and let me go to work. Right after the show, I promise you, I will turn the good doctor over my knee and give him such a gentle colonic he'll never even feel it."

"You are a great human being," said Clendennon with reverence. He administered a final squeeze to Ira's shoulder and returned to the control booth.

Ira reached his stool as his camera light went red. "You have just heard a powerful case made against food by Dr. Clara Silenko, a scientist of unquestionable eminence," said Ira to the audience. "I have with me now another scientist at least as eminent—in fact, a Nobel Prize winner in Medicine—whose views are completely the opposite of Dr. Silenko's. Ladies and gentlemen, meet Dr. Andrew McAndrews."

"Good evening," said McAndrews, pleasant, twinkling, comfortably erudite, wholly reassuring.

"Doctor," said Ira, "you heard Dr. Silenko. Do you have some answers?"

"Yes," said the doctor, "I have *some* answers. But I have a lot more questions than answers."

"For example?"

"For example," said Dr. McAndrews, "if you are the boss of a multimillion-dollar food company, what sense does it make to go around poisoning your customers? Next question: if female hormones used to fatten cattle induce sterility, how do you account for the population explosion? Next question: if flies and mosquitoes develop an immunity to DDT and other pesticides, why can't people do the same? Next question: if Americans are consuming poisons in ever-increasing amounts, why are we getting bigger, stronger, smarter, and longer-lived?"

"Excuse me, sir," said Ira, "but it's Dr. Silenko's contention that, compared to the year 1900, we are undoubtedly living longer, but most of us are walking around half-sick."

McAndrews chuckled. "Most of us, Mr. Shapian, are walking around with a Blue Cross card in our pockets, or some other form of group insurance. When we get an ache, we go to a doctor. Why not? It's free, isn't it? So that makes us a medical statistic—just the fact that we visited a doctor's office. . . . Now back in 1900, the only people who went to doctors were the very rich and the very nearly dead."

"Hmm," said Ira. "Never thought of it that way."

"Here's something else to think about: Let's take Dr. Silenko's indictment of pesticides. I won't argue that there haven't been a handful of deaths caused by pesticides, probably not as many as have been caused by aspirin, but, as I say, I won't argue. I will only make these points: in the north of Italy when pesticides were introduced after the war, crop yields increased by *one thousand percent!* Yes, young man, those are the actual figures. And here's more: Spain, which since the beginning of time, has been an importer of food, has become an *exporter* of food since they started using pesticides! Mr. Shapian, it is the business of chemistry to take intelligent risks. Yes, there is danger in pesticides—for that matter, there is danger in pie, in bathing, and in air-conditioning—but I say when you balance the benefits against the hazards, when you consider that every day there are millions more people who must be fed, pesticides are not only a risk science must take, but a positive duty science dare not shirk!"

Clendennon, sitting in the control booth, watching McAndrews' potent counterattack, beamed all over his face.

"Ah, shaddup," growled Jefferson Tatum.

Clendennon folded up his smile and tucked it in his conniving heart.

Dr. McAndrews, legs crossed, speech folksy, facts marshaled in long, serene ranks, continued his gently lethal rebuttal. Ira moved back out of camera range, figuring this wise old man needed no assistance. Behind the cameras, listening to every word, stood Dr. Clara Silenko, her handsome face a mask of battle. Ira took pains not to get too close to her.

"Now folks," said Dr. McAndrews, "let's take a look at antibiotics, which Dr. Silenko holds up as such a ghastly threat to life and limb. Of course, there is a tiny percentage of people allergic to antibiotics —we all know that—but do you have any idea what the adding of antibiotics to cattle and poultry feed has done for the production of edible protein? The increase is amazing. Fantastic! And this is a hungry world we live in, folks. Just because one man in fifty thousand gets a rash from aureomycin, should we go back to the good old days when half our farm animals died? And even the ones that lived were scrawny runts, compared to what we're getting today.

"And here's something else to mull over: Dr. Silenko showed us some pretty horrible sights, like cages full of mice dying of bladder cancer they got from eating butter colored with AB Yellow. Now, I don't doubt for one minute that Dr. Silenko gave those mice cancer by feeding them butter. But what *else* did she feed them? There's the question: what else did they eat besides butter? Any of you folks out there know a human being who goes through life eating nothing but butter? Me, personally, I'm going to be seventy years old next birthday and I never yet met a man who ate nothing but butter. Maybe if Dr. Silenko fed her animals a balanced diet, the kind you and I eat—and I include butter—well, maybe her experiments would have come out a whole lot different."

Ira held up one finger, warning McAndrews he had one minute left. The doctor acknowledged with a slight nod.

"One last point," said McAndrews. "First, let me state clearly and emphatically that Clara Silenko is a woman of sterling character and flawless medical credentials. I specifically exclude her from the group I'm about to name. . . . But don't you find it interesting that most people who write books and give lectures on health foods have one thing in common—a prison record?"

Ira signaled one-half minute.

"A few are doctors who have been arrested for malpractice; most are quacks who never saw the inside of a medical school. For every honest woman like Clara Silenko, there are a hundred pitchmen and snake oil peddlers. They're dealers in overpriced foods, phony machines, worthless cookware, but mostly they're dealers in *fear*. Be smart, friends. Don't swallow their sucker bait."

The final commercial went on. "Thank you, Dr. McAndrews," said Ira. "If you'll sit just where you are, I'll bring in Dr. Silenko and we'll wind up the show right after this commercial."

Ira hustled to Dr. Silenko's side. "Doctor, would you mind taking that stool right over here?"

Grimly, silently, she allowed Ira to escort her to a stool next to Dr. McAndrews.

"Good evening, Clara," he said amiably.

"Hi, Killer," was her reply.

Ira sat on the third stool and tried to think. In fewer than sixty seconds—no, in fewer than forty-five seconds now—he was going to perform the single most decisive act of his life. He was going to burn his bridges to commercial television beyond any hope of restoration; he was going to make his name anathema for all time wherever men gathered to use the public airwaves for profit. It was his Rubicon, his blast-off, his moment of truth.

Was he afraid? He did not know. His face, covered with tv makeup, could not show paleness. The hollowness in his belly seemed neither vaster nor smaller than when he first heard Gabriel's tape recording and made the fateful decision. He felt no hesitancy, and yet no eagerness. He had no clearly defined impulse either to advance or retreat.

But it was now academic whether he was afraid or not. The red light on the camera glowed brightly; the assistant director's finger was aimed at him like a spear. Even if he wanted to reconsider—did he? did he not?—there was, in any case, no time.

"When doctors disagree," said Ira to the camera, "what are we poor laymen to believe? Dr. Silenko, are you prepared to amend anything you said?"

"Not in the slightest!" she declared.

"Dr. McAndrews?" said Ira.

"I'll play my hand," said McAndrews firmly.

"Is there no area where you two great scientists can reach any common conclusion at all?"

"None!" they replied in unison.

Ira took a breath: now came the bombshell. "I recollect one occasion when you two were in agreement," he said. "You both, I believe, were members of the Surgeon General's Panel on Smoking."

"Oh, well, you're talking about cigarettes now, not food," said Dr. McAndrews. "Cigarettes are, of course, poisonous."

"And carcinogenic," added Dr. Silenko.

"Yes," said Dr. McAndrews, "and unquestionably our biggest single cause of heart disease."

In the control booth Clendennon was leaping wildly at the switches, tripping over himself, ripping his black suit on knobs and handles, tangling limbs with Jefferson Tatum.

But too late, too late. It had all gone out over the air.

"Thank you, doctors," said Ira softly. "This is Ira Shapian saying good night for—and *to*—the Star Spangled Broadcasting Network."

Ira slipped off his stool. Making a wide circle to avoid the personages exploding out of the control booth, he opened the side door of the gym and dashed into the cold night.

Chapter 20

While driving from Acanthus College to Boo's beach house, Ira underwent three dramatically distinct shifts of emotion. During the first third of the trip, he felt only pride—the pride of rediscovered manhood. It had taken real guts to close the telecast the way he had elected to close it. His job with Star Spangled was, of course, forfeited, and so was any possibility of working anywhere else in commercial television. He had branded himself an outlaw tonight, and never again would any lush tv berths be offered to him.

Yes, thought Ira as he drove the first miles to Boo's beach house, he had committed an act of indisputable courage, and all the more courageous because courage had been so long missing from his life. But now he felt assured that his native bravery had been only narcotized, not murdered, and he was properly full of self-esteem.

Pride, then, was the first of the three emotions that possessed Ira on the way to the beach. After the initial third of the trip, the second emotion took over: cool lucidity.

At last he perceived the consequences of what he had done this night. There was no choice now but to implement the plan which had heretofore been less a plan than a miasmic dream. He had to get a divorce, marry Boo, and go to work for Linus Calloway in Birmingham. That was the clear and single course of action open to him.

For the next several miles Ira's mind, clicking efficiently, explored ways and means. First, Boo would have to be told what had happened. She had spent the evening at the beach house where there was no television set, so she had not witnessed Ira's bridge-burning. Very well, he would fill in the details; he would describe the act and its sequelae.

He chose his words carefully. "Boo," he would say, coming at once to the point, "tonight I got myself fired from Star Spangled Broadcasting Network. Moreover, I so arranged matters that I can never again be part of commercial tv. I did all this for two reasons: first, because I wished to reclaim my soul while still I could; second, and more important, because I love you. We will be married now, my angel. I will take that job with Linus Calloway in Birmingham. I will walk tall again. I will rejoice in my work, and I will exult in the purity and strength of you. We have traveled a long, anguished road, my beloved, but our fearful trip is done. This is journey's end, the happy culmination of eighteen years when, more often than not, the flame of hope seemed quite extinguished."

Yes, nodded Ira, good words. Powerful, lovely words. Boo would be oh, so pleased.

He continued composing his speech: "My darling, kiss me on the mouth and tell me *au revoir* because I must return now to the Stonewall Jackson Hotel to ask for a divorce from—"

Now, suddenly, the third of Ira's three emotions seized him—clammy, paralyzing panic. Fighting for composure, he repeated the last line of the oration he proposed to make to Boo: "My darling, kiss me on the mouth and tell me *au revoir* because I must return now to the Stonewall Jackson Hotel to ask for a divorce from—"

The panic deepened, even clammier and more paralyzing than before. It was all Ira could do to hold the car on the road, for the incredible, terrifying, shattering fact was that suddenly he could not remember the name of his wife!

Ridiculous! Ridiculous! Ridiculous! he told himself, sweating frantically. I've known the woman for twenty-five years. Of course I remember her name! I know it as well as my own. It's right on the tip of my tongue. Let me think! Let me think!

He thought. Mary? No, that wasn't it. Edna? Elsie? Esther? Eleanor? Elspeth? No, none of those were even close.

He thought some more. Jane? Lottie? June? Alice? Jennie? Celeste? No, still not close.

Maybe if he could get the first letter of the name, it would come to him. But what was the first letter? He tried "D." Dorothy? Daisy? Dinah? Daphine? Drosophila?

Drosophila? That was a fruit fly, for Christ's sake! But wait a minute! Maybe there was a clue here. Fruit fly. The letter "F" twice. Could that be significant? Florence? Frances? Fanny? Felicia? Fifi? Faith? Fred?

Fred? He was going nuts, that's what he was going. Still, could there be a better reason for a man to go nuts than forgetting the name of his own wife? If such there was, it did not spring to mind.

Ira's eyes, though glazed with panic, observed that he had arrived at Boo's beach house. He pulled the car into the driveway. For fully five minutes he sat perfectly still behind the wheel, breathing deeply. It would be inaccurate to say that tranquillity had returned to him when he finally got out of the car and entered the house, but at least he was not trembling noticeably.

Boo was standing before the roaring driftwood fire as he walked in. "Good evening," he said and remembered to kiss her.

In his state he failed to see that Boo's color was abnormally high, her breathing rapid and shallow, her eyes overbright. Conversely, in her state, Boo did not note that Ira's stillness was of the kind that teeters on the very brink of hysteria.

"Hello, darling," she said. "Would you like a drink?"

"That would be nice," he said.

"What can I get you?"

"Whatever you're drinking."

"I'm drinking bourbon. You don't care much for bourbon."

"Bourbon is fine."

"Soda or water?"

"Any way you're having it."

"I'm just having ice."

"Excellent."

"Sure?"

"Positive."

She gave him a bourbon-on-the-rocks. "Won't you sit down, Ira?"

"Thank you."

"No, not on the couch. On that chair over there. I can see you better."

"All right."

He sat where she had instructed. She sat on the couch. For a moment they sipped silently.

"Your drink all right?" she asked.

"Fine. Yours?"

"Fine. . . . How long have you been drinking bourbon?"

"Oh, for about twelve years," he answered. "Actually, though, this is only the second time I've had it."

"Please, Ira," she implored, starting to rise. "Let me get you something you like."

"No, no, no," he said. "This is fine. Just fine. Fine."

She sat again, spent a minute of silence assembling her courage, and then spoke: "Ira, I wish I knew a more pleasant way to tell you what I have to tell you tonight."

"So do I," confessed Ira. "Frankly, I'm not having too great a time."

"You *do* seem a bit peaky, now that I take a good look."

"I've seen you a whole lot prettier yourself," said Ira. "No offense."

"No offense," she said without umbrage. "After all, a situation like this is hardly festive, is it?"

"I guess not. . . . A situation like *what?*"

"Perhaps I better start at the beginning."

"Good place."

She hesitated. "Ira, it appears to me that *you* have something to say too. Would you care to speak first?"

"Oh, no!" he cried. "Oh, no, no, no, no, no! You go ahead. Please."

"Very well." She paused again, then with visible determination, she began: "Ira, we fell in love during the war. After you left Owens Mill, though a whole continent separated us, we never stopped loving. And since you've returned, we've learned our love is stronger, deeper, and more compelling than ever. We know, both of us, that we would be ecstatically happy together, but we are kept apart for one reason. It is the same reason that has always kept us apart: we cannot bear to hurt Polly."

Ira bounded from his chair as though goosed. "*That's it!*" he hollered.

Boo, too, leaped to her feet, clutching her bosom in fright. "What's what?"

"Polly! My wife's name! Polly! Of course! Polly!"

She looked at him in alarm. "I don't understand, Ira. Certainly Polly is your wife's name."

"That's right—Polly!" His face was split by a grin of triumphant relief. "Polly Shapian. Yeah!"

"Are you all right, Ira? I do not ask the question idly."

"Fine, thank you. Just fine. Please continue." He sat down.

Boo looked at him nervously, but he seemed composed. "I was saying," she resumed, "that we have stayed apart because we cannot bear to hurt Polly—good, decent, brave Polly."

Now a brand-new form of madness fell upon Ira. All of a sudden, for the first time since Gabriel had played the tape recording for him, Ira was hearing voices in his head. He was, in fact, hearing the tape, every lurid word, loud and clear. Round and round Ira's skull the reel of tape spun, and the voices of Polly and Virgil blared forth.

Ira was on his feet again. "Brave Polly!" he shouted. "That's what you said, and you're right. She *is* brave! Her legs are brave. They *dare!* They *venture!* Even her ass is brave!"

Boo looked at him with mounting alarm. "Ira, what are you saying?"

But he was saying nothing. He was back in the chair, thinking silently, furiously, of Polly's brave buttocks. Damn it, he didn't need that double-crossing bastard Virgil Tatum to tell him about Polly's brave behind! He, Ira, knew! He knew with his eyes, with his mind, with his hands! How many times had he cupped those valiant cheeks in his palms? Well, maybe not too often in recent years, but how many times in the early days? How often, how joyously, had he felt the surge of Polly's butt, tight with passion, powerful with abandon, unafraid, unashamed, churning and lifting and *giving?*

"Ira," cried Boo with growing concern. "What's wrong?"

He shook his head. He did not want to talk. He wanted only to listen to the spool of tape whirling endlessly in his brain.

"May I go on?" asked Boo.

Ira waved vaguely.

"When you phoned today, I was on the verge of calling you," Boo continued. "Because all at once a great truth had been revealed to me. After eighteen years, I finally saw the tragic mistake we have been making. How can we hurt Polly? Is she weak? Is she vulnerable? Of course not. Polly is strong, vital, mature."

"Breasts," whispered Ira.

"What?" asked Boo, blinking. "*Breasts?* Is that what you said— *breasts?*"

He did not answer, for his whole mind was now focused on the tape. "*I can still see your breasts when you came out of the water— the thrust of them, the round perfection of them,*" Virgil was saying. And then he was saying, "*I saw your nipples, how the cold water had made them rise like two happy, eager things, ready for fun and play.*"

Then Polly was speaking: "*Twenty years have passed, Virgil.*"

She's got a point, thought Ira judiciously. Twenty years are bound to play hell with any pair of knockers, even a set as good as Polly's.

And yet, thought Ira, Virgil's answer covered the case nicely. "*The years have been kind,*" Virgil was saying. "*I look now at your breasts and I see the same vitality. I see more. I see tenderness, womanliness, passion come to full maturity.*"

True, admitted Ira. True and damned astute. Polly's balcony might not be something to inflame the pimple-faced readers of *Play-*

boy, but it had exactly what a grown man wanted: serenity without sag, comfort without pocky tissue, a snug harbor still totally serviceable.

Then, abruptly, a flood of rage washed over Ira. That sonofabitch Virgil! How dare he meddle with the breasts of Mrs. Ira Shapian? The gall of that lecherous, treacherous rat fink! College president, indeed! Prurient fraud, that's what he was! Depraved, corrupt, iniquitous, noxious wife-thief!

Ira's anger receded as quickly as it had arrived. He was mistaken to blame Virgil. Polly, that tiger, was not one who could be conned, beguiled, bamboozled, or even raped. The only person on earth able to put Polly Shapian in Virgil's bed was Polly Shapian.

But why? Why would she do such a thing to Ira? Okay, he had been less than ardent in recent months. . . . All right, make that recent *years*. But even so, was that any reason to put horns on a man? Didn't it ever occur to Polly that he spent long, hard, miserable days at the studio and when he came home he was just plain too tired for acrobatics in the bedroom?

A new spook came zooming in on Ira: Was Virgil the first lover Polly had taken? How about those long hours in Hollywood, those frequent nights when he didn't even get home at all? Who else had fondled those responsive breasts, those exciting legs, that nonpareil butt?

And if there had been others in Polly's embrace, could Ira blame them? The tape had now stopped spinning in his head; replacing it was a reel of motion picture film—pictures in three dimensions and living color, pictures of Polly's thighs and bosom and buttocks. What sane, healthy man would refuse them? Nobody! Nobody, that is, except a stupid, bemused, certifiable type like Ira Shapian.

"Why aren't you listening, Ira?" said Boo.

"Huh?" said Ira.

"Please sit down and listen," she said plaintively. "This is the hardest thing I've ever had to say in my life."

"I'm sorry," he apologized. "Really I am. Where were we?"

"Maybe I better start over."

"Good idea. And I'll try to pay attention, I promise."

"Well, briefly, I was saying that in spite of distance and time and separation our love is lovelier today than it ever was. And, my darling, it is in our power now to make each other truly, permanently happy. Why, then, do we hesitate? I'll tell you why: the same old reason: we can't stand to hurt a woman like Polly."

Ira, to give him credit, made an honest effort to concentrate on
Boo's words. But it was hopeless. The movies in his head started
running again, this time in Cinerama. Polly's naked body filled his
mind—filled the world! And all over Polly's body he saw an invasion
of clutching, male hands—strangers' hands, ugly hairy hands gleefully pinching and plucking the flesh that belonged to him—to Ira
Shapian!

A savage, roaring rage possessed him. Jealousy and hate descended
like a cloudburst. He rose—no, *sprang*—from his chair. "You're right,
Boo!" he cried. "You're absolutely right. You're a fine, decent woman
and I should have listened to you from the beginning. You're right.
We can't do this to Polly."

"But you miss my point!"

"A great woman is what you are. *Great!*" He gave her hand one
fervent shake and hustled toward the door. "Good-bye, Boo. You're
right. Good-bye. Good-bye."

She opened her mouth to protest, then closed it, for Ira was gone.
From the window she watched his car spraying gravel as it hurtled
out of the driveway. She allowed herself one small sigh, returned
to her seat, and picked up her bourbon-on-the-rocks.

Boo, said Boo to Boo, you are a goddam fool and you deserve
whatever you get. You are so idiotically enchanted with words that
you had to make a pretty speech, when all you needed was to open
your purse and produce the evidence. But that's not your style, is
it? Flowery talk and purple poetry—there's your style. And you'll
never learn to resist, will you, you big, retarded ninny?

Boo got up and made herself another drink. Her purse was on the
bar, lying open. With a melancholy smile she reached into the purse
and took out the evidence—the clincher, the hoop with which she
could have grappled Ira forever to her bosom if only she had not
chosen to deliver a long, rolling preface.

An envelope was in Boo's hand, a letter, postmarked Nashville,
which she had received that very morning. It was a report from a
physician, an old and discreet friend of Boo's, and it contained the
results of a rabbit test proving that Ira had once again made her
pregnant.

If Boo were not Boo, she would simply have handed the letter to
Ira when he arrived. But Boo *was* Boo. Roughness, naked and abrupt, was entirely outside her nature. She was flatly incapable of
giving Ira such a letter without first cushioning the jolt. She had,
therefore, prepared an eloquent speech, brimming with solace, to

precede the announcement of her new pregnancy. She did, of course, want Ira to marry her this time; the youth and energy which had bolstered her gallantry eighteen years ago were far too eroded to serve her again. But she wanted Ira to *want* to marry her, not to feel snared. She wanted him to believe in his heart that it was not a calamity but a blessing.

Toward this end she had carefully constructed an oration in which, with tenderness and truth, she would make the following points:

First, that Polly was a strong, proud, resourceful woman who would not die of heartbreak if Ira left her.

Second, that Ira loved Boo hotly and lyrically; whereas his feeling for Polly had long since cooled to dead, gray ashes.

Third, Boo's love for Ira was impervious to any hazard, including the greatest of all hazards: Ira himself.

Fourth, Boo was a very rich woman and could rescue Ira from his miserable entrapment in commercial television, whereas Polly could not.

These were the four points of Boo's sweet polemic. With such a quartet of arguments, arguments glistening with love and glowing with reason, she had reckoned to render Ira so happily amenable that the letter from Memphis would be almost an anticlimax.

Boo crumpled up the letter and threw it into the driftwood fire. She had no use for it now. Yes, she knew the letter still had great value. It could, if she chose, be the bludgeon that would force Ira to the altar. But the bludgeon was not Boo's weapon; in fact, seldom has any woman had so little ordnance.

"Well, flapjaw, what now?" Boo asked herself, sitting again. Abortion? No; not even thinkable. What then? Take a crazy gamble as she had with Gabriel eighteen years earlier? But how far can one woman's luck be stretched? How many bastards could she legitimatize in a single lifetime? Where, these days, could she find a bribable judge who would stay bribed?

A line of Scott Fitzgerald's came to Boo as she gazed into her drink. "Nobody feels sorry for a girl on a yacht," Fitzgerald once wrote.

Well, thought Boo, I am most definitely a girl on a yacht, and nobody is going to feel sorry for me—including me. I see nothing ahead but reefs, shoals, rocks, sea serpents, and hurricanes, but, nonetheless, I *am* a girl on a yacht.

Sail on, old salt, sail on.

Chapter 21

As Ira entered the suite, Polly was looking in a full-length mirror and merrily humming some popular airs of her girlhood, the kind of touching, heartfelt songs they seem not to write any more, like "Mairzy Doats," "Der Fuehrer's Face," and "Three Ittie Fitties in an Ittie Bittie Poo."

"You whore," said Ira by way of hello.

"I beg your pardon?" said Polly.

"Whore," he repeated at the top of his voice. "Don't give me that innocent bit. I know you were boffing Virgil Tatum this afternoon. Slut!"

"Ira," said Polly patiently, "I saw your telecast from Acanthus tonight, and I've been waiting for you to come home so I can tell you some lovely things. But if you'd rather fight instead, buster, I'm ready!"

"I'd rather fight!" roared Ira, advancing on Polly fiercely. "What's the idea of humping Virgil?"

"Well, look who's talking!" said Polly, placing hands on hips and standing her ground firmly. "How about you and Boo? Did you or did you not diddle her during the war? Are you or are you not *still* diddling her?"

"Don't change the subject."

"I'll change your face, you whimpering, sniveling breast-beater!"

"Yeah, *breasts!*" cried Ira. "You and Virgil had some very picturesque things to say about breasts this afternoon, didn't you?"

"I have no idea what you are talking about," she said aloofly.

"Like hell!"

"Excuse me, Ira. I believe I will go to the movies."

"You will stay right here! You will stay exactly where you are and answer one question: how *could* you? How could you do such a terrible thing to me? I've been faithful to you for eighteen years. Do you have any idea how much tail I turned down in that time—

young, gorgeous, *palpitating* tail? But I stayed faithful, and I didn't even like you!"

"Gee, thanks for turning down all that tail. How come you couldn't say no to Boo? Was it because her tail didn't palpitate?"

"Never mind Boo. We're talking about you and Virgil."

"*You* are talking about me and Virgil," she corrected. "I am talking about Boo—and a few collateral items. Your illegitimate son Gabriel, for example. And the picture of Boo you keep hidden in your wallet."

Ira blanched with fury. "When did you go through my wallet?"

"Today. Also your suits, your bureau, and your sandy shoes."

"You despicable sneak!"

"You philandering schmuck!"

Ira started to yell, then thought better of it. "Polly," he said evenly, "I do not like the tone this conversation is taking."

"You're absolutely right," she agreed. "We began on such a high plane: you came in and called me a whore. After that—I can't think why—it's been running steadily downhill."

He took refuge in dignity. "If you choose to treat this matter lightly, it is, of course, your privilege. You'll forgive me, however, if I do not find the subject amusing."

"Oh, shut up," she said without heat. "I can stand you shrieking with hysteria, I can stand you wallowing in self-pity, I can stand you blubbering with shame, but what I can't stand is you stuffy. So make up your mind: do you want to sit on your high horse or do you want to talk?"

"I want to talk."

"Good. So do I."

"May I talk first?" asked Ira.

"You always do."

"Tell me why you went to bed with Virgil this afternoon?"

"No."

"Do you deny that you did?"

"No."

"You admit it then?"

"No."

"Would you like to know how I found out?"

"No."

"It's a pretty interesting story. Don't you have any curiosity?"

"No."

"I see. . . . Well, then, to sum up, you won't confirm and you won't deny and you won't give me any information whatsoever?"

"Correct."

Ira shrugged. "Well, it doesn't really matter. I have all the proof I need about you and Virgil, so what's the point in pursuing it further."

"None."

"But let me ask you this: was there anybody *before* Virgil? And if so, how many?"

"Ira, don't *I* get to ask any questions?"

"Sorry. Please go ahead."

"Thank you. First question: Boo."

"What if I don't want to talk about Boo?"

"Oh, but you do," said Polly confidently. "You've got a big mouth."

"Yeah?" he bristled. "Well, maybe I do, but at least I don't drop my pants for everybody who comes down the pike."

"I ignore the insult and repeat the question. What about you and Boo?"

"If anything has happened between Boo and me—and, mind you, I don't for one minute admit that it has—well, frankly, it's not the sort of thing you would understand."

"You mean because it's so kind of—oh, I don't know—so kind of *ethereal?*"

"Maybe."

"It wasn't too ethereal to keep her from getting knocked up," observed Polly.

"That does it," he said with angry finality. "This talk is over."

"Balls! I'm just getting warmed up."

He raised a cautionary finger. "Stop, Polly. Please stop and think a minute. You and I, for better or worse, still have a lot of years left together. It won't be easy, but at least it'll be possible, unless we stand here and keep yakking away. Any second now, sure as hell, something is going to be said that can never, never be unsaid. We're in big danger of blowing a marriage right here, tonight. . . . So enough, Polly. Okay?"

"I agree."

"All right, then. No more conversation."

"Oh, no, Ira," she said hastily. "You misunderstand. I agree that we're in danger of blowing a marriage. I don't agree to no more conversation. And I'll tell you why: the world is full of marriages—and I count ours—that are held together by one dismal thing—default.

Husband and wife both know that if ever there should come an
honest exchange of words, the marriage goes down the drain. So the
words never get said. Look, for example, how long it's been that way
at our house, and look what a sickly, puny excuse for a marriage
we're left with. I say let's talk. It's risky, yes, but, on the other hand,
it might possibly be the transfusion we need. In any case, we can't
lose. If our marriage is killed, what's to mourn?"

Ira deliberated. "All right," he said. "Whatever else has happened
between us, I've never lost my respect for your mind. If you think
we should talk, I'll go along."

"You won't regret it," said Polly. "Or else you will. I can positively
guarantee one or the other."

"Swell. . . . Now to return to our dialogue, how come you laid
Virgil this afternoon?"

"*That* is one subject we don't discuss," said Polly, and there was
no mistaking she would not be moved.

"Great little game you invented," remarked Ira. "*We* talk, but *you*
pick the topics."

"Exactly."

"Seems fair. . . . All right, your slap-and-tickle with Virgil is out.
What's *in?*"

"You and Boo."

"You know something? I had that one figured. . . . Okay, what do
you want me to tell you?"

"Nothing," she said. "Try not to be disappointed, old friend, but
I'm really not interested in hearing you make a confession. You just
listen, and I'll explain all about you and Boo."

"*You* will explain?"

"If you'll only be quiet."

"Who do you think you are—the Oracle of Delphi?"

"No, I'm just the idiot who's wasted twenty-five years studying
you. So will you shut up?"

"I can't promise."

"I'll chance it. . . . Let's start at the top. Where are you from,
Ira?"

"What do you mean, where am I from? You know very well where
I'm from—Tenth Avenue."

"Precisely. Little Ira Shapian, the ragged Armenian street urchin
from Tenth Avenue. But an urchin with a big, beautiful dream. You
weren't entirely sure what the dream was, but this much you knew:
it was lovely and serene and peaceful and pure, everything Tenth

Avenue was not. Then the war came. You got shipped to Owens
Mill. You met Boo. And there stood your dream. There, alive and
glowing, the dream stood in front of your eyes. And how perfectly
mounted—the grace, the breeding, the portico, the paddock, the
jasmine! There it was, Ira, the vague, itchy, haunting dream all come
true in one exquisite package. No wonder you got knocked for a
loop."

"Thank you very much. That clears up my case. Now would you
be good enough to explain why Boo chose *me?*"

"Boo's motives are even simpler than yours. She chose you because
she's afraid of men."

"Polly, I've just reconsidered your brainpower. Not only are you
not smart, but you are a dithering dumbhead. . . . Boo chose me
because she's afraid of men? What am *I*—a panda bear?"

"Will you shut up and listen, or do you want to spend the rest of
your life ignorant?"

"Excuse me. Go on, please, with your piercing analysis of Boo."

"Yes, Boo. Scared to death of men. Maybe she had a father problem; I don't know. But I've read her poetry—I use the term loosely
—and it couldn't be more obvious: men *terrify* your elegant friend.
So this poor, gun-shy thing had the rotten luck to be born in the
South where masculinity is by far the No. 1 industry. And worse, she
had to pick Owens Mill where that old rooster Jefferson Tatum rules
the roost and all the others flap like crazy to keep up."

"*All* the others?" asked Ira. "How about Virgil Tatum? He seems
like a quiet, scholarly, cultured type."

"He is a quiet, scholarly, cultured *stallion*," replied Polly.

"Caught you!" yelled Ira triumphantly. "Caught you! Caught you!
Caught you! All right now, goddammit, what happened with you
and Virgil this afternoon? I demand an answer!"

"Oh, sit down," said Polly wearily. "Stop making like Perry Mason.
You are not going to find out about Virgil. In fact, if you don't be-
have, you are not going to find out about Boo."

"You are my wife!" he thundered. "I have rights!"

"I am your wife," she answered without raising her voice, "and,
if you will recall, I was the best pitcher at P.S. 189. If you don't sit
down in one second, I will start throwing lamps. After that I will
break the windows and fling out the furniture. Then I will turn on
the sprinkler system. This, I believe, will give me time to think of
something *really* destructive."

Ira took a step toward Polly. She picked up the nearest lamp and cocked her arm. Ira sat.

"That's better," she said. "Now to resume. . . . When war breaks out, we find Boo in Owens Mill surrounded by studs and trembling like a leaf. Now arrives Ira Shapian. Is he strong and silent? Is he stalwart? Is he a tower of power? No, not Ira. He bleeds and whines. 'Oh, God,' he cries, 'why hast Thou forsaken me?' But he is not always torn with anguish. Sometimes, all of a sudden, the gloom lifts. He frisks and gambols, playing in the sun, until, like a summer storm, the black clouds come rushing back. Boo watches his moods shuffle and shift, shift and shuffle. Soon a great, warm feeling of safety fills her breast. She knows Ira is not to be feared, because Ira is not a man. He is to be loved: he is a *child*."

"Oh, brother!" said Ira, groaning very loud. "Oh, brother, sister, cousin, and your father's mustache!"

"You don't believe me?"

"I believe you ought to be arrested for practicing psychiatry without a license. And what psychiatry! What crap! Polly, I'm worried about you. I mean really. You can't possibly mean what you just told me?"

"Every word."

"All right. Assuming you're not altogether beyond the reach of logic, answer me this: if Boo regards me as a child, how about all our activity in bed?"

"*Activity?* This you call *activity?* A few tumbles during the war, then eighteen years of nothing. Now a few more tumbles and probably, for the rest of your lives, nothing again. There hasn't been so much activity since Rip Van Winkle."

"How do you know what's going to happen in the rest of our lives? What makes you so sure I won't end up with Boo?"

"Because, you dope, it's *me* you love. Why else were you faithful for eighteen years? Why have you come home to me again? Why are you half-crazy at the thought that I might have gone to bed with Virgil this afternoon?"

Ira bounded to his feet. "*Might,* hell!" he shouted. "You *did,* and I know it! Break the lamps, turn on the sprinklers, tear down the goddam hotel if you like; but you are going to tell me why you put horns on me this afternoon, and you are going to tell me now!"

He was upon her so rapidly that she managed to fling only one lamp against the wall before he caught both her wrists in a grip of iron. "Tell me!" he demanded, ignoring the kicks that were slamming into his shin like a jackhammer.

"I am not going to talk about Virgil!" she said through clenched teeth, kicking steadily, twisting and flailing in an attempt to loose her wrists. "I only want to talk about Boo."

"I don't want to hear about Boo!" He held her wrists tight, pushed her backwards across the room, upended tables and chairs.

She tried to bite his neck, missed narrowly. "You don't love Boo, you fool! And she doesn't love you either. It's dreams you're both in love with, sweet, adolescent, impossible dreams. And deep down you both know it; that's why you've never done anything and you never will. You love *me*, you swarthy imbecile. Because I'm no dream. I'm flesh!"

"You're flesh, and this afternoon Virgil Tatum was pawing it with his big, hairy hands!"

"Goddammit, how long since you've pawed it with *your* big, hairy hands?"

"Too long, too long! But that's going to be corrected right now!"

They were at the bedroom door. Ira, finding strength he had never even suspected, lifted his wife and hurled her upon the bed. With three savage tugs he made rags of the blue Don Loper. Lingerie shredded like paper in his frenetic hands.

When Polly lay naked on the bed, he started ripping off his own clothes. He yanked off his lapels, tore his jacket in half, tattered his necktie, demolished his shirt.

"Ira," said Polly reasonably, "I'm ready and waiting. There's really no cause to ruin *your* clothes too."

"Shut up!" he snarled. "You're not talking to a child."

After lovemaking they slept. Only twenty minutes went by on the bedside clock, but when they woke, it was as though they had had twelve profoundly refreshing hours.

They looked at one another. They smiled. "Hi," said Polly.

"Come closer," he said.

She turned and snuggled against him. He stroked her hair, ran his hand gently down her back, stopped and nestled a buttock. Then, suddenly, he pinched.

"Ouch!" she cried, jumping.

"Yeah!" he sneered. "So what's all this big talk about a brave ass?"

"Okay, let's try yours," she said, and, before he could escape, she got in a sharp-nailed tweak. Then they rolled and wrestled, playfully grabbing, giggling, nipping. The frolic stopped as they found themselves face-to-face. Tenderly he cupped her chin in his hand and gave her a long, serious kiss.

He said, "You're right. I *do* love you, you disagreeable, feisty, contentious little hardhead."

"And the same to you, you road-company King Lear," she said, her fingers twining in his. "I love you so deeply that I ache with it. If our stalemate had gone on much longer, I think I would have cracked up. God bless this day."

"Yes, Polly, God bless this day. . . . And God bless Virgil Tatum who made it happen and who I am going to punch in the mouth first thing in the morning."

"I wouldn't do that, Ira, for two reasons: first, because when he hits you back, you are a dead Armenian. Second, I never went to bed with Virgil."

"My dear wife, honesty has just paid us an unexpected visit. Let's see if we can keep it around, huh?"

"I was about to suggest the same thing. Tell me where you got your information about Virgil and me."

"All right," he said and recounted the story of Gabriel and the tape recording.

"Why, that little bastard!" exclaimed Polly angrily. Then, remembering her manners, she said, "Nothing personal, Ira."

"Perfectly all right," he said. "Now will you kindly explain about that tape?"

"Yes. And I will also kindly explain what happened before and after that tape."

She did.

When she finished, Ira sat in stunned, glazed silence. "You *do* believe me?" she asked.

"Of course."

"Then why the funny look?"

"I am trying very hard to find something to say about you and Gabriel, but all I can think of is to run to the closet and tear up another suit."

"Forceful," admitted Polly. "Kind of a waste, though."

"Yeah. . . . Well, let's look at the bright side. Tomorrow we'll be leaving Owens Mill and Gabriel."

"And then," she said, "we return to Bel Air where Gabriel has bought the house next door."

"I'm afraid, old girl, that will not be a problem. We have to sell the house in Bel Air. You saw the telecast tonight. I can't afford Bel Air any more. I am out of a job."

Polly kissed him hard on the lips. "Yes, I saw the telecast, and I have never been so proud of you in my life. For that matter, I have never been so proud of *me*, because, in spite of everything, I never stopped believing you were still you!"

"Thank you. I will think often of your kind words when I am standing in those long lines at the unemployment office."

"Ira, tell me something: when you kicked away your job tonight, you must have had a plan in mind. What was it?"

A wisp of a smile crossed his face. "As a matter of fact, I did. I had a beautiful plan. Only trouble is, it won't work any more."

"Why not?"

"Because I just found out how much I love you," he answered. "Ironic, yes?"

"Very. Also enigmatic. What are you trying to say?"

"Actually, I'm trying *not* to say it. But this seems to be the hour of truth, so here goes: forgive me, Polly, you won't find this flattering, but I had a scheme laid out, neat and foolproof. I was going to divorce you, marry Boo, get canned by the network, and take that job with Linus Calloway in Birmingham."

"I see. . . . Well, me you're not going to divorce and Boo you're not going to marry, but why can't the rest of your idea work?"

"Because you I'm not going to divorce and Boo I'm not going to marry," he replied. "So how can I take the job with Linus? He'll only pay $100 a week. With Boo it wouldn't have mattered; she's loaded. But you and I living on a hundred dollars a week? Oh, come now!"

"We've lived on a lot less," she declared. "And happily!"

"Polly, don't lay there on your brave butt and talk brave nonsense. Sure, we've lived on less than a hundred a week, but we've picked up a few obligations since then."

"Don't *you* talk nonsense. Obligations, you say? Okay, let's count. Our two children and their bottomless bellies are now the responsibility of the U.S. Marine Corps. Our servants can be fired. Our houses, cars, jewels, paintings, and alleged *objets d'art* can be sold, which will give us a nice little nest egg to dip into if we should run short in Birmingham. . . . Only we *won't* run short, because we're going to rent a two-room flat and live on beans, plus I am going to learn typing and shorthand and get a job!"

She was shaking Ira by the shoulders, physically transferring her excitement to him. "You'd *really* do it?" he asked eagerly.

"What have I been telling you year after year?"

"I don't know. I haven't been listening."

"So listen now. Not only *would* I do it, but I will hold my breath until I turn blue if you don't let me. Clear?"

"Clear."

"Good. Now let's call room service and order our last expensive dinner."

"Constructive thinking," said Ira. "But first—" he pulled her toward him—"how about a reprise before chow?"

"Ira dear, I am naturally flattered, but remember you are not a young man. The strain on the heart, according to eminent medical authorities, is equivalent to running up twenty flights of stairs."

"What a way to go!" said Ira, biting her shoulder. "Come here, you."

"Yes, dear," she said, complying. "Yes, my lustful Levantine."

Chapter 22

The front of the taxi was loaded with the Shapians' luggage. Polly
and Ira were seated in the back. They were on the way to the
Owens Mill airport to catch a plane for Birmingham, but Ira had
asked the driver to stop first at Acanthus so he could pick up a few
personal belongings at his office.

"Be right out," said Ira to Polly as the cab parked in front of his
office in the administration building.

Into the building ran Ira and into his office. Quickly he stuffed a
briefcase with papers and left the office. He moved quickly down
the corridor, turned the corner, and bumped smack into Virgil Tatum, who was approaching from the opposite direction.

Both men stopped in their tracks. Both fidgeted. Both flushed.
Both were bereft of words.

A fine point of etiquette was preventing Ira from speaking. How,
he wondered, do you greet a man who has described your wife's
breasts and buttocks in such loving detail? What do you say to a
man who has kept the memory of your spouse's erogenous zones
evergreen in his mind for twenty years? Offhand, violence seemed
a proper response, yet Ira could not but consider that despite Virgil's
long-cherished honing for Polly's parts, he had, when they were
freely offered to him, found the strength of character to return
them unused. This, surely, was an act of renunciation to make the
heart swell with gratitude. But—taking another view—how grateful
can you feel toward someone who knows your wife's body as only
her husband and her gynecologist ought to know it? But—taking
still another view—was it not admirable that a letch as durable as
Virgil's should be held in bounds by something so fragile as princi-
ple? Yes, thought Ira gravely, an exceeding fine point of etiquette
was involved here, a thorny point, a many-splintered thing.

Virgil, to whom chivalry was as real and alive as a large flowering
tree, was vexed by a conundrum even more subtle than Ira's. He had

no knowledge of Gabriel's tape recording; therefore, he was not aware that Ira knew what had been said in the private dining room at Big Eddie's roadhouse. But he, Virgil, knew what had been said. Granted there had been no deeds, only words; but when words were so graphically horny, so hornily graphic, did they not, in themselves, approach adultery? Does a true gentleman make such a speech to the wife of a friend? Yet, on the other hand, could anything conceivably be more friendly than *not* having done what Virgil had not? A delicately shaded question, he thought, a puzzle Talmudically devious.

Meanwhile these two grown men stood and shifted from foot to foot and avoided one another's eyes and tried to think of something to say. Finally Ira was struck by a bolt of pure inspiration: he knew *exactly* what to say to Virgil. "Hello," he said.

Virgil smiled with joyous relief. Yes, that was the word all right. "Hello," he replied.

"Hello," said Ira again, and it seemed just as inspired the second time.

"Hello," repeated Virgil. Then, spontaneously, he added a refinement of his own: he offered his hand to Ira.

Ira seized it, and with the firm clasp of palm on palm, embarrassment vanished like smoke. They exchanged level looks, honest smiles of friendship.

"I'm glad I got this chance to say good-bye," said Ira. "Thanks for everything you've done—for me and for Polly."

"Me? Hell, I haven't done a thing."

"More than you know," said Ira. "And please say good-bye to your father. I hope he didn't take it too hard—what happened last night on the telecast."

"He's fine. They're letting him out of the hospital at noon. In fact, it's taking four strong nurses to keep him there that long."

"There was nothing personal in what I did. I'd like your father to understand that."

"Relax, Ira. Pa's cracked tougher nuts than you."

"Well, give him my best."

"I'll do that when I pick him up. Anything you want me to say to Clendennon?"

A smile lit Ira's face. "Is he in the hospital too?"

"In the crying ward," replied Virgil. "He got fired two minutes after the broadcast. Your Mr. Davies doesn't waste any time, does he?"

214   MAX SHULMAN

"Don't think me hardhearted for laughing about Clendennon,"
said Ira. "It's not as serious as it seems. He may lay off for a few
months, but in television sonsofbitches like Clendennon always manage to land on their feet."

"It's a property of sonsofbitches everywhere," said Virgil. "When
are you and Polly taking off?"

"Right now."

"Hollywood?"

"No, but we'll be in touch."

"You do that, hear?"

"I hear and we will," said Ira truthfully.

"My love to Polly."

"Thank you."

With a final handshake, Ira ran out of the building. Polly was
standing outside the taxi, waiting.

"Virgil sends love," he said to Polly. "And here's a little from yours
truly."

He kissed her briefly but seriously.

At this point a tall, gangling figure emerged from behind a nearby
oak tree where he had been spying: Gabriel. "Hi, Mr. Shapian," he
mumbled sheepishly. "Hi, Mrs. Shapian."

"Gabriel," said Ira, "you thought any about working for the FBI?"

Gabriel ignored the sally. "Sir," he said to Ira, "you know what I
thought I just saw? I thought I just saw you kissing Mrs. Shapian."

"So you did, boy. Here, I'll give you an encore."

Ira kissed Polly again, this time with passion.

"Well, I'll be dog!" said Gabriel incredulously. "Mrs. Shapian, you
seemed to *enjoy* that."

"It was heaven!" declared Polly and gazed adoringly at her husband.

"Kissing," said Ira to Gabriel, "is what Mrs. Shapian and I do most
of the time—often twelve or fifteen hours at a stretch. Do you know
why?"

"No, sir. I swear I do not."

"Because we are in love," said Ira.

Gabriel turned eyes full of disbelief on Polly. "Is that true, ma'am?
You're in love? *Both* of you? With *each other?*"

"Yes," she said, gently and honestly. "Yes, Gabriel. It is true."

Gabriel scratched his head, licked dry lips. "Something's wrong
here," he said helplessly. "I am confused."

"Confused is exactly what you are," said Ira, speaking quite without harshness, touching the boy's elbow affectionately. "Now, if you don't mind, we have a plane to catch."

Gabriel nodded. "I'll be going," he said.

"Good-bye, Gabriel," said Ira.

"I've got to rethink this whole situation," said Gabriel.

"You do that," said Ira.

Gabriel looked hopefully at Polly. "Have you got anything to say before I go, ma'am?"

"Just good-bye."

"Sounds pretty final," he said dolefully.

"And good luck," she added with sincerity.

He grew moroser. "Sounds even *more* final."

"Please don't think us unfriendly," said Ira, "but the airlines *do* have schedules."

"I'm sorry, sir. I didn't mean to be a nuisance. Only thing is, everything's so *strange* all of a sudden. . . . But I'll be going now. Lots of rethinking to do. Days, maybe weeks, of rethinking. Someone has blundered, that's for sure. But who? There's the riddle. *Who?* Good-bye, ma'am. Good-bye, sir."

Polly and Ira stood in silence and watched Gabriel shamble across the tree-lined quadrangle. Still silent, they got into the taxi. Ira turned his neck and looked out the back window at Gabriel receding in the distance. Nutty kid, thought Ira. Wild, exasperating, headlong kid. Volatile, mercurial, impetuous, precipitous, reckless, heedless, defenseless—in short, *my* kid. My vulnerable flesh and my unreasoning blood. Mine, and I can never let him know. Good-bye, my son. Good-bye, my seed, my self.

"Ira, are you crying?"

"Me? No. Something in my eye, is all."

"What a coincidence. It's in my eye too."

"Really?"

"Really," said Polly, and took Ira's face between her hands and kissed him tenderly.

"Thank you," said Ira to Polly. Then, to the driver, he said, "Airport."

Ira took one last look out the back window as the cab started away, but Gabriel was gone.

Epilogue

Linus Calloway's television station in Birmingham was housed in a converted garage—just barely converted. There was one single studio in which Ira Shapian, sweating happily, directed, produced, wrote, rehearsed, announced, and somehow made exciting viewing out of amateur talent, snips of noncommercial film, and provocative ad libs. There was no hint of professional gloss in Ira's programs; neither was there the fumbling of amateurism. What lifted the shows and made them leap was the unexpectedness and breath of life.

A plywood partition separated the executive suite from the broadcasting studio. Behind this barrier sat Polly Shapian, working as secretary, receptionist, and switchboard operator, and performing each function with exemplary good cheer and monumental lack of skill. Nobody, however, seemed to mind, or, for that matter, to notice.

At night Polly and Ira went home to their substandard dwelling, ate a meal that would cause multiple suicides at the Cordon Bleu Society, and made love to one another—sometimes vigorously, sometimes without any contact whatever, but always happily.

Linus Calloway spent his workdays in the least prepossessing office any executive has ever occupied—unpainted plywood walls, a desk bought from the Goodwill Industries, and two kitchen chairs. What Linus did mostly was write checks, never losing his brave smile though his bank balance raced like a whippet toward the precipice of overdraft. Not one penny of income accrued to Linus' station, until, to Linus' surprise and delight, a small, unexpected windfall came one day: the William Lloyd Garrison Foundation informed him they wanted to engage his station and his personal services to tape their annual Community Relations Award on the fourteenth of March.

Professor Linden-Evarts, chairman of the board of trustees of the

Garrison Foundation, arrived at Linus' station at ten A.M. on the morning of March 14th. Despite the professor's horrid personality, he got along famously with Linus because it quickly became obvious as they talked that both held the same views about race relations.

Promptly at noon the recipient of the Garrison Award appeared at the tv studio—Jefferson Tatum. He shook hands with Ira, Polly, and Linus, and then he addressed Linden-Evarts. "Professor," he said, "you are looking at a very surprised man. I'd have bet my bottom dollar you'd never recommend me for the William Lloyd Garrison Award."

"Why not?" asked Linden-Evarts.

"Well, first off," said Jefferson, "if you'll pardon my language, I had you figured for a sure-enough pissant."

"A natural mistake, Tatum," said Linden-Evarts generously. "Actually, you're in the right phylum; you've just got the wrong genus. The kind of insect I am is not a pissant—though I confess I do give that impression—but a *gadfly*. And believe me, Tatum, it's a useful thing to be in the academic world. You've no doubt heard universities described as the Groves of Academe? A grossly romantic misnomer, sir. *Swamps* of Academe is far more accurate. It is the little stinging, buzzing, swarming creatures like me who are best adapted."

"I didn't understand one word of that," said Jefferson. "But never mind. There's a more important reason why I never thought you'd give me the Garrison Award: you been calling me a tokenist every chance you got. You been saying I don't give a hoot in hell about colored folks; all I want is to keep my Negroes quiet and peaceable."

"And isn't that true, Mr. Tatum?" Linus interjected.

"I ain't saying," replied Jefferson cannily. "But if it is, it seems to me a pee-poor reason to give somebody a race-relations award."

"Mr. Tatum," said Linus, "there's no question that the Garrison Foundation could have picked any number of white folks who have a genuine feeling of brotherhood for Negroes. You, as Linden-Evarts says—and as I, too, happen to believe—just want to keep your Negroes quiet and peaceable. And how do you accomplish that? By paying a living wage. By giving equal job opportunities. By desegregating public facilities. By keeping a strict watch on police brutality. By denying the ballot box to nobody because of his color . . . Your motives, sir, are far from admirable, but your results pay off—for you and for the Negroes. Love is a beautiful ideal, and we should never stop striving for it. Meanwhile, enlightened self-interest deserves to be recognized."

"And it better be recognized damn quick," said Ira, looking at his watch. "Come on, Linus, Mr. Tatum. Let's get this presentation taped. I've got a show going on in six minutes."

Ira hustled Jefferson and Linus into the studio and placed them before a camera. "Roll it," said Ira and threw a cue to Linus.

"Ladies and gentlemen," said Linus, "the William Lloyd Garrison Foundation is one of America's oldest, most tireless, and most effective forces working for better understanding between the races. Each year the Foundation gives a Community Relations Award to that city which has made the greatest strides toward true racial equality. It is my privilege now to present this year's award to the city of Owens Mill. Accepting the award will be Mr. Jefferson Tatum, Owens Mill's most prominent citizen and most dedicated laborer in the cause of racial equality."

Linus handed a handsome bronze plaque to Jefferson.

"Thank you kindly," said the old man. "I ain't one for speeches. I only want to say this: I never set no store by the color of a man's skin; it's what's inside that counts. I'm real proud of this award and I want to announce, here and now, that first thing tomorrow morning I am sending one million Tatum Cigarettes, absolutely free of charge, to the NAACP."

Ira, torn between laughing and crying, made the throat-cutting gesture and the camera went dead.

"I done pretty good, huh, sonny?" Jefferson asked Ira.

"You were incredible," replied Ira.

"You wasn't bad neither, Mr. Calloway," said Jefferson, patting Linus' shoulder.

"You are too kind," said Linus.

"Let me ask you something," said Jefferson to Linus. "This here tape we just made—who's going to see it?"

"We'll run it on this station, of course," said Linus. "And the Garrison Foundation will supply copies to every other station in the country. Some will use it; some won't."

"Uh-huh," said the old man thoughtfully. "So just as a rough estimate, maybe ten or twenty million people might see this tape."

"Entirely possible," said Linus.

Jefferson grew even more thoughtful. "Mr. Calloway," he said, "can I talk to you private for a minute?"

"Certainly." Linus ushered Jefferson into his shabbily furnished office. They sat.

"Mr. Calloway," said Jefferson, "before I came down here, I done a little investigating about your television station. I'd say you was in pretty bad trouble. You've got no money to buy canned shows. You're putting your programs together out of spit and gumption. You've got no rating to speak of, and your bank account is disappearing like frost on a spring morning."

"All true," admitted Linus promptly. "Just the same, we *are* picking up a small audience, and my bank account isn't *quite* empty. I figure we still have a chance."

"Mathematically, I'd reckon about a ten percent chance."

"And I'd reckon you're pretty close to the mark."

"Slim odds, friend," said Jefferson.

"I never thought it would be easy," answered Linus.

Jefferson removed a checkbook from his breast pocket. "Would you like a donation of five million dollars?" he asked.

"Let me put it this way," said Linus. "Yes."

The old man wrote a check and shoved it across the desk. "It's yours."

Linus made no move to pick up the check; instead, he looked closely at Jefferson. "Forgive the question, Mr. Tatum, but is it conceivable that the Garrison Award has given you just a tiny attack of conscience?"

"I'm a businessman, Mr. Calloway. And I thought you was too. Us businessmen don't say words like *conscience*. What we say is *deductible contributions* and things like that."

"Quite right," Linus agreed.

"Also—I'll be frank with you, Mr. Calloway—Shapian gave me a pretty good kick in the head when he did that show up at Acanthus College. Sales been disappointing since that goddam program. . . . So I'm thinking this. You say ten or twenty million people are going to look at the tape we just done. I calculate a quarter of 'em, maybe a third, will be black. Right?"

"Probably."

"And when them black folks see me getting the Garrison Award, there's bound to be an awful lot of 'em switching over to Tatum Cigarettes. Way I look at it, I'll get this five million back with interest, and damn soon."

Now Linus pocketed the check. "Self-interest—God bless it," he murmured.

"I'd appreciate it," said Jefferson, "if you'd let this be an anonymous contribution."

Linus' eyes widened. "That, I confess, puzzles me."

"It shouldn't," said Jefferson. "It's my experience nothing gets talked about quicker than an anonymous gift. Ain't that the way you've found it?"

"It is," said Linus.

"Sure. So you get a double payoff. First off, folks think you're a mighty big feller for giving away so much money. Second, they think you're an even *bigger* feller for not blowing your horn about it."

Linus laughed deeply.

"Thoroughly enjoyed our visit, Linus," said Jefferson, rising.

"Come again soon, Jefferson," said Linus, offering his hand.

Barbara Ogilvie Owens Fuller, called Boo, thought long and hard about bearing Ira's second bastard in brave secrecy, and the longer and harder she thought, the less brave seemed the project and the more imbecilic. Even for a soul as exalted as Boo's, there is a point when nobility must yield to good sense. One day, during her third month of pregnancy, Boo finally reached that point. She invited Virgil to come by.

"Virgil," she said, "you have been asking me to marry you for more than twenty years. Would you marry me now if I told you I was bearing another man's child?"

"I can think of more ideal conditions," replied Virgil, "but yes."

"Do you want to know who the other man is?"

"Hell, no!"

"I feel I must be completely honest," said Boo. "It is Ira Shapian."

"I didn't ask you," said Virgil, "and I'd have been a lot happier never to know. Still, I will say this: I can't fault your taste."

"Ira Shapian is also Gabriel's father," said Boo.

There was a period of silence from Virgil. "Boo," he said at length, "I told you I'd marry you, and I will. But if it's not too much trouble, do me one favor: try very hard not to have any more children by Shapian."

"Yes, dear," said Boo.

"Now I'll tell you why I'm going to marry you," said Virgil. "Half of the reason is plain habit. I've been wanting to marry you for so long that it's become part of my life—like shaving every morning, or drinking coffee after dinner. I suppose if there was some compelling reason, I could grow a beard or switch to tea, but it seems easier just to go on shaving and drinking coffee—and wanting to marry you."

"Not entirely flattering," remarked Boo.

"Neither is the second half of my reason," said Virgil. "I want to marry you because I love you. I love you so much that it grinds me up inside when I see you doing a stupid thing like not loving me back. Don't you know how many years of happiness you've cheated yourself out of by not marrying me? Don't you know I'm the best goddam man you've ever clapped eyes on, and I specifically include Ira Shapian?"

"Now, just one minute!" said Boo, bristling.

"No, not one minute," replied Virgil firmly. "Not one second. I love you, I want to marry you, I will make you happy, I will cherish your children. What I will not do is stand and discuss terms with somebody who's in no position to make a deal. The justice of the peace closes in half an hour. Come, Leda, let us fly."

"Yes, dear," she said.

Now, last of all, Gabriel.

His suffering was sharp and constant for several weeks. Waking and sleeping, he agonized over Polly Shapian until he thought he must go mad. Then, quite by accident, one day in physics lab he noted that the girl at the next table had built a microphone smaller by two-thirds than anything he had ever attempted.

Love, joyous love, smote Gabriel instantly, though, it must be admitted, the girl was less than attractive. She had, for example, two goodly warts and spoke nothing but Finnish. Still, she *did* build beautiful little microphones, and her love for Gabriel arrived as quickly and fiercely as his for her.

They will be married come June.

ABOUT THE AUTHOR

Like a rookie who hits a grand slam homer his first time at bat in the big leagues, Max Shulman knocked it out of the literary ball park in his very first appearance—*Barefoot Boy with Cheek*, 1943—and he has been batting close to a thousand ever since.

Following *Barefoot Boy with Cheek* he delivered such solid hits as *The Feather Merchants, Sleep Till Noon, The Many Loves of Dobie Gillis,* and *Rally Round the Flag, Boys!* In addition to writing novels, Shulman has done more than 100 short stories for leading magazines. On Broadway he made his mark as co-author of *The Tender Trap*. In television he is represented by the long-run comedy series *Dobie Gillis*. His weekly humor column, "On Campus," appears in 350 college newspapers.

Shulman conducts his durable-joke business in Westport, Connecticut, where he lives with his wife, the former Mary Gordon, and their five children.